Maybe It's My Heart

by Abigail Stone

Lincoln Springs Press
P.O. Box 269
Franklin Lakes, NJ 07417

For my mother

I saw a painting last night by Vincent VanGogh. It was the last picture he ever painted. I think he may have finished it, touched it up here and there, put down his paint brushes and killed himself, though I'm not sure; he might have killed himself later in the week. Anyway, it was the picture of the wheatfield with the crows overhead...those terrible crows in his mind, something like Ethiopia and Phil Donahue are to me. The battering away, the bothersome, nagging thing in one's mind that forces one to do things one might ordinarily have avoided. Like painting or writing or killing oneself. That sort of crow.

> Ring around the rosey
> a pocket full of posey
> ashes, ashes, we all fall down.

My oldest daughter Regina used to sing that song when she was little. Now, at seven, she sings "girls just wanna have fun" and "two four six eight who do we appreciate?" while continously jumping rope. I can sit in the kitchen eating and watch her outside the window. She looks a lot like her father who visits occassionally...she has that long face, stringy blondish hair. I remember how I would play ring around the rosey with her in our little cabin in the woods. She had a hard beginning; we've all had a hard time of it. Now though, things are different. Of course it's important to recall in detail all the struggling you go through to reach a plateau of drab contentment, but it isn't always easy to remember the years in our cabin. Now with running water and electricity the past gets dimmer. Did we really share a small two room camp with the field mice? Did I really have twins alone in the hospital, did the twins' father really disappear into thin air a week before they were born? Am I thirty-one? Is it possible, after all this time of anguish to come down with Altzheimers disease and forget everything wrenching in my life? Well, no, it isn't. I remember it all in vivid detail. I haven't forgotten one second.

I remember my narcissistic lover, Lymon, who always looked in the mirror. He bought himself clothes and carried a briefcase and didn't have a cent, didn't have a job or a house or anything. And the skin on his hands was like a baby reptile, transparent and scaly. He had beaver teeth and red hair and his favorite word was INGENUOUS. He was always hugging strangers. With him, I had twins.

I remember the boyfriend with frizzy wild hair that said, "Whatever you say is revealing about yourself...see? Even that's revealing. No one says anything that isn't about themselves."

"Maybe that's just you," I said. The wild hair that frizzed around his white gay face.

"I sleep with men as an extension of my own energy," he said. "Women are energy sappers..." He carried a sketch book with him and disappeared in Nepal in 1972, and I never saw him again. "You see how you have a center to every picture you draw? It shows you are very sure of yourself. I can tell just by looking at this, that you have a permanent centered self."

When I am not thinking of myself, my faults, my attributes, my children, I think of my men. The short one who never stopped smiling, even while working at the graveyard. His big white teeth went around his face like a scarf. "I have a job," he told me, the firelight in his face, his naked grinning face. "I'm working the deadhead shift at the graveyard, midnight to seven. I can stay in the empty mausoleum. I can work on my poetry there. Gee, I'm so happy."

The one who took me around Europe first class, wringing his rich hands in misery. "They're out there, and they want me...but it's eluding them that I hate, y' know? It's the daily grind of escape that I can't hack much longer. I need to satisfy them with a sacrifice you know?" And his sharp thin teeth and huge blue eyes sank into me, frightened me, changed me, laid their permanent mark on me forever. I would never be the same and I might never even remember my old self.

* * * * * * *

Gee, it's a nice day! Maybe I'll try and muster up the energy to take the twins for a little walk. They've been so cheerful lately and now that we are living in this adequate house, I feel I ought to make a real effort to give them a normal life. Though this morning when I got up to make Regina breakfast before she went to school, I looked in the bathroom mirror...horror upon horror I saw looking back at me a grey woman with bags under her dark eyes, with limp hair around her wan face...it frightened me, I'll be honest. I was so scared that I cried in the egg water. I drank my coffee with a sinking feeling in my stomach. It's probably my heart.

Yesterday it snowed so hard that the driveway disappeared. Regina made a fort, the neighborhood kids went sledding in the streets. In the evening we all made cookies...and yet, while I sat by a window watching the snow fall, seeing the soft lights of the Christmas tree, I was overcome by the normality of the situation...even the family dog lying by the kitchen counter, true she has always had fleas... It seemed and still seems I might add, too good to be true...all except for the hole in my heart. That's what I've narrowed it down to. After the x-rays this week which haven't come back yet, I realized in a great flash that the fluttering sound was the edges of the hole in my heart flapping. The exhaustion, the grey ness, all due to the lack of umph in the old major muscle. That's it, I'm convinced.

This is a good neighborhood. Not too many Catholics, only two shacks on the street, nobody elite, an auctioneer, a gas station owner, a physical therapist, somebody next door dying of cancer...I ought to go over and introduce myself.

Yes, this is what it's all come down to...trying to make my oldest daughter happy, I have moved into a yellowish-green house on a nice street in a nice town so she can go to a good school, have nice friends, be invited to parties...etc. But what, now that I am in here, looking out the wavy glass window, am I supposed to do in this one-horse village? Not that I ever had much to do. I don't have a very long work record. My mother lives near by, not too near, about thirty miles and she visits. She's just as wild as she was twenty years ago, she still has goofy poets staying for weekends with her in her rambling unusual farmhouse. My sister lives in the next town over, married to a nice man who wears glasses and takes photographs. She has one son, a smart boy who is always dressed in primary reds and blues. He carries a book bag to his private school kin-dergarten. I have another sister who married a woodcutter, she has two children who ski and play soccer, she once said to me, "Let's pretend we don't know each other."

The twins can walk. So what.

Uh huh, almost Christmas and the old heart is popping holes, making aggies in my innards, gee whiz I'm scared. Not as scared as the time the whole family was on the *Queen Elizabeth* coming home from England where my father had pulled a fast one and killed himself, and they had a life boat drill, and my mother and my two sisters left me in the ship's day care door while they ran off in life jackets. I was five mind you, it wasn't an intellectual fear as my holey heart is, but I saw all the passengers, huge crowds of them rushing down the stairs by the day care door, everybody wearing life jackets, everybody breathless and yelling...and I said to the only other person in there with me, a young unpleasant girl who was the ship's babysitter, "Where's my mother?" and she said, "I don't know." And I tell you I was very scared.

Dying is another way of being left out of the life boat drill.

In this house there are two bathrooms. One in the basement off the family room, a large empty room with a cement floor where we are supposed to congregate and I guess play trivia, and the other bathroom is on the top floor with the three bedrooms. I'm very lucky to have this place. Several people have told me if it hadn't been for the perfect timing, the local references, the elegant outfit I wore to the interview, I might never have landed it. There is even a sink in the family room. On the middle floor there is a kitchen with a sink and a living room...the windows have inside shutters, like a camera looking out at the world, I can lower the f-stop if I want to be alone.

I don't have any furniture though and that bothers my landlord. I can tell when he comes over to put in a new lightswitch, he is casing the joint to see how desirable I am, rental-wise. And he sees that I have my Christmas tree up, good he thinks, that's efficient, get it up early, end of November's not a moment too soon. And he sees I have a red tablecloth on my kitchen table, uh huh, festive...and he sees I have a color television, very good...color TV is American. Black and white TV suspicious. And he sees I have an expensive stereo system...that's good, shows money. But the stereo system and the color TV are on the floor because I don't have an entertainment center. That's what they call those things that hold all your electronic equipment, entertainment centers...they are usually in the family room. And the landlord thinks, that's odd. And while I am at the grocery he slips upstairs and takes a peek in the children's room and he sees in Regina's room records, a child's record player, toy dolls, everything lying all over the floor and no bed. In the twins' room he sees two cribs, both covered with brown sticky caked-on goo. And the room smells of babies, urine and milk. The landlord thinks it's disgusting, it's weird...

Then he looks in my room and there is a futon on the floor and some clothes in a pile. That's it. He finds it all very strange. He thinks he might have made a mistake renting to me. He mentions when I return from the grocery, that he will be drawing up a lease. I smile. "Great!" I say, sounding like it's just what I've been waiting for. Dreading. Whatever.

Or another possibility is that it could be some kind of dread lung disease...other than lung cancer, because it would be unlikely my doctor said, for me to get lung cancer at my age and especially since I quit smoking two years ago. Unlikely, he says, but...not impossible.

Regina has gone over to the auctioneer's house to play with his daughter. She tramped through the snow in her pink snowsuit and blue Care Bear mittens, fushia hat on her head, good bright colors against the winter background. Twins are asleep, finally, taking their midmorning nap. Coffee's hot. Walls are paneling by the way, so the place isn't perfect. The dog's gone with Regina, everything's pretty much paid for, too bad I'm so sick, I might be able to really enjoy this total change of lifestyle. Altogether, there are four sinks in this house. Two toilets. One bathtub, one shower and a washer-dryer hookup. It just goes to show you how clean Americans like to be.

"We gave out whatever food we could spare," a female journalist said on the news. "We had to keep some naturally...but knowing that a piece of bread and a little water could sustain life among one of these people for a few more days...it was incredible...and Tom, I will never forget their faces, the way they looked at me." She was speaking, of course, of the Ethiopians.

Regina told me this morning, "Everybody in my class comes to school with wet hair." And I said, "They DO???? Why? Aren't they cold?"

"Mommy!" she explained, a little exasperated, "they all take showers every morning." I was, honestly, incredulous.

"ALL OF THEM?"

"Most," she said.

I'm lucky if I get around to a bath a week.

There is much to be said about change. How we human beings can really be made over in no time...I'm looking forward to changes I'll make in myself...like for instance, squeaky clean day in and day out. Big fresh fluffy towels, nice normal soap. Cream rinse.

Regina was two when I became involved with a man named Martin. On and off he made no sense but he was Italian and dark, he was funny, he liked my style, that sort of relationship. I moved in with Martin before I found out he was crazy. He had fooled me if you can believe that: he had introduced me to his normal mom and dad, he had showed me his brother at Cornell, he had looked up and up...I was perpetually dieting anyway so I didn't notice things like I notice them while I'm eating. "The organization has chosen *ME*," was the first indication he gave.

"What?" I said. I was buttoning up my daughter's coat. We were on our way to the little park.

"I have been selected. They are going to experiment on me. I dread it you know. But maybe even you are in league with them..."

"No," I answered, reluctant to hear what I was hearing.

"Obviously there is nothing I can do. I tried to force Lisa to take my pills, I wanted to see if she would...because I had the feeling she was in league with them...she kept crying." Lisa was his previous girlfriend. "I got four down her," he said. When Martin smiled he reminded me of a crazy man I once saw locked in a wire porch at a state hospital. I was there visiting a colleague who'd had a nervous breakdown and I passed under the wing for the criminally insane...the hopelessly insane. And there was a ferociously crazy man with horrible hair locked on a basketlike porch, laughing but his laugh was so terrifying...it was a scream. "They NEVER come out of there," my friend confided in me. I looked up as I was leaving...there was a tiny old lady with the wild man. She had her face to the wire...she was mouthing something. It looked like "help help."

"You better not try any dirty sex tricks," Martin warned me. I packed up my daughter's toys that night while he was at work and had my mother come and get me. My daughter didn't like the way he made her eat cottage cheese. "Eat little one, eat little one, eat little one," he would repeat to her. Then he would wipe her with a cloth after every bite.

I had a terrible fear of pregnancy. Every fifteen days or so I would go to the women's health clinic and have my blood drawn and checked. Those were odd places, those women's health centers. This one was run by—as usual—all women. Most of them wore old jeans and tee-shirts that read "Women's Caucus" or "Women are Wonderful." There was no doctor, but there was a black nurse, with a huge afro and a small girlfriend. Once they decided to examine me. "I have a feeling she's pregnant this time," the black nurse said to the girlfriend. They were standing around me in jeans while I lay on the floor. ("We don't need tables and stirrups," they said.) "By the size of the stomach?" "No," the nurse went on, holding one of my hands. "By the red flush on her hand here...see?" The girlfriend looked.

"Am I?" I called out.

"That's common in early pregnancy...the red flush along the palm here."

"Am I? O shit!" I said. "Are you sure?"

"We aren't sure, no," the nurse said, still with my hand, "but it's a pretty good indication. Do you want an abortion?"

"Shit this is awful," I said. "Are you positive? Can we draw some more blood?"

The black nurse patted the sheet I had on. "I'm going to go in and check. Would you like to watch?" The girlfriend rubbed her jeans with her little hands. I had a good view of all of their feet. The nurse was wearing leather thongs.

"Watch?" I repeated.

"Max can hold a mirror for you to look while I check. It's kind of fun to watch." Max was the girlfriend.

"No thanks," I said.

"See here? Look." They held up a little mirror that dentists use and I could view my cervix.

"Gee," I said. I leaned back on the floor. All I could think was how Martin would be mad.

The nurse pulled her glove off. "Feels about I'd say, six weeks," she said.

"Ohhh nooo! This is too terrible. I can't stand it. Are you sure?"

"Well, no." The nurse admitted to me, sitting crosslegged on the floor. "You could just have an abnormally large uterus. Do you know the size of it?"

I said I didn't.

"Well...," she put her arm around Max and they hugged briefly. "Let's get a blood sample and I'll give you some brochures on our abortion scheduling."

Max and the nurse left me to dress and while I was putting on my skirt, Martin burst into the room. "...How could you?" he shrieked. "Come to this place and not even tell me? If I hadn't been watching you I might never have known! Are you pregnant?" I pulled on my socks. "If you are you will simply get an abortion. I'll see if my father will pay for half and you can pay for the other half." I tied my sneakers.

"Just leave me alone," I said. I put my purse over my shoulder.

"Either you take the the offer or not. I won't pay for the whole thing. It's your fault afterall. I'm not the one who's pregnant."

"Come on in here," Max called to me. I had my blood drawn.

"My father will probably cover about half the costs. No more." Martin said.

We left the building quickly because the black nurse was angry. "There's no men allowed in here. We told you that...Get him out." Martin didn't have any money with him so we walked the three miles back to his apartment.

"Between you and the organization I won't have any life juices left," he said.

That night Martin took me out for a Mexican dinner. We went to a dance hall afterwards and split a gin and tonic. "My father ought to support me totally," he shouted over the music.

"Why?," I said.

"He's the one who hooked me into the charter chapter of the organization."

"What?," I said. "I can't hear you! Can we buy another round?"

"I'm broke. Anyway, you're pregnant. You shouldn't even have a little sip." He took the glass from me and drained it. "I won't have a child born out of wedlock," he said after we had gone back to his apartment. "And I won't have you getting rid of it at that lesbian hostel."

I had put my daughter to bed, we were lying on Martin's couch drinking wine. The phone range. "PAPA!," Martin said into the phone, his voice jubilant as always when his father called. "Muchalianoo! etc. etc." He went off into gesturing Italian and when I woke up it was morning. I was alone on the couch. I put on my same old clothes and went back to the health center taking my daughter with me.

"I'm here about the blood test," I said. The receptionist looked up. "Jusaminute...Judy! Ain't you got you' coffee yet? Come on girl take my place I wanna hit the streets." Then she looked at me. "What you want?," she said rather as a statement. "I had a blood test yesterday to see if I was pregnant."

"Jusaminute. I say girl, I'm gonna leave. The hell with you. Bitch." The receptionist stood up. "I don't know 'bout those tests," she said.

"My name is..."

"I'M LEAVING!," she shouted to the back room. The nurse's girlfriend appeared.

"It was negative," she told me leaning around the corner of a door. "Take a flyer there. We're having a fundraising vegetarian dinner next week, no men allowed, if you and some of your support group want to come it's ten dollar donations. I've got to get back to the sister in the other room now. "GOOD LUCK!" I didn't go to the dinner because that was around the time I realized Martin was sort of dangerous and I had to have my mother come and get me. Also, I didn't HAVE any support group to take to the fundraiser with me.

I don't resent Martin for his insanity. I mean he came to visit me many years later when I was married to my only husband who grew to remind me a little of Martin. My husband was at sea at the time and Martin arrived in his father's car though he wouldn't admit it was his father's car. "The organization assigned this car to me," he said, climbing out and standing in the road by my large house holding a paper bag. "All I have to do is collect material for their studies. They're doing a survey of abused homosexuals."

"Really!" I said. "What's in the bag?"

"Nothing! Just forget about the bag," he said.

No, it isn't that I resent him. Or the time I wasted with him. After all, I got good writing material out of him...that's what my mother says of all my horrible experiences..."Thank God it happened. Look what you've turned it into! Pure gold!" Or, "Oh honey, write it up, it'll be great. Laugh a little for Christ's sake."

It was hard getting rid of him after he found out where I lived. He locked himself in one of my large marble bathrooms and threatened to ruin the septic system which was really already on its last legs because my husband had already ruined it. "And don't try and get me to eat any of your cheese!" he shouted through the keyhole.

"Look," I said, trying to sound sincere. "Just eat what you have with you and leave. I'm not in the organization."

"This house is perfect for us! We must have it! You have to stay with your husband! We can eliminate him anyway. But he can't know we are here. Did I tell you I only eat seaweed and horse dung?"

"Please, Martin," I said. "Come out of there. I want you to go home."

"TO MY FATHER??????" he shouted.

I'd say resent was a bad word. I'd say more forget. I'd like to forget Martin ever existed in my life. I'd like to pretend he never lived with me, he never kissed me, he never holed up in my bathroom.

"I'm taking a long crap," he shouted.

I heard on the Donahue show that women are growing increasingly wary of men. I heard that they now say when asked out on a date... "Oh, why bother? It never comes to anything more than a struggle to get rid of the guy." And Donahue said to the crowd, head to one side, "But are ALL men like this?"

"You must make your mommy understand!" Martin shouted into the toilet. My daughter and I could hear him from the downstairs bathroom. It sounded almost as if he was trapped in the pipes that wound through my huge house that my husband bought for me to stay put in. "She has to keep the house for us. We need it to combat sodomy!"

"Why is he upstairs?" my daughter wanted to know.

"He's sick. He's saying these things but he doesn't know he's saying them," I said. I finally called the police but when they arrived he had already burst out of the bathroom and run terrified to his father's car, leaving his bag of seaweed and sawdust on the windowsill. I—knock on wood—haven't seen him in five years. But he traumatized me forever with his awful dance the night he had first arrived...he put on a record and had gyrated into my rug throbbing to the music, shouting, "no more faggots!" He was bigger than when I had lived with him, and his face had become denser. And he beat the rug with his fists and really scared me.

In fact, Donahue had two guests on who had written books on the new women and the old men. How men have been left behind in their attitudes. "Do you know that out of half of every divorce with children, the man, the father, pays no child support???" Donahue smiles. "And we'll be right back," he says.

Do I know that fathers do not pay child support????? I don't really know if Regina's father Richard is out there having fun exactly. He never appeared to be having fun the whole time I knew him. My sister once said he had no presence...that you could walk into a room where he was and not realize he was there. "He's invisible," my sister said. So maybe he is not out there having fun but merely just out there. Anyway, he refuses to pay child support. On the Donahue show today Rachel Welch said, "Ladies let me tell you children are wonderful they are just fabulous and when I had my children I was scared and I said gee whiz...but but, now I think they're just wonderful. Children are great."—So I feel guilty saying anything to the contrary...I would be a dog to admit putting them all in an orphanage had crossed my mind. "Miss Welch, what do you think of abortion?" one of the bobbed headed women in the audience asked. "What do I think?' Well, I think, let me say, children are wonderful...they really are..."

Regina Lee, light of my life, sore in my side, dream in my pocket, reason for myself, I am not sorry I had you but sometimes I am sorry I am who I am. Why couldn't I have been a smarter woman who held out for large sums of money from a rich husband? Why couldn't I have been a career woman who never had children till she was thirty-eight? Why couldn't I have been Rachel Welch?

Regina Lee and I sometimes go out for french fries at McDonalds. We used to do more before the twins were born but for each child, less time. Less space. Less money. Less energy. Listless.

Bitter is a good word I think for this. Bittersweet. People who live in mansions drink bitters. Some home decorators use bittersweet flowers in clay pots as doorstops.

So what. Who cares. Oh God let's not start THAT again. For everything there is a reason. Look at my first and only husband, Shel. It seemed at first there was no reason for our terrible life together, and then out of his intense jealousy and paranoia, I fled into the arms of a man whose grandmother was a twin. From there I had my own, and who knows...from these human bodies may come world leaders...great writers...another messiah. And so from the child of Richard could come something that later saves my life...could result in a nuclear arms freeze. I tell you, I'm open to the possibilities.

I want to get away from the subject of MEN but God it's difficult. There have been so many! My husband sticks in my mind as the experience that sums up all my encounters.

Shel was balding and overweight. He wore clothes that were a size too large for him so the shirts hung to, and the pants wouldn't stay above, his hips. He was a merchant mariner, rode the greasy waves on an oil tanker. He stressed that he tried to save gulls that had been sprayed with the oily water, he said he was more like Herman Melville than not, but what he portrayed to the world was a short hairless unkempt man who wouldn't brush his teeth and who was never seen without a beer in one hand and a cigarette in the other. "I'm tellin' ya," he'd express, "you're one hell of a beauty...hey, listen to me...I'm tellin' ya."

So what ever drew me to him? This borders the other question SO WHAT? Who cares?

I just want to say that after we had been married one month and had bought our luxury house and sports car, I became pregnant. Shel was at sea when the doctor diagnosed my condition so as soon as he called from port I gave him the news. "Awwwwooh," he said, sounding far away. He was calling from the streets of New Orleans. "So how far along?" he said.

"Oh, four weeks I guess. Aren't you excited? Oh, isn't this so great? We have everything," I said. I was leaning back on a blue velvet couch and twisting the phone cord around my finger...

"So whose is it?" he asked quietly.

"What? What?"

"Miss Welch, how long have you been married?"

"You mean this time?" she chirped.

I was four months pregnant when my sister and I went to an auction one Saturday. We drove there in my new Ford truck laughing the whole way about our husbands and this and that. We are really almost twinly; I bid on a baby carriage, a beautiful baby carriage made of elegant curves of wicker. My sister bid on old trunks full of antique clothes and while we were bidding merrily I began to miscarry. They even announced it over the loudspeaker as we hurried to the hospital. "Let's take a moment to pray for Mrs. Bertwein who apparently was having a miscarriage while bidding here today. And what'll I get for this Windsor rocker? Can we start the bidding at three? Who'll give me three hundred and can I have four?"

Ship to shore ship to shore...Shel Bertwein, swabbing the deck, standing watch on the clam waters outside Porta Wartha in Puerto Rico, his balding head bent in a subservient manner as it always was, he had no sense of self...no self respect. "I'm tellin' ya," he often said, "nobody likes me, but YOU...you have more people that love you than...huh! I'm not one for sailor dialogue but they'd call you on ship, a dish." Shel, in the hot sun, wearing long paint-covered jeans, embarrassed to show the other guys his white legs, long-sleeved shirts to cover his average arms, a hat to hide his head. He was a second mate which means he was assigned mostly to chipping paint from the ship and reapplying it. An orange bright ugly paint. "Those babies rust faster than we can paint them...They have us covering the rust with paint and then we paint the paint. It's a tub, lemmie tell ya." Ship to shore. Shel Bertwein your wife's in the hospital. She lost the baby.

"Did you do a blood test? Was it my blood type?" he asked.

"SHEL?" I shouted into the phone..."I lost the baby. It died. We can have another one," I shouted.

"Watch it Sweetie, we're on short wave radio here. Everybody's listening." For you Shel, they were all hanging over the sides, listening in, waiting to take it all away from you, because you were so undeserving.

"Listen, so how's Regina? How's your mother?"

"Shel??? I bought a carriage. I shouldn't have lifted it. What's that noise?" Waves cracking against the sides, rocking the hospital bed, Shel rowing home, rowing home. And just before he got back, a bunch of black ugly loud screaming birds flew down the chimney and bashed into the room where the carriage was stored. I had put an antique doll in it, and one of these birds flew straight at the doll and smashed its head with its beak. The doll's face cracked in half and split open, a head of paper mache and the bird died in the carriage. I thought they were buzzards, but the old lady next door said, "Oh heavens, those pesky starlings!"

"My daughter will be coming out of a coccoon in this particular movie and marrying an earthling," Rachel Welch says. I can certainly relate to that.

The actual ceremony was so simple...almost dull. I had thought getting married was an unbelievable exciting moment, something you can't forget...something that causes wild feelings, brings tears to everyone's eyes. "Such a lovely bride," the rabbi's wife repeated throughout the afternoon. "Oi, she's as pretty as the one we married this morning. Such lovely girls."

"Rabbi, a little something for your trouble."

"But I couldn't...this is too much!"

"No, huh! Too much! For what you just did nothing is too much. No it was a beautiful ceremony. You deserve this. Please. I insist."

"I thank you Shel. You two make a wonderful couple. I mean that in sincerity. And now we must leave. Ah! yes, we must..."

"Listen, let me drive you..."

"Oh, no! You stay with your bride, you two have much rejoicing to do. I'll have your cousin here take us back." The rabbi hugged my husband again and nodded his head at me and they went out the front door, his wife exclaiming "what a gorgeous day it has turned out to be! Oh and look at the flock of birds there. Simply lovely."

We danced the traditional Jewish hat dance or whatever it was, Shel was embarrassed of his dancing, he felt he wasn't good enough though I thought he was perfectly adequate. I feel a man should be the straight man so to speak for the woman in dancing. Because women are more limber, easier to watch. "I'm telling ya sweetie...you look good enough to eat," Shel said, downing a glass of champagne.

I gave him a book of birds. And for a joke I circled the number on the page on Buzzards, the chapter of flesh-eating winged creatures.

"Are you ever self-conscious about your bust? I mean...*honestly*, doesn't it ever bother you just a teenie tiny bit?" Donahue asks.

Rachel smiles. "I am an exhibitionist," she admits. The crowd claps.

"They like your attitude, Rachel," Phil Donahue says and points his microphone in the air.

"Has it always been just you and the three children?" someone asked me in a confidential tone recently and I said "Yes, it's me and Regina and the twins and my guitar, my typewriter..." Oh, but that reminds me of my horrible uncle.

I had an uncle once who was a lot like George Bush. He lived down the road from me when I was little, and he hated his mother. Some days, I guess it was rarely, he'd drive up in his boring green Oldsmobile and take me to town with him...and every day that he came I would be in the front yard playing, in shorts and bare feet. And he'd say, "NOBODY should EVER wear BARE FEET! It's disgusting." He said this, my mother explained, because he had been poor as a child and had been traumatized by the other little children in his neighborhood laughing at him. I think he had been so poor that he couldn't afford shoes. He had me put on sneakers and a dress and with dirty legs, I climbed in his car and resigned myself to the short trip. But before we left he'd say to my mother, "No kid of mine would EVER be allowed to run around in barefeet. It's not right and that's all there is to it." My mother would say, "Ohhhh, well, they like to take their shoes off..." And my uncle would snarl and we'd drive away down the mountain. My uncle during the five-mile ride explaining why my mother was such a lousy mother. "Now! If you're GOOD, I might get you some candy...would you LIKE that?"

"Yes," I'd say, "Can I have."

"I said MAYBE," he would say and while I waited in his strange smelling car, he would go into the garage and talk. My uncle reminds me now of Bush...he had very short hair, cut close to his head, and he was the same build...punky looking...not tall, not big...not exaggerated in any way...and he had a southern accent. My uncle was a democrat but he argued and complained and talked about blessing America like Bush. He had been shot in the leg in World War Two and I think it affected him sexually, my mother hinted at that, but she might just have been saying that out of malice. She hated my uncle Smithy.

Whenever I went to my aunt's house, my uncle would be sitting in front of the TV in a reclining chair saying, "Look here Ellie...lookie here hun at this idiot...c'mere, Ellie..." My aunt would be in her house slippers, all worn out, and a pair of old dark colored pants and a plain shirt and she'd be smoking.

"What?" she'd say, running her slippers along the floor as she moved to my uncle in his chair.

"Here, damn it, can't you see? Lookie there...what an idiot. Can you imagine making yer money doing THAT on television? In front of millions? Chhhhhhhssssss." My uncle would glare at the entertainers on TV and my aunt would laugh a short depressing laugh and go back to making dinner. She smoked Camels.

"And I am pleased to introduce to you ladies and gentlemen...BOY
GEORGE!" The crowd screams. Donahue points his microphone and
out from behind the curtain, Boy George struts onstage in a a blue
marching band suit. "Why do you dress like that?" Someone in the
audience asks him immediately. "I mean...my daughters love your
music but why do you dress like a woman? Don't you think you could get
your message across better if you dressed more NORMALLY like
other people?"

"I like the Waltons," my aunt said, sitting in her colonial rocker reproduction. "Smithy teases me about it but I love to watch them. I like
John Boy. He's sensitive."
"I hate the Waltons!" I said, "But I haven't watched them really...I
don't watch TV..." My aunt smiled and took a sip of tea. We were waiting
for Smithy to come down from upstairs where he was taking aspirin.
"Ohhhh ma leg," he said, limping down the steps. "It's my old war
wound acting up damn it to hell. Git outa my chair girl." He sank into
the recliner I had been in and was silent.
"Well," I said, "Thanks for letting me use the phone...I guess I
better go..."
"You get home already, honey? You want 'cher uncle to give you a
ride?" I said no. It was early winter and I walked home with the ice just
beginning to form on the trees. My aunt drank Salada tea. She smoked
constantly: she died of lung cancer when I was twenty-one. My uncle
remarried so he isn't my uncle any more and I didn't vote for Reagan, I
voted for Mondale-Ferraro. Why? So what? Because I didn't like my
uncle.

"You will forgive me for saying this but you seemed a little apprehen-
sive toward me before the show started," Donahue says, leaning over
Boy George who is sitting in a chair alone on the stage.
"Well, that's because you tried to steal my lipstick," he said.

I say so what. I say the world is set up unfairly. We should be helping
the Ethiopians and the children around the world...America is a rich
nation and Americans en masse decide the fate of the world's needy
children. My doctor, whom I visited two days ago because I was coughing blood...my doctor said of his vote for Reagan, "people don't want
to...give up...what they have...you know what I mean? They...aren't will-

ing to...share what they've gotten...."

"I know what you mean," I said, in an understanding confidential
tone. I figure if I humor my doctor, I wouldn't have such a bad
diagnosis.

"Look at the song of songs!" Father Greenly said. He had a calm
attitude but his eyes were slitted and beady. "That's extremely
erotic...many parts of the Bible are...sexual...." The crowd is frowning,
listening intently; they seem to be silenced by the unusualness of a liberal
priest. The camera moves to Donahue.

"And you will excuse me Father for interrupting you.... Far be it for me
to interrupt a priest...you must realize how uncomfortable it makes
me...but we have to pause here for a station break...."

Poor world! Oh poor world! Today in New Delhi they have lined up
dead children on the streets, for their parents to find...poisoned by a
chemical company; it was an accident, they said, on NBC. They were
reported as denying charges of negligence. "The company will meet with
the victims' families today to try and reach a settlement...."

Have you ever noticed how Tom Brokaw smiles while he says the
news? I know it's a job but how ghoulish to smile after film clips of dying
children. "Most of them were the elderly and children," he said, and
smiled. "In North Carolina today," he continues, his voice rising slightly
in an upbeat manner, "six are dead, thirty more are presumed so in a
poison gas explosion in a mine...."

I am sure they teach them in newscaster school to keep it cheery no
matter how gruesome the report. I suppose if the newsman looked stricken he might lose his audience.

"It's all packaging, isn't it?" Boy George says in his English accent.
"But I get so sick of people asking me why do I dress the way I do...why do
you dress the way you do? Can you tell me that one? eh? Can you?" A
woman stands up in the crowd. "I just wanted to say I don't care how you
look I like your music I like your message...It's okay with me if you want
to dress that way...."

I try and get away from the bad news. I want to remember earth as
sweet. I want it to be nice for a little while...just while I resign myself to
my illness...but maybe I don't even have an illness. It could be any number of reasons...this bleeding...this grey pallor....

"This is for Boy George.... I want to ask...do you dress like that for the money? I mean...do you get more money that way?"

Donahue takes the mike and says, "I think what she means is would you sell as many records in a suit and tie?"

"Who cares?" Boy George says and laughs, opening his purple lips.

"Well," Donahue says, obviously annoyed, "I think SHE cares. That's why she asked you."

They are shooting people one by one on a jet liner landed in Syria; some of them may be Americans, think of that. It is a group of terrorists doing it. They are demanding political prisoners from somewhere...and whenever they get particularly irritated, they throw another passenger's body off the jet. " And the death toll is rising," Tom Brokaw says, looking into the camera with a professional stare. He is one of the new young Republicans I'm guessing. Why though am I delving into this? You have a TV...you can watch for yourself.

Yet I have put my typewriter and my guitar and my piano all away. They are gone. Instead, I hunker down before the blinking neon black dots congregating portable color television set. And I watch "Gimmie A Break" and "Different Strokes" and "Scrabble" and "Love Connection" and "Days of Our Lives" and Tom Brokaw and every morning at nine right after the "Today Show" I watch Donahue. He hurries up and down the aisle in a grey suit, his hair is grey, he scratches his head a lot, he carries a portable microphone, he says "What's your opinion?" to a woman in the audience, wearing neat jackets and pants. He says, "THEY think you're all at home watching daytime TV eating chocolate covered cherries...and are you going to stand for that?"

At this point in time, when I have turned grey and sickly, I'm not even sure where my suitcase it.

Yesterday I almost passed out cold when I coughed a little more blood. It wasn't so much the actual blood, it was the waiting for it to happen. I knew it was going to happen again. I seem to be bleeding all over...and I'm weak. I'm exhausted. I have this sinking realization.... I called my doctor at home; it was Sunday, naturally, nothing happens during the week, and he said, "Hmmm, could it be coming from your nose do you think?"

"I don't think so," I shouted into the phone. I was afraid he wouldn't be able to hear me: I was in a phone booth because I never paid my last phone bill a year ago. They say I have to pay that bill before they'll give me another phone. "Shall I come into the hospital?" It was a cold day;

the wind was whistling around my legs and my kids were all crying in the truck.

"Are you having your period?" my doctor went on, seemingly unmoved.

"NO!" I shouted. "I'm finished with it."

"Hmmmmm," he said. Silence. "Was it a lot of blood...or just a small amount?"

"I don't know.... I don't know. I'm so scared...maybe I should come in???" My son was beeping the horn. BEEEEEEEEEEEP. It was Sunday but there were people around in the parking lot staring at my truck. BEEEEEEEEEEEP.

"Runny nose? Sore throat?" my doctor asked.

"NO, NO, nothing. I'm not sick, I'm dying...," I said. "Did the x-rays come back yet?"

"No, they didn't yet. Why don't you come into my office tomorrow morning, okay?...and if it gets worse today, call me."

"Am I going to die?" I called into the receiver.... I was panting from the breathless feeling that goes along with my illness.

"No, I don't think you are," he said. BEEEEEEEEEEEP.

So that was that. I went home and lay on the couch in terror till around five. Then I had a whiskey sour and went to bed. My mother came over to help with the children. "Honey, have they eaten yet?" she called to me.

"Ahhhh," I said. I could hardly breathe. The illness is strange in that way: it's almost as if it is a lung disorder. Possibly a lung cancer or maybe a form of heart disease. You hear all the time on TV how heart disease is a Number One killer. It has to get SOMEBODY.

Seven point seven Ethiopians are dead from starvation and thirst. It is so hard to imagine. SEVEN MILLION! That's as many they say as died in the gas chambers in Germany...and it is so hard to believe...when I see the film clips on television there they all are, in huge brown crowds, sitting before the NBC cameras with pitiful horrified faces, all wearing torn brown rags holding naked starving babies...the ground is dust. Brown dust. They are probably already dead by the time I view the news. So what is so unusual, what is so upsetting about one measly human being dying in America: in Vermont, mother of three, poor, thirty-one, big deal...so what...who cares, compared to SEVEN MILLION?

"Honey? Are you all right? Did you cough any more? Honey? Why are you looking like that?" my mother holding her heart, standing in the kitchen looking at me lying on the couch. The x-rays came back negative. "Your lungs look good," my doctor said as I sat down in his office.

He had a pamphlet in his waiting room called "How to Check for Cancer On Your Own" and inside it said: "a lump or thickening in the breast or elsewhere...." Well, that was me all over: I have a cholesterol lump on my eyelid. Bingo. "A change in a wart or mole." "Unusual bleeding or discharge": bam. I could hardly breathe and I was afraid I would start screaming. "Change in bowel movements"...well, that could be me. I had diarrhea this morning...God, I had it yesterday, too.

"The doctor will see you now," the nurse said and I went into his office and he said, "X-rays are normal. Lungs look good." He had on a yellow suit, rather natty for him, and he had just taken a shower. I could tell because his hair was still wet.

"I have all these symptoms," I said, holding up the red pamphlet.

"Have a seat," he said.

"Those who are lucky enough to still have family able, are taken off to the dying huts." I thought about that all night.... What are dying huts? Are they like the Bubonic Plague wagons where people were either put on dead or almost dead, and carted away? What a grisly way to go. I am grateful that I will miss the nuclear war.

Speaking of nuclear, I saw on TV last night a thing on the nuclear night. According to Sagan and other renowned scientists, we would as a species never survive a nuclear night which would bring extreme cold to the planet for months along with other horrible things. So this new discovery will now go to the board at the Pentagon and they will mull it over.

I don't think it will have anything to do with what will happen, though.

My doctor did a cardiogram. This is when they put you on a bed and strap electrodes to your wrists and ankles and put something which looks like a microphone on your chest. The machine then writes using lines, and the doctor can read how your heart is doing. I had that done on Wednesday—Wednesday afternoon they called my sister.

"Have your sister come in again," they said. "Something...ah... technical problems with the machine...we need another reading...." I knew right away when I heard that that they had discovered a discrepancy in my heart. Of course. It all fit suddenly like a puzzle. My heart! It was riddled with disease. That accounted for the shortness of breath, the blood, the exhaustion.

It was with shaking hands that I returned to my doctor's office. "Is he here today?" I asked, as I climbed back into the paper johnny you have to wear when getting tested.

"He'll be in at noon," the nurse said. She strapped my ankles.

"So, it was a technical error? What? The machine didn't come on?"

"Ohh, it came on all right," the nurse said loudly. I sank into the operating table.

"It just gave a wild reading, huh?" I said.

"HA! Yes it certainly did. Doctor John said to get another reading because that one would have meant that you...oh boy, let's see, this goes herrrrre." She fiddled for a minute with a strap and then turned on the machine. I lay there freezing, crinkling everytime I moved, awash with fresh terror. "Okkeee-dokey," the nurse said, removing the electrodes. I crept out of the office once I had put my jeans back on and my tur- tleneck...I asked at the receptionist's desk if the blood work had come back, but they didn't seem sure what to answer.

"Bye, bye," I said at the door, like an idiot. I am always reduced to about age five when I get frightened. And I drove to my mother's house for reassurance.

* * * * * *

My mother. Evil, possessed, sweet woman with her canvas bag full of old clothes and books, her leather purse a poet gave her on a trip to New York, her v-neck sweaters, red and grey hair in a bun, big sad hurt 1920s' eyes that can narrow into cynical, condescending. My mother. Always on the verge of seventy, living in her rambling dream house, a house of dreams, there's almost no house left anymore. In her beat-up Buick Le Sabre with the dripping asbestos ceiling and the shredded seats from when she put the dog in the car: Mom, Mom.... I call her mom but I never write mom. I write mother. I am formal in my approach to her. My mother, poet, man-hater, woman-hater...ego maniac, generous—so generous she will live in abject poverty and filth, she will drive a broken hunk of junk so I can have a new car, a new house, a new skirt.... She will babysit. And clean. And repeat herself and quiz me on the children's health and insist on being the fire inspector, the safety inspector, the nutritionist, the head of household, the moneylender, the great Mother.

Once she was my mommy. And I called through our dream house: "MOMMY????? I'm hungry." "MOMMY????? I'm going to the bathroom!!" I remember the brownies we ate at night, the fudge, the fireplace, the cold house, the dress with recipes on it that she bought me...how she offered to buy me presents if I wanted to stay home from school...how she popped up in front of me sometimes...opening a door she would be in the room sitting in a chair...she missed my father. My mother. How do I get to the center of her? How do I reach the essence of what she is? Her knit outfit she only wore once...her material for curtains. Her enthusiasm, depressions, heartpains, arm aches, fear, worry, her anxiety.

My boyfriend with the frizzy hair, the guru, said, "She's a Gemini, right?" and I said, "Right, how did you know?" and he said, "I always know. You'll never get along...She doesn't get along with Cancers."

There's that word. That awful suspect word. Sounding lumpy, swollen, distorted. It could be me. I could die, and my mother would either go crazy or stay the same. Who would get my children? Where would my stuff go?

Mother, why is it I can't remember my childhood? Except for the fact that I hardly went to school; when I did, I never had lunches like the other kids. They had Bologna sandwiches and baggies with chips in them. I had a dark brown banana, a cream cheese sandwich on two heels.

Mommy can I, mommy can I, mommy can I? Apartments, new rooms, closets, places where we lived. We were always moving. She was always getting another job.

"GUESS WHAT?" she'd say, waving a letter in front of us...a letter of acceptance. "I got a job in Wisconsin, kiddies." "In Illinois, kiddies. In Cambridge. In Indiana....This is it kids." "Ten thou!"

So what. From Cambridge to West Newton to Wisconsin to Illinois, I didn't have any friends to leave; I had no roots to uproot. No wonderful room to desert. I chose a large closet as my room when we'd move into a house. "Dibs on this room," my sisters would say. My mother would take whatever was left...and I would choose the room with the biggest closet.

"Mommy? Where are you? The dog pooped on the floor."

She never had a boyfriend. She was beautiful and smart. She was funny. She had good jobs. Beautiful daughters. When I was six a man used to shovel out our driveway every morning and I said, "Mommy, why don't you marry Peter Brite?" and she said, "He doesn't like women." Later she said, "He's a homosexual."

When I was in second grade a dumb man in Vermont used to stop at our house in the evenings with eggs from his chickens and tell me my mother was so beautiful. We used to hide when we saw him coming.

In ninth grade a professor from a snazzy university stayed overnight

but in the morning my mother confided to me, "He's too aggressive.
Oooh, he was awful...I just couldn't...."

Sixth grade a man came to our house and broke our door when he'd
had a drink. My mother stood outside by the currant bush and cried for a
long time. "Why don't you marry him?" I said.

He's not Walter," she said. "And besides, he's insane. Nobody is like
Walter," she said.

"Mommy!!!!! Mommy!!!!! Here I am! I was just kidding. Did you
really think I fell out the window?"

She lives in the same summer house we always stayed in from June to
August. The same front porch, the same back porch, the same kitchen
ceiling caving in, floor sliding away, big black cook stove taking up the
view from the window.

...The same long living room, the fireplace that was tricky, no one else
could use it but her...the bathroom, claw-footed tub, window to the back
yard...where the apple trees bloomed in spring and then bore wormy
hard apples with patches of red on them. And the playhouse she had
built for us...by a strange guy. The brook where we weren't supposed to
play way down because the toilet let into it; further up we played in the
tunnel under the road...sitting at the tunnel entrance in our shorts, the
cold water rising against our backs.... I was scared every time...get
ready...we're going to stand up...get set...let it get a little higher.... GO!
And we'd all stand together and the water would rush out, and knock us
all over.

"Mommy? Mommy, there's nothing to eat." My mother. Everybody
has one. She was mine.

I read recently in a *National Enquirer* sort of newspaper that Donahue
was moving his show to New York City to be closer to his wife Marlo
Thomas. She's the actress who has that peculiar appealing voice, star of
"That Girl." I wonder why she never acts anymore. In the paper it said
Donahue had SEVEN MILLION viewers. I was astounded. Seven
million! Why that's as many people as have died in the famine in
Ethiopia.

I can't bear to watch the ads of Oxfam, save the Ethiopians. My
daughter watches them while I close my eyes and hum and she says, "Oh,
mommy, look...did you see that baby and they were so skinny."

I remember when my mother used to pick me up at school for lunch
and we'd drive over to McDonalds, then a new fast food place. It had a

sign blinking on it that said "OVER ONE MILLION SOLD!" Later it was changed to "OVER SEVEN MILLION SOLD"...viewing, dead, starving, whatever.

Mother—I don't remember her reading to me. My sister said, "Oh I loved the *Wind in the Willows*.... I remember when mom read me that," and I was angry. She didn't read it to me. Or, my sister said, "That one was my favorite.... I loved it when mother read it to me."

"I did too," I said, but I had never heard it.

Mommy my mommy my mother, my strange angry weeping figure, who sometimes appeared in the barn, crying on an old Victorian couch...mother who invited to our house all the children nobody liked...one with a withered hand who was dying of some disease, a fat girl named Beverly Broucher who threw up in my purse, a nasty girl whose parents were divorcing.... I never knew them till they arrived, carrying overnight bags, ready to spend a week at our summer house, their thankful parents nowhere in sight. "This is Kit, Arelia, Leslie...why don't you show her the orchard?"

My mother who tried and failed. Who didn't try and then succeeded. Mommy, the hamster died.... Mommy, the Guinea pig won't stand up anymore. Mommy can I go to town? Get out. Get out get out of here mommy. Leave me alone. Just leave me alone I hate you.

Donahue had a fat lady on his show yesterday   She weighed almost four hundred pounds and all these thin pert female New Yorkers sat in the audience saying, "Now you can't tell me you're happy because I know I wouldn't be happy looking like that.... I couldn't stand to weight that much. I get upset if the scale shows a pound gain."

"But she says she's happy at this weight," Donahue argues.

"Well,...JjjjjSS! I sure wouldn't be. And what about your health? Have you considered your health?"

"I just want to know do you have to work hard to keep all that weight on?" The fat woman is holding the arm of her chair, her huge pale face looks injured, her husband, a member of FAT ADMIRERERS is glaring into the TV lights.

"I never said I tried to stay fat," she says, slowly, a worried look spreading across the dough....

"She's just learned to be happy with who and what she is," her husband interjects. "She has a body that insists on being fat...so now she is happy with herself anyway. That's all."

"So be it," Donahue says and a commercial comes on. It is a Diet Pepsi ad. "One calorie one calorie one calorie...MMMMM." A skinny beautiful model skates across the screen, holding a can smiling, then many skinny models slide by smiling, wearing leotards. I stare into the bleeping colors, watching the can of Diet Pepsi go from one beauty to another. Then there is an ad about S'mores candy bar.

"We have with us...a woman who lost sixty pounds after her divorce. And what we want to know is...does marriage make you fat?" New York women after shopping, on their morning out, sitting in rows before him, while he scratches his head in front of seven million viewers.

"I think the key word is exercise," a tiny dark-haired woman in pearls says.

He moves the microphone. "I want to ask the fat lady, does she have trouble getting through doorways? I mean, wouldn't she be happier if she dieted and exercised as this lady here suggested? And I just wanted to say that I agree with that other lady: if you care about yourself, you'll find a diet that suits you and..."

"But she's happy," Donahue says of the fat lady. The camera shifts to her sitting on stage with her husband. They are now holding hands.

Mommy? I'm sick. My throat hurts. My eyes ache. There's a big dot and a little dot fighting...the big dot is covering everything...it's covering all the white space...obliterating the little dot. To this day I hate *Heidi* because while I was in a coma in the hospital after a bicycle accident, my mother had it. I was unconscious but whenever I would come out of my sleep I would see it in her hand. Blue and red and yellow shiny cover...an ugly little girl skipping up a mountain...my mother hovering over me...get out of here. I hate you. Mommy? I think it's dead.

She had a big school bell that she rang when she wanted me to come home. Ding ding ding..."Better go home," the kids would say, laughing at me. "Your mother's ringing...you've gotta go now...." I remember the dress with recipes. Orange and black and brown: add one cup of flour, one teaspoon salt. Mother, why can't I remember?

"I'd like to know," a thin blonde average woman says, standing up and pulling her sweater down around her slim hips, "do you have any children...?"

"No," the fat woman says.

"Well, if you had children, and they wanted you to lose weight, would you?"

"No," the fat woman says.

"You wouldn't do that for your CHILDREN?" the woman says, incredulous. The audience is waving their hands...they all want to ask the fat woman questions. They all are incredulous.

I had a fat boyfriend once. His fat was so soft that he could pour himself into small clothes and look like a regular person but with fat seeping from every available opening—he ate three boxes of cereal each morning.

In Ethiopia, one dollar will feed five people for a week.

Mothers. What would any mother do for her child? Of course we know the stories...Mother lifts truck off baby—saves its life. The mothers that sang to their children in the lines to the gas chambers. The mothers that rock their starving children in Africa, hold them to their empty hollowed breasts, trying endlessly to soothe. The mothers who give all their money to their ungrateful children. Like my mother does for me. And that Iranian mother who worked every day for a pittance and gave it all to her son to buy his fancy clothes. The mothers who work all night, slave all day, to feed and clothe their children. And the children. Who leave home after all that and sometimes never come back. The ones who don't call. The ones who hate. Who are indifferent. The ones who turned their parents into the Nazis.... HERE they are! Hiding in that corner there...come out Mother. Come out Father. The ungrateful horrid little brats who want want want. The mothers' faces in the newsreels...feed them the faces say. Please feed my children.

My mother when we fought...the fights were ongoing...shrieking, door-slamming...my mother would say, clattering the silverware drawer like she was getting out a knife, "no wonder the kids don't like you in school! You aren't likeable!" and then she would retreat to the bathroom with a handful of sharp instruments, locking me out: she was really going to do it this time.

I can't remember, but so what, who cares. What does it matter whether you recall your entire childhood or not. Maybe I have Altzheimers disease.

When hypoglycemia first came out, my family each secretly decided they had it. "I can't eat potatoes," my sister explained, "I have hypoglycemia!"

"I've got to go home," my other sister said, "I'm hypoglycemic. You must have put sugar in the spaghetti sauce...because I'm dizzy...did you?"

"No.... A little wine," I said.

"You don't know how awful it is to have hypoglycemia," my sister said.

"Oh boy I sure know," mother called out. "I've got it. Dizzy? Tired?

Overeat? That's me all over. I've got it. I bet we all have it."

So what if I can't remember the daily life of being the youngest in my worried anxious family? We were all constantly on a diet. On a budget...our money never lasted through the month. We all loved salad with Italian dressing. We all had long hair. Why then do I feel I am blocking out a whole chapter of my life? Repressing an important part of my history? Why is it I am left feeling like I have Altzheimers disease?

Mother, mother, what could I do? I loved you, dearly, and yet, whenever we meet, whenever we met, our jaws clamped, our hearts were sore. But at night, age nine, I would lie awake thinking about you. Worrying that you were so unhappy...that I was the cause. Was I really? Poor mommy, with your dead husband, and all that guilt! Nowhere to put it and no one to blame...and how we blamed you. One of us would say, "you killed him." But how worn out those words are now. You killed him. Look at it this way, mother, he was only one human, made of flesh who took his own life, a no-fault divorce sort of death—think of it this way, and then you will see the insignificance of our father's little dying. Or perhaps my own illness, of all our meager passing one day or another.

* * * * * *

Let me get reacquainted here briefly. I show a space to represent time lost. There is no Donahue spot to fill it in, no story of a hot night in Spain...blank space will have to do because I have been ill you see, once again, ill and then busy and this piece has sat in a closet looking ugly and getting further away from me every day. First I put the Christmas lights on top of it, in the closet space, I knew where it was—I just had to put the tree trimmings away. They were driving me crazy at the kitchen table. Then two new Pampers that had fallen out of the box and I couldn't find the box so I threw them in the closet. Landed on top of this piece, this novel grovel, hovel, whatever. I opened the closet door days later and thought I would move the writing. I reached in for the patchy-looking pages, old hairless dog that it is, and I felt this queer sensation. When I turned around sure enough, there was a man standing in my kitchen.

* * * * * *

Reagan has done something to this country. He has changed where no other person has been able, he has conservatized those who were unconservitable; he has wiped away nearly all signs of difference. We stand, the

American people, together in a great arcade hall, shooting stars, dressed alike, loathing all the right things: poverty, Communism, education. And poor dressers. I always considered myself unchangeable but now I go to the arcade. And I hate poverty, and I dress every morning with caution...would this REALLY go with the green? Are these the right slacks for the occasion? No but I mean REALLY????

So I was buying a new skirt in an elegant store when the shoemaker who once had my boots for two months and never fixed them, came in. "Well hello," I called out, cheery because I was spending fifty dollars on a linen skirt, the kids were in the car, I had missed the Donahue shoe...who knows? Maybe my mother is right: maybe Donahue DOES upset me. "How's business?" I asked.

"Very slow," he said. He had a beard and mustache and long blonde hair—not too long—but nicely long, and he wore teddy bear clothes...the sort like corduroy pants, Dunham boots, soft foresty-green sweater, grey turtleneck underneath; he looked cozy.

"Well, slow is it? Maybe I should bring my boots back...."

"Bring them back. I'll fix them right away," he said.

"Really?"

Then he followed me out of the elegant store and into the street. "Is that your car?" he said. I said it was. "Don't forget to bring in those boots," he said.

I said I wouldn't. Then I sailed home with the children in the back seat calling "mama? mama? mama?" because that is so far the only word they know.

I took in my boots. And he fixed them and when I went back to pick them up he said, "We should have lunch sometime." Or something like that. And I nearly passed out with joy; he was very cute: I can't explain—where does one begin? It has been so long.

But when I got home the kids had torn up the kitchen. Regina was watching them, and she had fallen asleep in a chair and they had torn out all the stuffing from pillows, had emptied drawers, the little boy was running through the living room holding the turkey carver: fortunately it is dull; the little girl (these are my children of whom I speak so distantly) was without her diaper; she was peeing quietly in a corner. "Mama? mama? mama?" she said. She waved once and then looked down at herself.

I picked Regina up into my arms and danced through the kitchen. "Somebody likes me," I said, "somebody cute likes me," but really what I was saying after so long was, "I finally like people again." Then I thought

I'd move my novel so it wouldn't get hurt and the funny feeling came over me and I turned around and there he was, the shoemaker, standing in my kitchen...whatever for?

"How about tonight?" he said.

"Oh, this place is a mess," I answered, I was, well who cares what I was, so what.

"I've seen plenty of messes before," he said and picked up my son. "What's that?" the shoemaker said. "What's that? A knife? You could hurt somebody with that," he said. "You could hurt somebody...."

Whew! Was that an understatement.

* * * * * *

I don't want to leave out Ali Mahzlehanii, a Tehran, Iran, newspaper artist. I met him in a bakery called Ali Baba's in the seventies. He was dressed in a thin suit and had a sheaf of papers with him. "I am sitting here?" he said standing beside my table.

"Oh sure," I said. I had been in Iran for a month and knew very little farci.

"You are Amreecan."

"Yes. What's your name?"

"I am this...this." He showed me the papers.

"You draw?"

"I am draw, yes."

"What's your name...?"

"Oh yes, Ali Mahzlehanii. I am artist. What you call?" He pointed to my small glass of tea.

"That's tea."

"I am artist, yes. I draw and draw. Look." He unfolded the papers and showed me a girl sitting on a flower with a balloon above her head that said "MAKE LUV NOT WAR" and there was a man in the picture with his arms spread out. "This is good," Ali said and patted the paper. The waiter brought him a glass of tea and he paid for mine as well. "You are veddy veddy nice girl," he said. "Some nice...some...you are telling me...."

"Some aren't so nice," I helped.

"Yes. Botttttt, you, veddy nice."

"Well, thank you," I said, sucking a sugarcube.

"Look. In Iran we are this..." and he put a sugar cube in his mouth and picked up his glass of tea, drinking it through the sugar. "You see what I am telling you?"

I said yes, I could see.

When I went back to where I was staying in Tehran, I left Ali in the office of the *Teharn Journal* where he worked. There were some other men there who were impressed that he could speak some English and that he had discovered an American. "You are going," he said, smiling at me. "Yes, yes you are going," and he seemed quite pleased. Later that night however he had managed to find where I lived and when I answered the door, there he was, still smiling. "I am Ali Mahzlehanii," he said, stepping inside.

"I remember," I said.

"I here...bottt, because you veddy nice girl. Annnnnnnd, out..." he pointed out the window,"...veddy bad."

My sister came up and stood behind me. "What's going on?" she said. It was her house I was visiting. She and her husband both worked for the Peace Corps.

"Hello. I am Ali Mahzlehanii."

"Is he bothering you?" my sister said. I shook my head no. "Because if he is all you have to say is your father is burning in Hell and he'll go away. It works on everybody over here. I'll teach it to you in farci later...."

"I am Ali. Hello." Ali held out his hand and my sister said, "This is my house." For a moment I was unsure of what I should do and then Ali, still smiling, said: "I now going. I see you."

"Maybe you could come back tomorrow?" I said. He continued to smile as we closed the door.

On the hot sultry desert nights of Iran. Once, I let Raza Shaheem, one of my lovers, take me by taxi through the wild mountain roads way out-side of Tehran, on and on endlessly, and at last the taxi driver, leering at me in his rear mirror, let us out by the side of a cliff. It was dark. We looked down below, thousands of feet straight down, and along the ledge were lights and when my eyes became accustomed to the dark there were brown shapes...huts and children...I could hear voices but I couldn't ask Shaheem Reza what they said because he didn't speak English at all and he refused to listen to my pidgin farci. It was almost supernatural, as if we were on the edge of a witches' conven...looking down into the brown Asian night.... I was so afraid we would have to try and climb down the cliff...there didn't seem to be any other way down...but then along the road came a Citroen car, like a little orange jeep, no top, and stopped beside us. "Get in," the driver said in English to me. We climbed in and continued on through the night, Reza sitting in the back seat with me, clipping my finger nails matter of factly, feeling the rough spots in the dark, saying nothing to the driver. Just before the sun rose completely, the driver parked his car, and we climbed out. Reza was tired but I had slept on his shoulder. It was dim out...things were visible but it was not yet morning. There was a door near us, and we went through it. It seems now that the door was cut into the side of a mountain. Inside was dark and smelled of Iranian food. There were men suddenly all over Reza... "Salam! Salam!" they were shouting...hello, hello. They sat us down on tiny stools, and we ate some sort of strange stew. Reza talked for hours with them...a man handed him a large wad of bills; he looked at me then, pocketing the money, kissed me. A woman came into the room; she was all bent over and wrapped in their traditional raggy clothes, a chedora on but not covering her face...pants under her skirt, soft ragged slippers. She motioned for me and then hit me on the arm in a cheerful way, urging me to follow her. The men watched. "Reza...," I said. He walked out of the hut. The woman finally gave up on me and brought out a hooka from another room. The men pointed to me.... "REZA!" I called louder. I opened the door and saw him climbing into the car with the driver. "REZA!! REZA!!" I screamed, and ran after him. Once in the car, we all sped away, Reza at first angry and then laughing and throwing his arms around me. "HA HA HA!" the driver called from the front seat. They were very pleased with the whole thing.

Ali Mahzlehanii wanted one thing and that was for me to marry him so he could get to America. We sat together in one of the foreigners' bars drinking glasses of beer. Most Iranians don't drink because of their religion but Ali was willing to do anything to please me. "Obi Joe, aurah," he would say when we were seated. "Beer please, waiter," and the waiter would look at Ali disapprovingly and I would notice but Ali would not. "You see," he'd begin, taking the salt and pepper shakers in his hands, "Her is you." And he put down the pepper. "Andddddd...this is Ali," and he shook the salt. "You are going going going—this is okay. I am okay." The salt tilted in his hand, as if he were waving goodbye to the pepper. "Boddddddd, Ali is not going going. You are going going. Ali is...here."

I drank my beer. "Aurah? Can I have another one?" I called.

"You always come back ALI, yes? You see?"

"I see," I said. I patted the salt shaker. "Hi Ali," I said to it.

"Yes, yes. You are going going...this is good this is okay. I am Ali. Butttttttt you come to Ali, okay?" He was moving the pepper all over the table now, his eyes on the path he was making; then he let the pepper stop beside the salt and drained his beer. "Make love...not war," he said and smiled at me.

Reza was always trying to sell me for a couple of bucks. Whenever he pushed me into a car and climbed in behind me, carrying a fingernail file and a hairbrush, I knew I was in for another struggle. They were terrifying experiences yes, but I always escaped unharmed. One night he dragged me up four flights of stairs to an empty apartment where three large pale men lay on the floor smoking opium from a hooka. None of them spoke a word of English but the same old transaction occurred between them and Reza Sheheem. He brushed my hair in front of them, and kissed me, I adored him for some reason: I thought he was so cute, and then he stepped back away from me and they handed him a parcel of bills and moved toward me. "REZA!" I shouted, knocking over the hooka. Reza slipped down the stairs and the men circled around me. "REZA!!! You bastard," I yelled. I plunged through the ring of fat men and rushed downstairs. It was late at night; Reza had disappeared. After that I wouldn't let him see me anymore. He sat under my window, his face tragic and his hands clasped behind him. And waited. He stayed there for two days but I wouldn't come out. Sometimes I drew the curtain aside and looked at him, equally tragically, but I never went outside. My sister said, "Why's that guy hanging around in the kuche?" A kuche is an alley. "Shall I call the police or is he one of the creeps you're always picking up?"

Tehran is the city that I lived in with my sister but we often took little excursions to neighboring cities and once we went all the way to Shiraz, where the women don't wear black veils to cover their faces but brilliantly colored ones, that fall all the way to their feet. Purple and pink silk ones. And on the way to Shiraz we stopped in Gomn, the city of gold, where there is a huge dome made of gold that shone in the sunlight. We weren't supposed to get out of the car there because it was a holy city and the Iranians might have gotten angry but we got out anyway and walked a little way down a dusty street. There were things flying through the streets it was so windy, and along the edges of the town there were huge salt deposits...the roads were just pathways through the desert; it was all very wild. When we were in Shiraz we stopped at a palace-like hotel where the walls and ceilings were covered with tiny mirrors and the floors were hand inlaid...but we ended up spending the night in a flea-bag hotel where everybody slept in the same room and nearly in the same bed; there were hard mattresses all over the place. We heard noises during the night and my sister slept with her shoes on. The country was so

unbelievable...the desert and the mosques, the huge churches all hand-
made by slaves; the churches were covered in gold with tunnels
underground from the palaces to the churches so that the royal women
need never see the light of day. The tunnels were for times past, of
course, but the women in Iran were covered from head to toe when they
went outside and they never went anywhere alone and they married who
they were told to marry and they never smoked or drank or cursed or
walked beside their husbands: they walked ten paces behind as Reza
Shaheem tried to teach me to do.

He stopped me on the street and hit me. Then he walked on and I stood
there crying and wondering where we were...then he motioned for me to
come. I rushed ahead to catch up and he grabbed my shoulders and
rooted me to the spot. Then he moved ahead again. Then motioned for
me. Then he threw his arms in the air in exasperation when I hurried to
stand beside him again. "Koocheloo," he said stroking my hair. Means
honeybunch. "Koocheloo." It was the only time he ever spoke to me
directly.

When I left Iran I didn't leave any easier than I had lived there. I put
my yellow suitcase on a plane going to Moscow and I got on a plane
headed for Syria. It was all accidental. I had met a pilot...a handsome
pilot who flew for the Syrian Arab Airlines and while we were talking and
walking toward the terminal, he said casually, "I'll take you up with
me...have you ever been to Arabia?" I said my plane was already leaving
for London with my bags on board. "We can send for them," he said, not
urgently, but very casually...as if none of it was of any importance. "We'll
go to Damascus. You can ride with me, in the cockpit. I'll even let you
drive! Ha, ha, ha!"

Oh buzzards, the lot of them. Buzzards hanging over my body, wait
ing for me to give in so they can come in a horde and pick my bones.
Great black birds with an enormous wing span...once in Turkey I saw
them swooping down on a baby goat that hadn't yet died....

My love, my lovers. The heat of the nights and the cold of the rejec-
tions, and the pain of childbirth and sorrow of death and the joy of oneself. Thank God we all have ourselves.

World traveler. Risk taker, meat eater, pathfinder, love seeker, those
all fit my description. I am that. Yes, I was at seventeen living in a com-
munal situtation for disturbed adults, and that's where I met my rich
boyfried, and where I saw people who believed they were horses. And
ones who thought they were presidents. I met a girl there who carried
around a clay head calling it Sidney. At sixteen, I ran away from home

with a girlfriend and spent an eerie night in a murderer's mansion in Greenwich, Connecticut. Murderer? Yes, we were convinced he killed his family. He picked us up hitch-hiking and took us to his stone fortress, showed us to our room three flights up, with a balcony overlooking the gardens. He was a nervous man, who wouldn't be after what he'd obviously done? "Eat whatever you like, girls," he told us, as we stood in his massive kitchen. "All the help is away for the week...my son will be returning...soon." He then took us to a room where there were photographs on stands. "That's my wife," he said, and pointed to a young woman. "That's my daughter...." We said, "Oh!" but we were interested in finding dinner. "They will be back...soon." We laughed and looked at each other, my friend and I...the guy was an old coot we figured. He left us in the kitchen and we opened both refrigerators but there was nothing in either one.

"That's weird," I said, opening empty cupboards. "Maybe there's a freezer in the basement...." We went down the stone stairs and found several freezers filled with brown packages. "We could have hamburgers...let's see...this one says..." and I tried to read the writing on the paper: "Looks like it says the dog...weird." And we laughed. Oh ha ha ha ha, we said, and read another one: "Anna...that says 'Anna'...There are big packages. Let's get out of here!..."

We turned around and saw something at the top of the stairs move. For the rest of the evening the man had disappeared. We went to bed in our huge room, and locked the door. "I can't sleep...listen to the barking...." Outside our window dogs were howling...then someone was turning the doorknob...slowing...slowly...but it was locked...they turned and turned...pressure on the door...then whoever it was went away. We stayed up all night in terror, and once more someone turned the knob and went away.

Yes, me who has escaped certain death, crawled through incredible disasters without a scratch, yet it is I. And what insights do I now have? I would sooner stay home, I guess, than go to Bulgaria, where I was almost arrested incidentally, for not having a visa and it was a good old American twenty-dollar bill that saved me from rotting in a Bulgarian jail. I would sooner stay home; I would rather watch Donahue at nine than ride a black horse along the shores of the Caspian Sea: I was not alone mind you, a Baghadadian followed me on a white steed.... I would not do it again. "Killer dogs in there!," the Baghadadian shouted to me when I rode my horse through the water..."Stay away. Stay away. The dogs...."

In fact, today they had a radical priest on who said God could be a woman or a man, that sex was only one sin and not THE sin and a woman called the show and screamed, "You are a pervert Mr. Priest. You are no priest, you are a pervert and a devil in sheep's clothing...."

Donahue scratched his head.... "Well," he said, pausing, "the woman is certainly entitled to her opinion...and Father, what...what...how are you feeling right now after this onslaught?"

Never again to the French quarter of New Orleans with my rich boyfriend who had by then gone completely mad.... Where we sat on the dock and watched enormous water rats come and go under the boards. And he said, "It's not all just beer and pizza...." And I said, "I'll eat whatever you do. I'll go wherever you go," but it was too late: I couldn't follow him there...he was determined to leave me behind. I'll never ride another plane again...once we lost an engine over Frankfurt. Once my window cracked 35,000 feet in the air...once I flew over Syria in a cockpit with a drunk pilot...and I will never go by hovercraft to the Isle of Wight again: no, I'll stay home. I prefer now a quieter crowd. Say, for instance, the crowd in the NBC studio during a Donahue show taping.... The worst of them saying to an Indian immigrant: "Hey listen...I think if you don't love this country then why the Hell are you here? Why don't you just go back to wherever you came from if you don't love this country?" And the enthusiastic clapping and Donahue saying, "Yeah, but where are you from?"

"Ohio."

"No, I mean originally? Where are your parents from...where are your grandparents from? Ireland? Italy?"

"We're Italian."

"I see," he says. "So should you go back to Italy?"

"No," the woman says, confused..."No, because I love my country...."

"Which country?" he asks her. And people titter.

"I am always loving you," Ali had said to me, when we stood together in the Tehran airport. "You are going going I am always loving you. They say hello Ali what you want? I tell them I love but she go like this," and he soared his hand through the air. "I am waiting for you." I sometimes think of where he is now...does Khomeini affect his life? Is he still alive? And I know I will never know, and so what. Who cares?

* * * * * *

Yes, shoes, shoes, shoes that I could have repaired for free!!! Imagine! Free service on shoes! And I have no shoes. He fixed my boots, we agreed in a laughing sort of way on a bill of fifty cents, payable when we quit seeing each other: isn't love exciting? Doesn't it beat all? And don't you think it is elusive? One minute it is there, sitting on your lap like a bag of popcorn at a theatre and the next, it is out the door, be right back I have to go to the ladies room, but there it goes, out the double doors, into the dark wet streets, leaving with the jujubees and buttery flavor no salt. Wait! Wait love, wait...down an alley, into a passing car, slumped in the backseat, making out with someone else. You think you can do without...then you think you will die without. You think it will come without asking, and then you think you have to force it out of wherever it is. And it's there, and it pops up, and disappears, and reappears and when you finally have it right where you want it, in your room late at night with the lights out and the futon rocking under the weight of it, you realize what you REALLY want is to BE loved, or to FORGET love, or to go to sleep. The aching gnawing agonizing feeling that is love in its peak is driving you insane...it keeps you up it won't let you live, you live only to be in love, you live only because you have forgotten everything, even where your boots are. Let me remind you. They are with Charles, the shoemaker.

* * * * * *

Donahue, upon moving his show to New York, took the TV audience through the motions he was going through when he first came to the new studio. "And here is the main door...see that? NBC. Donahue at nine...and through these doors here...oops, 'scuseme, okay, through these doors here...." He had on a New Yorker's black leather jacket. The kind you see Yoko Ono wearing on the cover of *People*...or like John and Yoko used to wear posing outside the Dakota in New York. It is a sign of a tough skin. A brutal shell, unbreakable. Oh well, the world is shot.

"Here are the mikes and the stage here where I'll stand and grind out the questions that are so...so...essential to our society...the whys, the wheres...the audience, you the audience I should say, will sit here...." His back is to the camera.... I watch the creases in his black leather coat, the...what are they called...the cracks, the sign of a coat not just purchased, the sign that he has been a leathery-skinned man longer than I imagined. His wife has that cute crunchy voice. When I was little I worshipped "That Girl." I always wanted to be Marlo Thomas.

The audience appears suddenly on the screen. Everyone begins to cheer. I look through them, maybe I'll see someone I know...maybe one of them will look familiar...but they are a New York crowd; unlike the Chicago crowd they seem wealthier, less like the average and more like the upper crust—interested in seeing this odd man in his black leather jacket. He takes his jacket off: "Welcome to the new Phil Donahue Show," he says. He's wearing a sweater. God, he puts it on like Mr. Rogers, "and we'll be right back," he says. He lifts his microphone. The crowd continues to clap. They are still mostly women but they have on furs, can you believe it? —furs instead of polyester, and elegant purses and shoes and chunky jewelry, and pearls. I want suddenly to be there. I want to be in Studio Eight or wherever it is, waving frantically to Phil, wearing beautiful things.

Hello Phil, welcome," I want to be there too but I can hear the babies crying; they've thrown all their graham crackers out of their room and are standing at the gate, shrieking.

"MAMA MAMA MAMA!" I am glued to the commercial. "Really satisfies you...diet pepsi...FREEEEEEE!" It's that word free that gets me. It's the word that gets me crying. Shit, wasn't I that way too? Once, I mean?

Of course we all know why he moved because there was a big write-up in *The Star* magazine about it: Marlo said either you come to New York or you can kiss our marriage goodbye Philly. I wonder if she calls him Philly. Philip? And does he grill her in bed?

But what about that, Marlo? Was that good darling? Or is it the fact that we're so used to each other that we automatically think it's good without really looking into ourselves? He might say: "Far be it for me, Sweetheart, to criticize such a firm and wonderful actress as yourself, but were you faking that swoon? Was our love-making perfect? There are some questions that come to mind. And I'll be right back...."

I think my novel is deteriorating.

Yes, the reason Phil Donahue moved his successful Chicago show to New York I think, is because his wife, Marlo Thomas, was unable to live in Chicago (all her connections were in New York) and Phil is wild about her and willing to give up almost anything to be near her; she's probably unsure if she wants the marriage to continue anyway: she has that cigar-smoking father who cares about children doesn't she...yes, so he has moved the whole sheebang to New York where according to the *Star* newspaper he has failed twice before to capture the rawness, the realness, of American women on their morning break. I thought the Chicago women were much more American. New York women are too foreign, don't you think?

Charles, the shoemaker. Weird eyes. Blue or green. Lines all around them, blonde hair, beard, moustache, thin, five eleven, age 37, reputation? Miser. And love. Does love enter into it or is it as usual, a combination of lust and loneliness?

Van Gogh had troubles too. Ostracised, dirty, lonely...Mozart, he was always in bed with somebody....

So now I have quit watching television all together...no news, no Donahue. I am retreating into myself. Into something...I am Rachel Welch's daughter coming into and out of a cocoon in my latest movie. I am the victim of multiple personalities, with a darkened face on Phil's show, with my psychiatrist in the audience saying, "Yes, she has thirty-three different personalities. Well, thirty-four, counting herself." I am a starving Ethiopian child, clutching soft brown sandy dirt, holding onto my dead mother. I am the cat I keep forgetting to feed. I am my children, my shoemaker.

Spring is here. The snow is melting off the roof. It falls in huge clods, anything underneath is crushed. The icicles are gone. I take out my sister's skis and put them on. They are wooden. I wear them into the woods, push-push-push glide. Push glide. I trudge up a hill and turn around. I bend my knees. I am going to go down. I am sure of one thing...I am going to go down. In the woods it is silent. Earlier today I dropped my twins off at a day care center and my older daughter off at her school and my shoemaker disappeared into his messy shoe shop to glue heels and sew leather and curse his customers, his machines. His green blue-grey eyes are very clear, the skin around them is soft and lined: he is handsome. His own boots are a wreck.

I put my dog out. I let my cat creep onto the clean counter and look furtively for food I don't have. I ate peanut butter on bread and then, cool as ice in my Diet Pepsi, I sat down at this machine and tapped lightly on the letters. Hummmmmm. The machine clatters to me. Hummmmmm. It is my sex. It is my center. It is, it is. Gauguin left his wife and children to paint. I leave everything. I leave it all behind me in my head and go into myself...not to paint or to give the world anything...but just to step away from the reality...and become disembodied. Just until noon when I have to pick the twins back up at the day care. They will have eaten their macaroni and hamburger soup. They will have fresh diapers on and be rosy from the heat of the room. They will take their chilly bottle full of milk and lie down in the dark room upstairs and sleep. Just like I am doing at this table...a calm retreating into the world of vacancy.

I read an article mentioning Donahue.... It said there were no men left like him...that he was not macho enough. That when women were offered two men: "Who would you rather leave a party with?", the article asked a survey of women..."Phil Donahue or Clint Eastwood?" Ninety-eight percent said Clint Eastwood. That amazed me. I thought everyone LOVED Phil Donahue.

Nobody loved Van Gogh either. Except his brother, Theo. I think maybe the more wonderful you are the more people detest you. Probably has something to do with jealousy. Although far be it for me to say anything against Mr. Eastwood. After all, I loved the movie he made with the gorilla. It was a little confusing but good, nonetheless. He lived with his nutty mother and a big gorilla and he would go at night to this bar and listen to this woman sing whom he seemed to be interested in, but whenever she came over to his table he would slam his beer bottle and walk away. Then she would follow him and get in his old beat up truck and the gorilla would lick her and she would try to get Clint Eastwood to talk to her. In the end of the movie I think they were together but it was hard to tell because they were both very hip and didn't say much.

I rather suspect my shoemaker is like that. He is quiet except when I say something, then he repeats it...it's very erotic. Like this: "Charles?" And he says, "Charles?" And I say, "Charles, look..." and I hold up a painting from a book of Impressionists and he says, "Look what sweetheart?"...and I am limp with affection. I like to hear my own words poured back into me.

I was with the shoemaker for almost a week before we actually made love. It was an eon. He'd come over after work and knock on my door. The children I sent to bed early; I had cleaned up the little kitchen and would then be sitting in one of the red kitchen chairs I painted to match the Christmas tablecloth. "Oh well hello," I'd say.

"Oh well hello," he'd repeat. My heart would race. He would look straight at me with his cool blue green-grey eyes and I would look away because who knows? Maybe experience shows in one's face...maybe my eyes would tell him how *lived* I am. How all emotions and all experiences from here on in are merely repeats of what has gone on before. Although I'd never known a Charles before, nor a shoemaker. I thought shoemakers were something from the nineteenth century. I thought there were only a few left in Holland, wooden shoe repairmen. I liked the fact that he was in such an obscure business. That his small shop on the corner of a quiet street was full of strange pieces of leather and bits of the sides of ladies' shoes. I suspect my father would have approved of him. God knows my father would have died a thousand times over if he knew of my wild life.

"Do you want some tea?" I said. He took his soft blue parka off and laid it over the top of my great round-backed wicker chair.

"That would be nice," he said. He adjusted his wire rimmed glasses, and handed me a pin which said "BREAD NOT BOMBS." I put the pin on the counter and turned on the tea water. My cat leaped up and sniffed the pin.

"I've got to buy cat food," I said. Charles sat down and stared at me. He had his beeper with him. A beeper is a thing that looks like those old transistor radios we used to have in ninth grade at the lake. We took them with us swimming—my girlfriend and I—we'd lie on the beach in our HORRIBLE two-piece suits and try to tan but I never got brown. I got some freckles and my thighs would get red.

"I'm on call," Charles said. I gave him his tea. His beeper made a whoosh noise and then a woman's voice came on.

"Hospital to beeper ten. Dr. Bill please call the lab. The bilirubin count you want is in. Beeper ten, please call the lab..."

Charles turned the beeper down. "Why's she doing that?" he said.

"What?" I asked.

"What?" he repeated. I sipped my tea. After we had finished our drinks we then went into the living room and I put on the tape of Mozart and we sat together on the couch and he kissed me and said, "God you are pretty," which should have made me elated but I was after all BEAUTIFUL—not pretty. "So, Sweetheart," he said, as a statement.

"Mmm," I said. He put his hand on my face and pressed the skin of my cheeks back, pressed the tip of my nose, put one rough finger in my mouth. "Mmm," I said again.

"Mmm? Mmm what?" he said. It was all very erotic. He came over every evening and we did the same thing. Monday. Tuesday. Wednesday. Thursday. Friday. He always had his beeper with him; it usually went off in a whoosh sound and a woman's voice would come on saying someone should go somewhere, do something...and he would tell me I was pretty and we sometimes had two cups of tea before we retired to the couch to kiss.

Once in a while the beeper woman would say "Beeper fifty-one, code three...woman fallen downstairs, possible head injury...code three," and he would say, "Shit," and stand up and put on his soft parka and say "Goodbye Sweetheart" and walk out to his car, and drive away.

He is an ambulance driver, and studying to become a paramedic. He once said when the beeper called his number and he had to leave, "Gotta put on my superman suit...."

A friend of mine said scornfully of the ambulance rescue squad, "Oh they all think they're Marcus Welbys without a degree. You see them running all over town looking important."

"Charles, that feels good," I said when he ran one hand along my body, down my hand-knit cotton weave sweater, down my jordache jeans size thirty, almost to my argyle socks that needed washing.

"Charles that feels good?" he repeated. "Good, huh?" I could hardly stand the way he did that, touching me and feeding my words back to me; it hit me like Percodan or some heavy syrupy drug...it made me lean back into the couch, wishing he would hurry up and and...

"So it's not sex women crave as much as the loving embrace, the bouquet of flowers, the dinners with candlelight...am I right in this assumption? Let's see what the survey shows. Slide six please?" Donahue looks up at the TV on the wall of Studio Eight in New York and they showed the survey. "Seventy-eight percent of all the women surveyed say YES, sex is unimportant...we want more affection, more displays of emotion, less...how shall I say it?...get on and get off method." The audience laughs. I shake my head and lift my bottle of Diet Pepsi Free. One calorie. Free. "Do you agree with this? I mean, you're the ones they're talking about...let's let YOU decide." He holds his microphone to a woman in a neat sweater and pearls around her neck. She wears matching pearl earrings and has on dull pants.

"I want more flowers, candy, dinners, whatever...I want hugs and kisses, I want to be SHOWN that he loves me by what he does not just an 'oh I love you hun, roll over,' you know...and" she pauses to laugh. The audience is strangely quiet. I tense up in front of my own little TV. "I'm sick of just sex without love."

Donahue pulls the microphone back: "So your husband should be more attentive to your needs?"

"Yes," she shakes her silvery blonde hair affirmatively.

"I see...uhh, does he kiss you good morning?"

"Oh yes," she says.

"Does he call when he's going to be late getting home? Does he kiss you when he gets home at night?"

"Oh sure...."

"Do you go out?"

"Oh, we go out," the woman says. Her pearls look real. I recall almost getting a strand of pearls with my rich boyfriend in New Orleans once. He had them in his thin tanned hands; he almost pulled out his American Express card, and then I said, "I'd rather have an emerald," and he put them down on the counter.

"Yeah, let's split," he said.

"So your husband isn't one of these let's have sex and forget the rest, kind of guys?"

"Oh no."

"Okay,...well, uhh," Donahue moves down the aisle while he speaks: "What is it then? Is it candy you all want? I mean, chocolate-covered cherries or what?" The audience rustles excitedly. A woman stands up and grabs the microphone from Donahue's outstretched hand.

"I want love and you get love by giving love...by making him nice meals and looking nice for him...not being a nag...not leaving the house a mess...you know men need to be shown that you care, too.... I mean,...am I right?" Some people clap. I drink more Diet Pepsi Free and wish wish wish that I could be in that audience. I wish I had pearls that matched my earrings. I wish I had not wished for an emerald when I could have had pearls.

* * * * * *

Charles told me about his mother one night. We were on our second cup of tea and I wasn't sure if maybe he was getting bored with my kisses; he had touched my knee once and then stood up and walked around the room. "Yeah, my mother was a wonderful woman," he said, sitting back down and bobbing his cranberry cove tea bag up and down in his cup. "Hardly ever complained, brought up all the kids, kept the house neat and clean, baked bread. I was her favorite." I smiled. Charles looked very alone all of a sudden. I wanted to put my hand on his knee but I hesitated. "She died oh, eight years ago...ten, huh?... He let his breath out in a quick sigh.

"Did they ever fight?" I asked. I always like to know if people fight or not. Somewhere in my mind I'm afraid I'm the only person in the world who gets mad.

"Oh yeah, they fought. The kids would always hide on the stairs and listen to them. Yeah, they fought. Well, my mother hardly ever yelled at my father. He was the one did all the yelling." Charles shook his tea bag.

"How did she die?" I said.

"Well, breast cancer, sort of...she had breast cancer and they removed her breast...then I guess it spread...anyway, she never complained about it. I didn't even really know she was sick for a time.... I remember the day she passed away—" He stopped and I thought he might be crying. It looked as though there were tears in his eyes. It was strange to me...seeing a man emotional about his mother.

"Was she blonde?" I asked, stupidly.

"No. She had brown hair...like yours." Charles looked at me then and I was quite sure he had tears in his eyes. They were greyer, and he looked so unutterably sad and alone. "And my father passed away a few years after that on the very day she had." He took one of my hands and held it, turned it over, rubbed my fingertips. "She was a strong lady. You have strong hands," he said. "Then, after that, why there didn't seem any reason to go home any more after she passed away.... I quit seeing the family, quit visiting.... I really ought to go to Montreal and visit all my cousins...haven't seen them in ages...."

I rocked back and forth in the red kitchen chair. "I couldn't stand to lose my mother," I said. "You must be lonely at Christmas...what do you do on the holidays?" He looked at me and I thought he looked angry for a minute. I have a habit of saying rather brutal things.

"Oh I go up to my sister's, sometimes...for Christmas. I remember Christmas at my grandmother's house. We'd take apples and core them and put brown sugar on the middle and set them on the big wood stove in the kitchen...don't know whatever happened to that stove...and we'd play all through the big old house. My father and mother would come in and my father would go off with my uncles while my mother'd pitch right in helping my grandmother...and there'd be so much food on the table...never saw so much food. Homemade pies and bread and in the wintertime, we'd have pea soup and jonny cake; summers it would be strawberry shortcake." I watched Charles' face. He was cheering up.

"Do you want more tea?" I asked. His beeper went off.

"Beeper fifty-one...code three. Possible seizure...." And he put on his coat.

"Goodbye Sweetheart," he said. I watched him climb into his silver volkswagon with EMERGENCY MEDICAL TECHNICIAN stamped on its hood and drive away. Pea soup and jonny cake. The Shoemaker and I were very different. When I was growing up we had spaghetti and salad. My mother had red wine. And she always put a lot of red wine in the spaghetti sauce. We'd have the table all set, with a white table cloth and candles lit and wine glasses...then we'd eat and fight and at the end of the evening there was spaghetti sauce stained on everything and wax from the candles dripped all over. My sister and I would take the burning candles and drip the wax onto our outstretched palms. There was something excruciatingly painful and wonderful about that feeling. The hot wax dripping onto my skin, making round pools all over my hand...and then we would show our mother and she would scream, "OOOHH don't do that! It's not good for you! It looks like leprosy!" and we would shriek. The tablecloth would have wax all over it. The candlesticks would look like they had been dunked in wax. Or other nights, especially at the end of the month, we'd have no money and my mother would make tuna fish casserole which we all ate nervously because she had a phobia about tuna fish and then after we ate it someone would say they didn't feel good and my mother would pump us all with red wine or if she was out of that we might get sherry or vermouth. I don't recall ever having pea soup except maybe Progresso. We got a lot of Lipton Chicken Noodle from those packages. And Saltine crackers with unsalted tops. And liverwurst which was almost as bad as tuna fish. I still don't understand why my mother gave us liverwurst and then lay awake all night worrying about botulism.

The babies like the day care center. When I pick them up they have a fat look about them, as though they have been playing with someone else's toys and have temporarily turned into someone else's babies. They look up at me when I first come in, and their faces show nothing...then we recognize each other and they both begin to cry.

"There's mommy," the day care girl says. They call her a "caregiver" there. "They had fun," she says, and hands me the little girl. I take her outside into the spring day and put her in the car in her car seat. Then I go back in for my son. He is screaming. "There's mommy," the caregiver repeats. I pay her and we drive away. Other babies watch us from the window. I think briefly of stopping by Charles' store but then I don't because I don't want to spoil anything. I am afraid of doing much at all about him for fear of spoiling my delicate feelings. After so much torture in my life, I am chary with joy. Why, even my coughing blood has diminished since meeting the shoemaker.

Yes, how did it all turn around just like that? One wonders. Suddenly after years of obesity and sorrow, of crying into my futon and bleeding from all over, of dirty whimpering babies and awful illnesses and such poverty it would challenge Van Gogh, I am instantly in a pretty life. Almost bourgeoise. New car (gift from my mother), little rented house on a little ordinary street (even the woman with cancer next door has been out twice today walking her miniscule dog), lost thirty pounds suddenly (could be the disease...) and a lover, one with grey-green eyes who could, if I had any and they broke, fix my shoes....

* * * * * *

As it happened yesterday was March 11, the day my father died, twenty-six years ago. Gee whiz, you think I'd forget by now. No, every March 11, I think, well today's the day. How did he feel I wonder? There he was, in a little rented room in London, with the rain drizzling outside his small open window (the coroner said it was open) and his papers on Keats lying all about the room. His narrow bed where he would lay his narrow body every night, probably a chair somewhere, and his landlady, coming slowly up the stairs checking to see who would be in for tea? A stout woman, all the landladies in London are stout. They all drink pints of Newcastle Brown Ale at home in front of their coal fires. This was in the fifties when they still had coal. Now they use coke and the nice ladies have half lagers at the pubs on a night out. My father. He would probably have finished his day's work, he had just called my mother earlier and they had talked of going to Paris, he wanted to see France...he said his novel was not going well...in fact, it wasn't going at all, and the publishers who had advanced him such a large sum were on him to hurry. I wonder if he had anything to drink...there was a door naturally, to his room. The window...open...it was March 11, 1959...—or was it '58?—when he died. But so what? Who cares? It has been twenty-six years and surely by now I should have forgotten.

Yesterday, on March 11, 1985, I went to my doctor once again for my two-week check-up. "He'll see you now," the nurse said, coming into the waiting room to get me. I followed her obediently. One always feels like a child following its mother in these doctors' offices. You are so at their mercy. They can at any moment give you the terrible blow: "Yes, you're dying...maybe three months...four at the outside...." they can do with you what they will.... "Lie down, roll over...roll up your sleeve...give me your blood...your bone marrow...stop smoking...eating...drinking." They are the eternal parents by whom you must always abide. My doctor ushered me into his back study and sat down beside his desk. "How are you?" he asked me, looking through my files.

"Better," I said. "But see here? My finger is still funny...the nail is lumpy." He took my hand and held it gently in his...then he ran one finger very softly along mine...and stared at me. I let him.

"I think you're going to be alright," he said, still holding my fingers. Then we suddenly let go of each other; the rest of the visit was quiet. He wrote in his files on me, I watched him. All around my doctor's office are ducks and paintings of ducks and cups with ducks on them. Mallards. He hunts. This always bothers me about my doctor. I have often argued duck hunting with him.

"I can't sleep," I said.

"Okay," he said, taking his prescription pad.

It's funny...I get this way sometimes...when I'm creating. I lie awake at night...I fidgit a lot. I guess I'm wicked." Then I looked down at my boots that Charles the shoemaker had repaired for me and felt utterly embarrassed that I said that. He laughed and was silent.

When he tore off the prescription for me he said almost pouting, "Now don't smoke." And I went out. It was still spring outside. It was warm, my car was full of warm children all ready to burst out of their seats and clamber over me.

"Mommy, did you get me anything?" my daughter called as soon as I opened the door.

"Mama mama mama," the twins said. They were sticky from cupcakes. The inside of my new car was beginning to look like a wreck. When I pulled out, I imagined my doctor standing at the window of his study, looking at me. I imagined he was still thinking about my fingers.

That would have been cheering. The whole office visit was silent, slightly erotic, everything is slightly erotic since I began sleeping with the shoemaker, but all in all it would have been heartening to walk out of my beloved doctor's office with a prescription and a softly spoken "I think you're alright," from my doctor. But just as I was leaving, I had to drop off the sheaf of papers on my case with the nurse. My doctor had said "Here, give these to Linda," and I had taken them to the front desk. And the folder had fallen open and there was a letter from the nose and throat specialist.

"Dear Jeff, thanks for recommending me...I believe there is more to this than I am able to diagnose. I am a broncoscope specialist and have worked with lung biopsies for years; however, I don't have the machines here to do the work that I feel is needed. I believe I saw some bleeding below the trachea, and we should confer on who the patient should be referred to for a broncoscope study. The case is unusual."

"And so is the patient," I said aloud. The nurse was looking at me. "Is it all right if I read this?" I asked.

"I don't know," she said and took the file. Then I left and the children clamored on me in the car and shouted "mama mama" and I had to drive to the drug store and buy them all gum for being so good while I found out I was dying.

Charles once said to my dog, "Take care of your mama, she's precious." I will always from now on, forever into eternity, be a mama.

So now what? Religion? Gauguin died in Tahiti of leprosy. His whole house, according to Maugham, smelled of his rotting body, and the walls were covered with his paintings. He even painted after he went blind. What a genuis. I think they have brail typewriters. I should look into that in case my disease takes that sort of turn. But I don't think I can turn to God. Not that Gauguin did. He didn't turn to anyone. He hated. Van Gogh had Theo. Gauguin had his Tahitian teenager. Lautrec had his whores. Dylan Thomas had his shrieking wife. Sartre had De Beauvoir. That was in the great age. When writers and artists were wild with desire and genuis and lived on wedges of bread and soup lines. When they could stay with one another and work work work on what they loved. No one had to live on welfare.

The shoemaker is interested in going to Africa to help during this present famine. He says he has some medical skills and that he is writing up his resume. "Can you type?" he asks me one day, while we are sitting up in bed. The futon is littered with TROJAN packages, empty, I know it's sordid to talk about it, but one had to get into the feeling of the room.
    "I can type," I assured him.
    "I'd sort of like to type my resume sweetheart, for that Africa thing." I rub his arm. He sighs and pats my head roughly, turns away. "I've got to get that done...."
    Speaking of Africa, he took me to a movie last week, and it was "The Gods Must Be Crazy," about a tribe of bushmen and other African tribes and dispersed through the whole film was a silly love story about a blonde guy who fell down all the time. What struck me most about the movie was the audience watching it. They were shrieking with laughter most of the time and talking loudly through the most meaningful parts, of which there were, I admit, few.
    "Look at the butts! Look at the butts...oh jess!" I could hear all around me people shuffling in their seats, bending forward and laughing... "Looket there...everybody's buck naked!" On the screen a tribe of bushmen hurry through the sand carrying a Coke bottle. The whole movie made fun of Africans and the audience made fun of the movie and I felt very raw and humiliated for my race. I felt as though I had been in some sort of shameful show. When it was over, and the whole thing was out of focus and blurry so my eyes hurt, the room emptied out into the lobby where other theatres were letting out....
    "So you thought Solidary didn't really kill him? Probably just jealous that's all...." someone said.
    "You've got to see 'Witness.' It's all about this Amish kid...." I wandered toward the glass doors and saw myself in the reflection, alone, on a

planet of people; we were all congregating but...even though we had all come to the same point and were dressed alike and each had a mate with them, we were all by ourselves. I opened the doors and the cold air rushed in to me. Charles was further behind; I could see his reflection, too, and he appeared to be glaring at my back.

When I stood outside in the wintery almost spring, he came up from behind and said, "Leaving, Sweetheart?"

"No," I said, "I'm not leaving.... I was just waiting out here." He was rigid, his hands in his pockets. He began walking down the street.

"Well?" he said. I went along.

"Can we dance?" I asked.

"Sure, you wanna dance right here?" I said nothing. He was in a bad mood.

"Are you in a bad mood?" I said. He said he wasn't. I turned around and looked at all the people leaving the theatres. They went off in different directions, arms around each other, some of them were laughing. I saw one couple fighting.

"Are we going to go?"

"I said we would," he answered and marched on glumly. The wind was blowing and I had gone out with a light jacket. I always wear what looks best, not what the weather wants me to wear. I had on my linen skirt that I had bought when I first met him, and a pale sweater, light grey jacket, the boots he'd repaired.

"Look if you don't want to go then let's just forget it," I said. He was walking far away from me close to the shop windows, his hands were out of his pockets now, the wind was blowing his blonde hair back and I could stare into his beard, his moustache: I wondered what his face looked like.

"Do you want to go or not?" he said.

"Yes! Yes, I want to go dancing, but you always get mad when we dance."

"I'm not mad sweetheart," he said. Then we crossed the street and went into the place where every Saturday night they have a live band. My mind was still on the bushmen. Charles paid the cover charge while I looked around the room. Maybe an old boyfriend would be there ...maybe somebody I would recognize would come up to me...make me more important by acknowledging me.

"Hey there, Charles," somebody said.

"Hey there," he said back. I began to get depressed.

In Africa, according to this movie, there are actually people alive who don't know what Coke bottles are. They have never seen civilization.

They don't have houses to live in. I wonder—do the babies wear diapers? How many years do they breast feed? "Sweetheart!" Charles repeated, "What do you want to drink?" The waitress was standing at our table, looking bored.

"Oh...well...let's see...can I have a Lite beer...no,...a white wine, please?"

The waitress repeated what I said: "White wine?"

"Yes," I said.

"Do you have tea?" Charles asked. The waitress shook her head. "A Coke then," he said. I sighed. Charles doesn't eat meat, or milk. He lives a sparse quiet life with a lot of sports. He plays hockey and skis and skates and has volleyball and ambulance meetings. "I'd like to go to Africa," he said. I had a feeling I wouldn't be dancing much.

Really? Not me," I answered in a gay tone. I was trying to e upbeat. "No, I'd rather live in England...or Paris. I wouldn't mind visiting Africa. About three months. But I could never live in a hut for the rest of my life."

The waitress returned and set the drinks down. "Five dollars," she said.

In Iran people lived in the sides of mountains...under what seemed to be piles of sand, they would creep out when the Critroen passed, pouring exhaust into their world, and me sitting on the back of the open top car, holding my guitar and letting the wind carry my voice away, they would climb out of the sand dunes and watch us: they never waved. And in Turkey, the boatmen who rowed the foreigners from Europe to Asia, a river separated the countries, lived in the sides of hills. My rich boyfriend and I went home with one of the boatmen; his name was Bier Becken, and he spoke no English and we spoke no Turkish. The whole way to his house we tried to explain that we wanted a hotel.

"Big...house...very big house with many rooms," my rich boyfriend shouted, waving his arms to show all the rooms of a hotel. Beir Becken looked interested but said nothing. We ran along beside him, my camera bumping against my hip. After running through tiny Turkish streets in Istanbul, the boatman came up to a row of taxis parked along a curb. He shouted to one of them, the man got out and they hugged and we all climbed into the backseat, where there were five other Turkish boatmen. They began jabbering excitedly to Bier Becken. He looked serene and profound. He would answer them and then put his hand on my rich boyfriend's shoulder and smile. My boyfriend, Eddy, smiled back nervously and then in a low tone said, "I don't like this one bit." The taxi roared off, and we were pinned to the backseat.

"He's nice," I said of the boatman. "Maybe he knows we want a hotel."

"HOTEL!" Eddy shouted again. He always shouted when he spoke to foreigners. "Sleep...." He put his hands against his face and began to snore. "SLEEEEP," he repeated. The other boatmen in the backseat laughed and shook their heads.

"ENGUSHTA??" one of them said, pointing to me. Bier Becken motioned to the driver and the taxi lurched up onto the sidewalk. People jumped out of the way; they were all men walking along the streets now, going home from work, dressed alike, in raggy-looking shirts and soft raggy pants and slippers for shoes. Some of them had such big holes in their slippers you could see all of their toes. Our boatman leaped out of the taxi window and rushed to a little hut. He pointed to the taxi and a man came over and peered in the window. When he saw Eddy he smiled an enormous smile and showed all of his gold teeth. Then he gave Bier Becken two apples and he climbed back in the taxi window. It roared off again.

"Shit, this is a screwed up man! Where the hell is he taking us? WE WANT TO GO TO BED!" Eddy yelled. He was beginning to look the way he looked when he freaked out.

"It's all right, baby," I said, patting his knee.

"Don't tell me that," he whined.

"It's okay...this boatman seems nice. He's probably taking us to a hotel outside of town or something." The taxi stopped suddenly and we were all thrown into the back of the front seat. One of them got out. They all shouted goodbye and we moved forward again. The streets had been lit up at first with bars and flashing photographs of Turkish women and wailing music coming from restaurants. Now the streets narrowed and were dark. Everything outside was silent except for the sound of the taxi bumping ferociously over the cobbled streets. Bier Becken clutched his apples close to himself. Slowly we let off all the other boatmen; they got out in what seemed the middle of nowhere, disappearing into the black Asian night. Then we were let off and Bier Becken gave the driver some ripped paper money. Eddy leaned forward in his seat: "I'll get that," he said pulling out his wallet. The boatman pushed Eddy's hand away. He took us along a dank pathway through what felt like dirt and stopped at a hillside. I could see lights in the hill coming from hollowed-out places and women looking out. We went into a tiny door. The boatman's wife was in the middle of the room bent over a huge banana leaf on the floor mixing some awful thing in the center of the leaf. She looked up and dropped her spoon. He spoke rapidly to her. She stared at us and said something to Bier Becken. It sounded angry. He showed her the apples and she grabbed them. Then she was smiling and three other people appeared from a back space. They circled us and stared. "Howdy," Eddy said. I put my purse and camera down. They looked at my camera. "This ain't no hotel," Eddy said in a low tone to me. After a minute the whole place was full of Turkish men. Bier Becken's wife was slicing the apples and laughing. They began to point to my hand.

"Engushta?" they said and lifted up one finger.

"Say what?" Eddy said.

"Engushta? Engushta?" I shuffled a pack of cards I had with me and they all clapped. Then we sat down around the banana leaf and some of the people left. They motioned for us to dig in: they were grabbing the mushy stuff in the center of the leaf with their hands and shoving it into their mouths. I ate an apple slice. For most of the night they repeated the one word to us and kept pointing to my hand. We thought they might be asking if we were married so we shook our heads yes. They all laughed uproariously and repeated the word. Finally Bier Becken led Eddy to their only bed in another little room made of dirt, and we lay down together. The bed was so damp it was almost wet. Eddy wouldn't even take his shoes off. "I want to be able to run if necessary," he said. He slept with his hand in the pocket of his jeans where he kept his wallet. In the morning he tried to give them money but they acted very put out and wouldn't take any. They wanted my camera. Now when I think back, I realize how poor they were but at the time I didn't think much about it. I offered them my cards but they kept pointing to my instamatic. I wouldn't give it to them. We took a picture of Bier Becken sitting in his little wooden boat. I thought he had been smiling but when we got back to the states and had the film developed I looked at the picture and he was frowning, almost glaring into the sunlight. His face was lined and he was very thin. All the other boatmen had circled their boats around his and they were blurred in the background. The water was shimmering. "Look, here's Bier Becken, the boatman," I'd said, and showed Eddy the picture while we sat in a restaurant having dinner.

The shoemaker surprised me with how well he danced. When he finally pulled me onto the floor we danced for four or five consecutive songs and I noticed. They say you can tell if someone's good in bed or not by how well they dance. I floated back and forth to the music...I'm almost too Egyptian in my dancing, my arms take on movements of the sphinx, the bent elbows, and my body sways more than moves.... I looked at other people out there among us; most of the guys were standing stock still, not moving their feet and bumping back and forth with their hips. The women they were with were all over the place banging into each other and snapping their torsos in sometimes obscene gestures. I tried copying one and lost the rhythm of whatever the song was. Charles glanced at me now and then but he never smiled. He was still in a bad mood. Or I thought he was. That's the funny thing about people. We don't all act the same on the outside even if we are feeling the same. For instance, when Charles is feeling romantic he might put his hands around my neck and squeeze. He might repeat whatever I've just said to him. When Regina's father was angry, he would play the banjo and not speak for hours. When I am mad I scream. When Phil Donahue is mad he just takes his microphone away. "Ready to sit down sweetheart?" Charles said, coming up to me finally and putting his arm around me. My hair was all wet underneath. I hate that. I hate sweating and all those human faults. When I went to New Orleans with my rich boyfriend, I was so hot I sweated for seven days inside and out, everywhere we went. And it looked as though I was the only hot person in town. Everyone else looked cool as a cucumber.

"Takes getting used to," Eddy had said, trying to make me feel better.

Charles always takes note of my little faults. "Got a spot on your sweater, sweetheart," he says. Or, "Lemme see your teeth." He used to be a dental assistant; in fact, he even drilled people's teeth when he was in the Air Force. His own teeth are perfect, white and clean and lined up just so. He said he had braces when he was little. "Yeah, I used to hate those things," he said looking closely at me. "Open your mouth, sweetheart; let me see your teeth."

If I ever get rich, of course I can have all these problems repaired. I can take my mouth to an orthodontist and have them redo all my teeth; I can have my body revamped: breast surgery so they will be pert again, and I don't know...maybe they can reduce your shoe size—I'm not sure.

"What about me when you go to Africa?" I said to Charles, once we were sitting down at our little table again, me sipping my third glass of wine and Charles finally on beer.

"Well, you can come with me," he said.

"Oh, follow you to the ends of the earth, mending the cheesecloth to cover us with to keep off the tsetse flies? I'd have to leave my children," I said. "I couldn't put them through that." We were speaking of Ethiopia, not bushman country. Where the bushmen live it isn't starvation they face, but the civilized world coming into theirs...Ethiopia, with its hunger and war and sorrow. With its government and its terrible train wrecks. All that gruel they eat...and camps where they all sit day after day waiting. "If I leave my children what good will it do? Leave one bunch of kids for another bunch of kids?"

"Yours aren't starving," he said. He swallowed his beer and made a face, almost as if to say beer was awful and I was awful for taking him to a place where he would order it.

"Well, then I'll go. I can take Regina," I said. The band was playing some familiar tune.

"We're gonna wrap it up now...get out here and boogie, people...and tip that waitress. She's been good to you," the lead singer said. Charles looked at me.

"This waitress is a bitch," he said.

"She is?"

"She is?" he repeated. We left. Charles said he would take the baby-sitter home. "Can I come back?" he asked before we went into my house.

"Oh...yes," I said. I found the babysitter in the living room half asleep on the couch with Regina. She is a big teenager with black hair and a bland face.

"They were pretty good tonight," she said, stretching.

"Oh were they?" I asked. "Did they wake up?"

"Well, the boy did. He woke up the girl too then. I went up to get him and she starts bawling and then he gets going." The babysitter lumbered into the kitchen after me, and looked around blankly.

"So they were a little trouble," I said, urging her on.

"HE was. But I rocked him and then he went right back, Regina got in the girl's crib and she went back..." It was sometimes hard to understand the babysitter. "Then she went back too." I handed her her windbreaker.

"Well, thank you so much. Charles will pay you," I said, laughing and looking at Charles. He glared.

"Yup, they weren't too bad," the babysitter repeated. She held her windbreaker but did not put it on.

"Ohhh," I said.

"Regina and I drew rainbows all night. Then we wrote about fifty questions...I wrote fifty and she wrote fifty-five. What's your favorite food? Who's your best friend...wasn't too bad."

"Regina asleep?" Charles asked peering into the living room where

Regina was snoring on the couch.

"Yup...guess so. I nearly was too...then I came back...then he woke up...I don't know." She shrugged her big shoulders and pulled the windbreaker on over her head.

"Well thank you," I said opening the front door. "Charles is going to take you home...is that all right?"

"I don't care," she said.

"Goodnight," I called as they went out.

"'Night," the babysitter said. And Charles, leaning in the door said, "I'll be back, sweetheart."

Sure enough, he was back that night. And every night when he wasn't playing volleyball or going to ambulance get-togethers where the squad members as they are called have meetings on where the new ambulance shed is to be located and what the interior will consist of...where the next meeting will be held, etc. He was back and when he came back I would be in bed with my flannel nightgown on, *Cosmo* always said flannel nightgowns were a no no but the shoemaker liked it...and I would have tea with me and a book on Van Gogh or Gauguin...and he would put my book down and say, "What are you doing sweetheart?"

Even though the children are in day care I can still hear them upstairs saying "mama???????" and rustling around. It's probably just the cat, lurking in hopes of a mouse. Poor thing, I've got to get it some food today.

I went in the shoemaker's store to show him a new outfit and he directed me to the back room where I could try it on for him. An older woman was standing at the counter holding a pair of shoes. She watched me disappear into the back with a disapproving look on her face. "I can always return it if you don't like it," I called from the wreckage. He had boots all over everything and books on writing and shoemaking and repair, there were clothes in heaps everywhere and a bottle of clorox next to a broken sink. Charles turned on his heel cutting machine and my voice was drowned out. I put on the white cotton pants and striped shirt. When I came out, the woman was still holding her shoes. She looked at my outfit? "Do you like it?" I asked him.

"Do I like it?" he said. He turned off his machine and kissed me. The woman put her shoes on the counter. "I'll see you later sweetheart...you better take those off before they get all dirty." He put one hand on the white pants and I looked into his face.

"Should I return them?" I said.

"No. I like them very much," he said.

My god, the cat just caught a mouse. I can't stand looking. Now it's letting it go...and catching it again. I've got to get out of here. I can't bear it. What brutal animals cats are. I put my feet up. I don't feel well. I've don't feel well. I've been feeling poorly for a few days now. It must be all the excitement of Charles or something. I wish that cat would just kill it and eat it. Maybe torturing it makes it taste better.

In bed Charles takes my nightgown off. "No" I say, protesting just a little. I'm very shy despite all I've been through. "Don't take it off."

"Don't take it off? Why not sweetheart?" he asks me, pulling it over my head and throwing it aside. Then he kisses me and I can't answer him. "What is it?" he says. He touches my nose, my eyes, runs one hand along my arm and down.... "No what?" he repeats but he isn't really looking for an answer. He is searching for something else.

Of course my feeling ill could be the same old illness acting up again. It could be the chest thing...the heart...the bleeding. But instead of bleeding too much I don't bleed at all. I'm two weeks late and for me, that means it could be a tumor. It could be any number of things but probably it means I have been careless with Charles and now I'm pregnant. Oh damn it. As Regina says when her ink pen runs out before her picture is done, Oh shoot shoot shoot.

"I can't!" I call out.

"Can't what? What can't you do?"

I can't be here. Can't have all of everything I want. Can't be dying. Can't be pregnant. Oh I just can't, that's all. Doesn't that make sense to you?

"What is it?" he croons in my ear. "What can't you do?"

I don't trust that day care, not one bit. They have a rude little woman working in the toddlers section who arrives at nine-thirty with her bratty son and tape player. She sets up the tape player on a windowsill and says "Well hi there" to one of my children. Her son pinches my little girl's cheek.

"Don't do that," I say.

"Jonny!" she says in a complacent tone. "Come here Jonny." The day care room is dull, with ugly carpeting and milk cartons full of blocks. She is already cleaning up the toys my childen have taken out. Jonny follows my daughter around the room, glaring.

"I'll see you at twelve," I say to the caregiver. She nods her head and I leave, because I can't bear to watch. Just like the cat with the mouse. I would rather not know. Just now I have pushed the car outdoors and the mouse runs crazily around the room, all disoriented and probably internally injured. It is not my place to rescue the mouse but I can't bear the mewing from the cat. What I find peculiar in this case is that the mouse hasn't squeaked once. It seems almost unmoved by the whole awful experience.

I'm moved by almost everything. Charles once said to me..."I don't mind you going out with another man...if you want to just talk. But I know if he lays a hand on you it's all over...you'll just melt in his arms. Right?" and I laughed but it did make me uncomfortable to know this was obvious to others, not just to myself. Yes I melt. I fall apart like papier mache under water pressure. I am only human, am I not? So if I am pregnant I will probably sob all the way to the women's health center.

Today I am full of questions. Would another child be good for my health? Does the caregiver secretly burn my children with cigarettes? Is the mouse going to die? Did I really gain seven pounds since yesterday morning or is it just water weight? And as for Charles, is it perhaps the flannel nightgown that has cooled his desires or the fact that I cried and said "I don't want your dumb baby?" Or maybe because he is broke from taking me out so much. Some men are like that. If they have a lot of money they are very erotic and if they are broke they are cold as ice and don't even kiss you. Am I getting too fat for him? Does he really love me or is it just another shoe on his shoe tree? I saw my dentist yesterday and had my teeth cleaned so when Charles says "Open your mouth sweetheart" I'll be able to open it a little. My dentist is terribly nice to me. He put one hand on my face and stroked my cheek. "You're very pretty," he said. I thought that was really something but apparently it was no big deal because the dental hygienist was sitting right there and she didn't act at all surprised.

When I told Charles he said, "What the hell's the matter with these people? You see your doctor and he holds your hand...you see your dentist and he puts his hands on your face instead of fixing your teeth ...what's wrong with these guys?" He stomped around the kitchen making tea and I watched him. Was he jealous? Was my dentist doing something out of line? Should I hit the mouse on the head with a hammer and put it out of its misery? Am I pregnant? Am I? And if he WAS jealous, does that mean something significant or not?

"I mean sweetheart!" he said, putting a cup of cinnamon rose down before me. I looked into his face. And I could see his beard, his mustache, his green-grey blue eyes, his blonde hair, his glasses, but from there I didn't know what else.

One time I had to go to an oral surgeon to have my wisdom teeth removed. I always wondered why they are called wisdom teeth. Maybe because you get them when you are supposedly grown up. I was twenty-one at the time and very immature for my age. The dentist knocked me out with a shot and a mask over my face. I remember saying, "No no no! Take it away...I can't breathe. Wait, I'm not asleep yet!" And the last thing I remember was the dentist snarling, "I know you're not asleep yet, damn it" as he shoved the mask on harder around my nose and mouth. When I woke up I called out, "I'm not asleep yet," only I couldn't really talk and no one paid attention to me. In fact, there was no one in the room. I looked around at all the instruments lying on tables and saw drops of blood here and there on the floor. My mouth was full of something. After half an hour or so they let me go, I weaved and fell through the door, staggering downstairs and out into the street. My mother took me home. Right away it started to hurt. The dentist prescribed demerol. I lay in bed with my face swelling up and wasn't sure if I was on the ceiling or on the floor. The pain never really went away, it was just disguised in a great cottony mass. I went in and out of sleep. After ten days my dentist refused to prescribe any more demerol. "She's just faking," he shouted to my mother on the phone.

"Oh, I don't think so—really, can you see her? She doesn't look well at all...her face is all swollen. I don't recognize her. Are you sure this is normal?"

"You don't recognize her because she's drugged out of her mind. NO more demerol!" and he hung up the phone. My mother sat by my bed while I cried. I cried all day. The tears welled up around my eyes because I was lying down and my cheeks were so swollen they went way out over my eyes. My whole head looked like a painting of square-faced Henry the Eighth after one of his huge banquets. My mother finally called my doctor and he prescribed more demerol but he said he wanted to see me. I cried bitterly and said I couldn't go...I have been in love with my doctor since I was nine and couldn't bear the thought of him seeing me look like Henry the Eighth.

"She's got to come in," he said when my mother explained that I didn't want to get out of bed. "Bring her in now and I'll take a look." I was still theoretically on the ceiling, at least I thought I was theoretically on the ceiling...the whole room was distorted and wavering. We drove to his office and I went in, wearing a brown paper bag over my head. I had to sit there in the waiting room with several local Vermonters staring at the bag until they said "you can bring your daughter in now." When my doctor took the bag off my head I burst into tears. He stared at me as though I were suddenly visible for the first time...as though he too loved me and didn't want to see me looking like a sixteenth-century painting. "Jim," he said on the phone to the oral surgeon. "Listen, this wisdom tooth extraction is very infected. Did you know?" I let the tears pour out and over my cheeks, streaming down into my lap. My mother looked worridly at me. When he hung up the phone he wrote out a prescription and I put the bag over my head again and we left. By that night the pain was all gone. One could almost see the real shape of my face again.

"No what, sweetheart? Why no?" This is why. This. Because the crows have come out of the sky and are flying around, swooping down, maybe one will carry my cat away. Because it is spring...and I have just found a day care for the children, have just applied for work at a local restaurant. No because I was years getting to his little surburan house in this boring little town. NO! No I have lived in a trailer and I don't every want to again. No. No. No I won't have this baby.

"You don't know," I say, frowning at Charles. "Babies cost a fortune. The twins cost thirty-five thousand dollars just to be born."

He shakes his head. "Okay, no," he says. But then again maybe I'm not. Maybe it is just all the excitement of having a new relationship. Having a little fun. Maybe it's nothing, this nausea and dizziness. Or, on the other hand, it could be the fatal illness again, bucking its restraints, rearing its cancerous head. Maybe it's just a li'l ole tumor. A doctor in Kentucky might diagnose it as that—"You'll be fine...it's just a l'il ole tumor is all."

My face swelled up a few days ago, almost like when I had my wisdom teeth extracted, even my hands were swollen and I had a fever. My sister saw me and said, "Oooh, you look terrible." And the shoemaker didn't come over for lunch, men are shallow like that. Inside my mouth was all swollen...then yesterday when I called the women's health center and set up an appointment for the you know what, I looked in the mirror and there were spots all over me, blistering. I have chicken pox.

The cat spent the night in the basement. I found a tail this morning of what looks like a mouse. Welcome to the maison de fous!

The shoemaker took me to a museum to look at the Lautrec paintings. Lautrec was a friend of Van Gogh. They drank together in Lautrec's studio. At the museum there were other paintings of impressionists. I love Monet. I had Charles hold my camera and I stood next to the "Tulip Fields at Sassenheim near Haarrlem" by Monet so he could take my picture. But I fell against the gilt frame and the alarms in the museum went off. The sound was deafening. Everyone else in the museum came in the room to look. Someone turned off the alarms while a guard in a green wool suit said, "What did you do??"

"I fell into the frame a little. He was going to take my picture...I'm sorry."

"Which frame?"

"This one," I said, pointing to the tulip fields. In the background there is a calm sweet house with three chimneys. And all around is a gentle color of tulips.

"Did you touch the paint?" the guard demanded. I said I didn't. They watched us the rest of the time, whispering among themselves in their hot wool suits. Later on, in the Lautrec room, while I looked at the actresses he loved to sketch, the shoemaker sat on a bench and chatted with the woman who had been particularly mean. I could hear her laughing and when I peeked out and saw them, he was seated on the bench and she was standing with one foot on the bench near his leg. I went to the bathroom. The museum was large and the bathroom difficult to find. I wandered through rooms of realists, halls with elegant writing tables against the walls. I was careful not to go too close to anything, for fear of setting off another alarm. When we left, Charles was silent— sometimes I think he would rather be with a guard or an ambulance driver. Sometimes I think he would be just as happy with somebody else. He drove my car along the pretty tree-lined street. "They were nice pictures," he began, turning a corner too fast, "but after a while you can't take in any more...."

I held onto the dashboard. "Will you slow down?" I said.

"Will you slow down?" he repeated, but he didn't. "So. Did you like that?" We came to a red light and I took out a reproduction of Mary Cassat's "The Red Hat" which I had bought at the gift shop in the museum.

"You mean the paintings or the fact that you flirted with that awful woman who was so nasty to me?" Charles leaned back and laughed. He always laughs when I accuse him of flirting.

"HER?? The ugly one?" he said stepping on the gas. We went on down the street.

"Maybe you set your sights too low." I went on, "You ought to find someone a little better than that if you're going to do it right...."

"Oh okay...you find me someone then," he said. He kept laughing. "I don't believe you," he said. "What a little brat."

* * * * * *

Here at home the children are upstairs, woozy from chicken pox, and I am trying not to scratch my face. That would be the limit, wouldn't it? To be scarred all over from the chicken pox, pregnant with the shoemaker's child? Well, when I have a run of bad luck, it runs as intensely as my good luck runs good. But I'm trying to remember when I had a string of good luck. Was it when the twins were born and nobody died, despite all the doctors' predictions? I remember lying in the hospital bed for two weeks while they pumped ritidrine into my veins, a drug that relaxes the uterine muscles and keeps you out of labor but at the same time whoops up your heart, makes your hands shake like mad, causes you to pant instead of breathe...and while I lay there and watched movies on TV and drank coke, nurses would patter in and out of my room. "Boy are you big...wha'cha got in there? Twins?"

"Yes," I'd say and they would come over to my bedside.

"No kidding...you poor thing. Did you go into labor too soon?"

"Yes," I'd say, flicking channels and waiting.

The nurses smoothed the sheets and blankets around me, checked my i.v., took my pulse, my blood, my blood pressure. "I had a cousin once had twins. Boy she had her hands full. But she always said God meant for woman to have 'em in twos...otherwise why'd he give us two breasts?" The television came in perfectly and it got ten channels including a strange channel of the inside of the hospital chapel. All day long it showed an altar with candles burning. Sometimes there would be a priest and music on, too. There was a French channel that had Bugs Bunny cartoons in French. At night a nurse would bring me seconal to put me to sleep and I would drift off, trying to keep my eyes on Clint Eastwood as he roared through another lonely town with his girlfriend. But the drug always won out, I slept until four a.m. when the nurses returned to check my vitals. They call them vitals, blood pressure, pulse, those things the nurses do when you are bleary-eyed and confused. "Open your mouth...and your tongue there. Uh huh. Very good." Back into sleep, wake at seven when the breakfast tray boy came in looking nervously at my enormous stomach and setting my tray down. He never said a single word to me in the three weeks I was there in my double room. I guess I got a double room because I was having two babies...I was at the end of the hall, with a view of the parking lot, I could sit up in bed and stare out at my little yellow truck...I had a phone by the bed, my own bathroom which I wasn't supposed to use but I did anyway. They wanted me to be totally immobile. When my liver took a bad turn and they had to take me off of the ritidrine, I went right back into labor. "We'll try for one," the doctor had said.... "We'll hope for both of them but we'll count on one, shall we do that?" By then I knew all the nurses and doctors. They called to me when they passed my room.

"How's those babies?" And "You gonna give one to me?"

At four a.m. I told the nurse, "I'm in labor."

"How long have you been?" she asked. I said about an hour. I had wanted to be sure.

"I need to take the picture my sister gave me to the labor room," I called out as they wheeled me away. They brought the picture to me. It was done in silk, of a little girl with sad eyes...eyes that throughout my labor stared at me in sympathy. They looked like the eyes of God.

"Doing good," the nurse in the labor room said. "I've called your coach and she's on her way...it'll take her about an hour...." I watched the silk girl. I thought of my daughter, Regina, pulling a sled with the twins on it. "That woman in there needs a nurse while she waits for her coach," I heard someone in the hall say. "She doesn't have a husband...." There were machines all around me. They had fetal monitors strapped to my stomach, two of them, one for each baby. Someone in the next room was screaming "I can't! I can't! It hurts! Mom, help...help!" for hours.

I finally said between contractions, "Can't they give that woman something? She sounds like she's in agony."

"We can't give her anything," the nurse said, whispering to me, "she's only fourteen."

I watched the silk girl. I looked at the eyes. I stared into the silk. Regina pulling a sled with the twins on it. Snow. Everything cold and white and frozen. Frozen lake. Regina pulling a sled with the twins. The girl in the next room was wheeled to delivery. "Mom, mom."

"Stop that," I heard the mother say.

"Mom, mom, I can't, I can't." Ten hours later when they wheeled me away I was saying much the same thing.

"I can't...god I can't," but of course at that point you have to. You have no choice. That is the way it is with women. You have to. And even though you don't WANT, you do. My son was born first. He stared at me when they handed him over. I said, "I'll take you sledding. We'll have a good life. I promise to make your life as meaningful as I can." There were ten doctors all around the delivery table, anesthesiologists, nurses, they all had on green cotton suits and masks. They looked like people from another planet. I began to have chest pains. I couldn't breathe. They covered my mouth with an oxygen mask and did an e.k.g.

"Baby's heart rate just dropped," someone said. "We've got to go in and turn it around...."

I said, "My chest, my chest." They were all over me, all around the table, my son had been taken to intensive care, they were like moon people, hovering around the mother ship.

"Forceps...get me those. I've got to go in and get it...almost no reading now."

My coach was somewhere in a green suit saying, "You're doing real good. Didn't he look beautiful? Wasn't he a beautiful baby? Now they're going to get the other one out. They don't want to wait too long...you're doing a great job...." When they brought out my daughter, she was dark and silent. They put her on something out of my vision and talked to each other for a long time, pumping and suctioning...I could hear them saying "come on..." as if someone wasn't trying hard enough...I looked down at my stomach...it was gone, the huge mountain that had been with me for so long, and what was left was a dull pain and a coach saying, "What a good job! Boy you are terrific..." and my own little memory of a sleigh ride.

* * * * * * *

The shoemaker said "Maybe you have small pox" this morning when he dropped by to have his eight-thirty coffee before work. He looked into my face and I tried not to cry. I get so emotional when I'm sick.

"The cat caught a mouse," I said.

"Good girl!" he said to the cat. "Good Minnew."

* * * * * *

I sat in the intensive care nursery beside the incubator where my son lay and held his foot through a little plastic door. "He's the irritable one," a nurse said, brushing past, holding a baby the size of a large mouse. "Why don't you visit with your daughter there? Do you want a picture taken of her? We have an instamatic." They took a picture of my son through the plastic of his incubator and one of my daughter. She was strapped to a large open table, naked, with tubes down her throat and what looked like microphones attached all over her body. "These burn her skin a little because they have to be applied with water and they are hot...but those burns will go away...this is the respirator for her RDS and this is the machine where we read her oxygen levels to try and prevent problems arising from too high contents of oxygen in her blood. In the old days that was one of the reasons many of these babies went blind. This is some cream if you'd like to put it on her...." I looked at my daughter lying totally still on the table, her face scrunched up from the tubes down her throat, her body swollen with edema and a burned red color. She had thick black hair on her head. A man in gray woolen trousers came over to my wheelchair and put a hand on my shoulder.

"She's a very, very, ill little girl," he said to me. "I'd like to talk with you downstairs."

The nurse gave me the photographs and I smiled. "Thanks a lot," I said, looking once more at the isolette where my son lay. He was crying.

"If you'd like to express some milk for him..." the nurse said.

"What about her?"

"Oh she can't have any...." The man in the woolen trousers wheeled me back to my room.

* * * * * *

"Volleyball tonight..." Charles said, looking at his watch. "Well I better go...got a lot I have to do today." I started crying.

"Here I am going to have an abortion tomorrow and you're playing volleyball. You're so busy...you don't even care. You haven't ever said a thing to me about any of it...."

Charles touched a chicken pock on my face. "I love you sweetheart," he said. "I don't talk about it because it makes me feel bad."

"But what about me?" I said, still crying. I must have looked terrible. Pregnant, chicken pox, crying. "I'm the one who has to go...."

"I'll go with you if you want,'" he said airily. "Are you always this sensitive when you're pregnant?" I looked in the mirror at the spots on my face. At least the swelling had gone down.

"Oh get out of here," I said to him. "I hate you...I'll never have your child. Even if all my kids were in college and I was rich I wouldn't have your child...."

"Oh yes you would," he said. He was sitting in an arm chair in my kitchen, tapping his hiking boots lightly on the floor. "You'll have my children...sixteen of them...and you'll be happy."

"I hate you," I said.

He laughed. "No you don't. You love me." Charles stood up and put on his blue down coat. "Have a good morning sweetheart," he said. The cat went out with him.

I thought chicken pox were unpleasant-looking little bumps here and there on your face and chest but not so. They have driven me nearly to distraction with terrible itching and burning. I have been in constant torture for two and a half days now. I had to drop everything yesterday and lie in Regina's bed in the dark, with the children screaming in their cribs, my face damp with witch hazel, almost beside myself with the overwhelming desire to scratch the features off my face. Disgusting, but accurate, and on top of it all, I know this is an old song, but I'm pregnant. Pregnant to boot. And when I heard the shoemaker saying "well gotta go to volleyball tonight..." I sort of froze over and locked all the doors to my house. Then in the morning, while I heard him tapping lightly on the window downstairs, I turned on the Donahue show. It was difficult at first to guess who would be on. Donahue was saying, "This man...has been dubbed at the box offices as.... he brings in more than any other...." I thought it was going to be Eddie Murphy but it turned out to be Liberace. He came out on stage wearing a rather ordinary suit and they didn't ever really bring the camera in close to his face but there were some closeups of his rings. One of them was a diamond-studded piano and he showed us a matching diamond-studded watch.

"I never asked the price," he said.

"No, but tell us...how much are your costumes?" Donahue said.

"Over three hundred thousand apiece," Liberace said. He smiled through the whole show. They showed clippings of him getting up in the morning putting on an ermine bathrobe, walking through huge rooms full of clothes.

"Do you ever feel guilty?" someone asked him. "I mean what with all the starvation and whatnot in the world?"

Liberace sat by a Baldwin piano with his hands in his lap. "I think...I've paid my dues," he said. The audience clapped. The audience always likes a working man.

Charles went around to the back door during a commercial. I could hear him try the lock, knock again, and then the sound of his Volkswagon starting up. My whole face was on fire so I poured some more witch hazel over it and wrote Charles a note while Liberace played "Chopsticks."

"Dear tech thirty-eight" I wrote. That's his number on the ambulance squad. "Please cancel the abortion for me. I am too sick to go. Please get me some calamine lotion. I don't want to see you for awhile. I hope you enjoyed your volleyball game." Then I wrote I love you in seven or eight different languages (I've known a lot of foreigners) and pinned the letter to the front door.

"I have a piano done completely in Austrian rhinestones," Liberace was saying when I crawled back into bed. Even the insides of my ears were full of chicken pox.

* * * * * *

The man in the wool trousers at the hospital was the attending physi-
cian for the twins. He was the first doctor ever to use lung surfactant on
newborn infants. There were articles about him hanging in the intensive
care nursery. "I don't want to be optimistic with you and raise false
hopes," he began, when I had been helped back into my hospital bed.
"Your little girl is very very ill. She has a problem with her
circulation."

"She does?" I said. I didn't understand what he meant. "She's going to
be all right though...they said she was doing all right," I said. The doctor
sat on my bed.

"She's not doing all right," he told me. "Her blood won't go to her
lungs to be oxygenized...it keeps going around and around, bypassing her
lungs...she's working as though she is still on the placenta...."

"Well she is bigger than a lot of the babies up there," I argued. "She
isn't the sickest one in there, is she?" The doctor took my hand and
squeezed it. I felt a wave of fear come over me.

"She is the sickest one in intensive care now," he said. "She may die
within the next day."

"Are your sure?" I shrieked, sitting up in bed. "Is she absolutely going
to die? Does she have a fifty-fifty chance?"

"Not a fifty-fifty...I'd say a ten percent chance.... I don't want you to
get your hopes up...but I do want you to keep visiting with her. I noticed
when you put cream on her arms her oxygen level went up considerably
on the machine.... And it's important for you to know her...even if she
dies. You and she both need to know each other...."

I was sobbing. "They said she was doing all right..." I repeated. The
man in the wool trousers put his hand out to me.

"I'm really sorry to tell you such bad news...but I didn't want you to
think everything was going well when it wasn't...I want you to prepare
yourself," he said, and then he left with me a book on dying children, and
how to live through it.

* * * * * *

At noon the shoemaker was back, in his silver Volkswagon. This time
he parked along the road, thinking I wouldn't see him so he could sneak
in. But the doors were still locked. I watched from an upstairs window as
he tore the note off the door and went around to the back. I knew he was
peering in the kitchen window because my daughter said "jay! jay!"

which is what she calls him for some reason. Then the sound of the car roaring away. I went downstairs and sponged up the children's lunch. They had thrown rice and hamburgers all over the floor. It must have looked suspicious to Charles when he peeked in. He might have thought I was neglecting them. "Mama?" the little boy said. I changed their diapers and went back to bed. My face was still itching like crazy. I wondered idly if it would help to drink the witch hazel instead of just pouring it on my face.

Regina came home at four from school. I made her a snack and sat in the darkened living room waiting for the twins to wear themselves out. "We had to watch another sam goodbody movie today, Mommy," Regina told me, sitting down beside me and eating a granola bar.

"You did," I said. I was nervous from wanting to scratch my face and worn out from fever.

"Yeah, it's really gross. I get sick when I watch these. Have you ever seen a real liver?"

"No," I said.

"Yuck," she went on, picking up her glass of milk. "I asked the teacher if I could sit next to her because I was really afraid. The movie scares me."

"Oh," I said. "Did she let you?" My daughter shook her head.

"No. She said she thought it was disgusting too but we had to watch it anyway. She said I had to go sit down in my seat. I don't like peanut butter granola bars anymore. Next time get me chocolate chip ones...."

Six p.m. Charles began knocking politely at the back door. "Don't let him in," I said to Regina.

"Regina," Charles called through the window, "open the door."

"Tell him to go away," I said.

"She says go away," Regina called.

"Tell her to come here," Charles said.

"Tell him to write me a letter," I said. Regina relayed the message.

"Okay," Charles said. He disappeared. I came into the kitchen and turned on the light. Charles was at the door again. "Let me in," he said. I screamed and went back to the living room. "I need a pen," he called to Regina. "Open the door and give me a pen."

"NO!" I shouted. "Don't do that, he's tricking you! He'll come in if you open the door."

Regina searched for a minute and said, "Can I give him a crayon?"

"No," I said.

"Open the door Regina and give me the crayon."

"Regina come out of the kitchen...he'll go away," I whispered from the living room.

"No, I won't," Charles said. He sounded very close.

"Please go away. Find somebody else," I said.

"I don't want anybody else," he went on. He was fiddling with something on the door. "I want you."

"Well you can't have me," I said, sounding a little weaker.

"Oh, yes, I can," he said. I went over to the door with the lights off.

"What are you doing?" I asked him.

Regina came up behind me. "What's he doing, mommy?"

Charles said, "I'm taking the door off." And when he said that, he lifted the door away from the hinges and stepped inside.

"Now that you have wealth and fame and all that, is there *anything* that you really want to do? Anything you just love doing?"

Donahue shakes his white hair. "Good question," he says approvingly. "How about it, Lee? What do you do with all that money?"

"Well," says Liberace, "I love dogs.... I like to pop my own popping corn and watch TV...isn't that funny? Yes, I love watching TV. And of course my dogs. I love dogs, uh huh." He is still smiling, the show is almost over, the women in the audience seem as layed-back as I am, with my head full of codeine to help the itching and my hands wrapped reverently around the bottle of witch hazel.

"Do you mind being recognized?" Phil wants to know.

"OHHH HEAVENS NO! better recognition than anonymity...oh heavens!" The audience laughs. They are bored. I can feel it. If I was in the audience I would ask if he wrote any of the stuff he plays. "I do all my own shopping," Liberace is saying. "I can whiz right through...I know just what I want."

"Please, Charles," I said, "don't turn on the lights."

"Oh is that it?" Charles asked, still not touching me, "you don't want anybody to see you ugly?" I wouldn't look at him. I stared instead at the paneling on the wall. "I'm going to stay and take care of you," he said.

"No," I said. My whole body was crying. It was calling out, in the dark kitchen, help help, get this stuff off me. Get rid of these chicken pox.

"Sweetheart, you made me cry today," Charles told me. He had brought a chair over to mine and he took my hand.

"I don't want to love you," I whispered.

He sighed. "I'm not leaving," he said finally. He took his blue coat off and kissed me. I was thinking how sick I've been. How for so long, months and months, I've gotten one illness after another. Maybe it's my immune system. It could just be that...my whole immunity system is breaking down and any old bug that comes along attacks me and I fall prey. I am weak as a kitten.

* * * * * *

It was November 1983 when the twins were born. There was snow outside the windows of the hospital and Thanksgiving was approaching. I was able to walk to the elevator that took me straight to the door of ICN (intensive care nursery) where my two new children lay waiting. I expressed my milk and the nurses let me hold my son and feed him drops of it from a preemie bottle. There was a lot of jargon used...preemies, RDS. I could stay as long as I wanted. My son cried and got better quickly. I have photographs of me holding him by his isolette with rows of other ioslettes beside us, nurses passing, i.v. poles and monitors, a huge x-ray machine in the background. "She's having a blood transfusion now," the nurse told me when I walked to the other side of the room to see my daughter. "We're almost done here...after this would you like to put some cream on her arms?" I watched my daughter, swollen and brownish red. She was utterly still but there was a tear rolling down her cheek. "We have her on a drug called pavulon," the nurse explained, turning down a machine, adjusting some levels. "It keeps her from fighting the respirator so much.... she was really struggling for a while...so this drug keeps her totally immobile."

"Can she still hear?"

"Oh yes," the nurse said, "she can hear and she can feel all the pricks and pokes too. She just can't move." The tear dried on her hot skin. I sat by her table holding one soft puffy foot, and I cried with her until midnight. It was hard to tell what time it was; in the intensive care unit there are not windows, only bright sharp lights overhead and humming machines. Sometimes a beeper would go off and a nurse would check one of the babies' heart monitors. Sometimes the x-ray people would come in and call out "X-RAY!" and we were all supposed to leave the room but I never had time. I would rush to the door and by that time they would be finished. I was the only mother who was there almost all the time. I wore a gown and mask and washed my hands over and over in milky brown liquid, drying them with paper towels. The man in the wool trousers sometimes came in and looked at my daughter, sometimes said "hanging in there...." The nurses avoided me. My son was moved to the regular nursery downstairs. He had a touch of juandice and weighed four pounds but he was almost ready to go home. One night at eleven, my daughter's night nurse came on duty and while she rubbed her with cream and checked her machines, she told me about her mother. Her name was Minuet. "My mother had me six weeks early," she said, with a slight French accent. "We were in Canada then, my mother said I was as small as a mouse...I weighed two pounds. The doctor couldn't get to us because of a snowstorm and we were so far out in the country...but my mother expressed milk from her breast and forced it drop by drop by drop down my throat for two weeks, and when I would start to die, she plunged me into cold water to make my heart speed up, and then back to the drop by drop feeding. She kept that up day and night 'til she was sure I'd live. Everyone thought she was crazy." Minuet put a tiny drop of water on my daughter's chest and re-applied the little electrode device they used to check her heart rate. Where it had been was left with a round burned mark, like a stamp. "Tonight is the night," she said pointing to my daughter. "We'll know if she'll be all right, tonight...." Minuet was chubby and warm, she often patted me while she talked, and had me wash my daughter's hair while we sat together into the night. When I went to bed it was two in the morning. My daughter had not changed.

In the morning, at six-thirty I woke up and ran to the elevator hoping to see Minuet before she went off duty. She was coming out of intensive care when I arrived. "She's made it, honey. Your daughter has turned the corner...she's going to live."

I remember how I just fell against her and said, "Thank you, Minuet. Thank you for saving her." Then I stood by my daughter's table and looked at her. They had given her a diuretic and all her swelling was gone. She was a lighter color, her oxygen levels and her breaths per minute were down. She had one eye open. "Hello honey," I said. "You're going to live!" Her one eye closed. The doctor stood beside her table and stroked the soft furry hair on her head.

"She's a real fighter," he said. "We're taking her off the pavulon slowly...a little at a time...so she may open one eye now and again today...maybe tomorrow she'll open them both. Boy she surprised all of us, I'll tell you! I had been on the verge of trying the surfactant treatment...it's only legal in babies under four pounds though...but she came out on her own...miracle baby. To be honest with you, I didn't have high hopes for her." I, of course, was still crying, in my old blue nightgown with a hospital gown over it and my hands scrubbed raw, I was still standing over my daughter with tears streaming down my face.

"I've been spared something really terrible," I said. The priest who had sat up with me one night came in and shook hands with me.

"God loves you," he murmured to all three of us.

* * * * * *

With chicken pox, one has to remain indoors for seven to ten days, according to my doctor who I called at the very start of my spots. "Are you sure they're chicken pox?" he said over the phone.

"I think so. They're all over me. And they itch." I was in a phone booth with my coat turned up around my ears so no one would see my face.

"Are you blistering?"

"Yes," I said.

"Yeah, that sounds like chicken pox. You have to be careful in someone your age," my doctor went on, "because of pneumonia...that's the only worry."

I listened carefully. "Is there anything I should do?"

"Stay away from other people so you won't infect anyone," he said. "How's your chest?" I thought for a minute.

"It's okay," I told him.

So for seven days I have been inside, doing a little reading of *Dear Theo*, a book of Van Gogh's letters to his brother, and watching a little TV.... Last night I saw "Night Rider," a show about a car that drives this cute guy around. The guy is always meeting beautiful girls and the car is always telling the girls how wonderful the guy is so the girls will trust him. Personally I can't believe some of it...I would do almost anything if a cute guy like that came up to me in a talking car. Earlier in the day I watched The Phil Donahue Show. It was on USA For Africa, a record made by lots of famous musicians all singing together. Kenny Rogers and Paul Simon were among those sitting there...and Harry Belafonte. My mother always loved Harry Belafonte. She used to buy his records in Harvard Square when we lived there, and she'd play them all evening. Sometimes she'd play Al Hirt too.

"I think the song's great, fellas, and I really think it's nice what you're trying to do for Africa...but what about here at home? Are you doing anything for *our* country?" The crowd claps enthusiastically.

I'll let our manager answer that one," Harry Belafonte says, pointing to a man in the crowd.

"Okay," Phil says, "go ahead sir. Not much time left."

"Ten percent will go to our hungry children in America...we don't have the kind of mass starvation here in the United States like they do in parts of Africa...hundreds of thousands of people aren't dying on the streets here...."

"Uh huh," Phil says. "But...and I don't mean to be all negative...but how much...just how much of the proceeds do actually get to the people?"

The man, who looks Italian, he's short and chubby and rather blase, says, "Seven dollars and fifty cents from each record...." Kenny Rogers is eager to talk. He says,

"Hey listen, I've laid my reputation on the line." They do a close-up of his face. He looks uncomfortable.

"Well," Phil says, leaning on one knee in front of Paul Simon at the end of the hour, "No one, sir, will ever accuse you of hogging a talk show." Paul smiles. He is terribly cute. He explains that he doesn't know much about the money part...he was just invited to be on the show. "You are considered on of our most important poets," Phil goes on. Paul says nothing, shifts a little in his seat, the camera moves to Harry Belafonte again.

"We're trying to get people AWARE of the problem...you see." The audience sits quietly.

"It is certainly a a a...GOOD cause," Phil Donahue says. "And we have to break here." I look away from the television. I'm afraid they are going to show news clippings of all the starving children they are hoping to help. I feel like a heel but I can't bear watching them anymore. One feels so helpless being fed movies through a box in your home of agony ten thousand miles away.

* * * * * *

Fever. Spots. Backache. Neckache. Vicious headache. These are symptoms of chicken pox. If you have these symptoms, do not take aspirin and see your doctor immediately. This is MY advice.

Once I saw a show about reyes syndrome. It is caused by taking aspirin when you have certain kinds of flu and when you have chicken pox. So when I got chicken pox the first thing I thought of was, if I start hallucinating or smashing my furniture, I have reyes snydrome and should be carted away by the shoemaker's ambulance team. I should attach a note somewhere in the kitchen telling them it is probably reyes, and to treat me for that, not for hysteria. On this show I saw, they thought the kid that had reyes was just freaking out on drugs so they tied him to a bed and beat him up and he died. I'm terrified of that happening to me.

Last night the shoemaker didn't come home 'til very late because there was an awful car accident in town and a teenager was killed. Charles said this morning, "We had to take two vehicles up, and another run later. Boy that kid's parents must be taking it hard. They were a close-knit family."

"What happened?" I asked him, taking a bite of an apple turnover. I've given up on dieting until the spots go away.

"Oh, I guess they were driving too fast, probably drinking...there were a lot of kids involved...and the car exploded...I don't know, sweetheart...did you get me a cheese croissant?" While we were eating, Charles read this book on defibrillation, whatever that is. He takes notes which I can't read and uses abbreviations that I don't understand. This is very erotic to me. I love being in the dark about things, being with someone who knows all this secret knowledge that I'm not aware of...it gives me a feeling of security.

"Your face looks better," Charles said before leaving for work.

"Oh, don't go," I begged. "Stay another hour...." I was thinking how he wasn't the first Charles I'd known after all. I had just remembered another Charles I knew in England. He worked for a nightclub where I sang. He was a bartender. At first I didn't realize he was slightly crippled. He stood behind a great wooden bar serving me gin and lime, which is as close the English get to a gin and tonic, at least in the northeast of England where I was living.

"How about a date this weekend?" he asked me, while I downed another glass. They don't use ice in their drinks either.

"Sure," I said. The room was dark and full of English teenagers and men from the works.

"All right then," he said, wiping around my drink with a cloth. "I'll take you to meet my mum." I said great, then went up to do my last set for the evening.

When he picked me up at the bed and breakfast house where I lived, I saw he wore a large shoe on one foot. "You gotcher purse and all?" he asked waiting at the door.

"Yes," I said, turning to my landlady.

She gave me a disapproving look and said, "Where'd you pick IM up? EEE what a mess." We walked outside and took a bus to his mother's house.

"I live with my mum of course," he explained, as we went down a little path to his front door. He lived along a row of houses all identical. They looked as though they were made out of cement. He rang the bell and a stout woman in dreary clothes answered.

"Charles pet where have you BEEN! I've been worried sick about you I have."

"Mum, this is the girl I was telling you 'bout. She's come to listen to some records." Charles pushed past his mother and limped to the couch, covered in plastic.

"Well let's take that off, then," his mother said, trying to pull the plastic off.

"Oh, I don't care," I said, but they were already yanking the cover away. Underneath was an ordinary print sofa. We all three sat down.

"You work here?" the mother asked me, while Charles put on a record.

"She sings at the club mum, I told you that."

"I'm asking HER, Charles. Eee but he's very cheeky, isn't he? Well then I'll just go start your tea Charles...." The mother left the room and Frank Sinatra came on the stereo... "Strangers in the Night"....

"I love Frank Sinatra," Charles said. I was still looking at his large foot. "See here...I have every recording he ever made...he's the world's finest, is Frank Sinatra...." Then he limped to me and put his hand on my leg. I noticed how thick his glasses were, how his dirty hair hung over one eye. "I can sing like him," he told me. He was beginning to paw my leg. "What brought you to England?"

I stood up. "Don't do that," I said, sounding as American as I could. "It's very rude."

"Do you love Frank Sinatra?" he repeated. He seemed almost as if he were in a trance.

"Well...he's nice," I said. Actually I hated Frank Sinatra but I didn't want to hurt his feelings. He had a club foot.

"I'll take you home...here sit by me awhile. Take yer coat off, pet...my mum will make us some tea." I said I didn't want any tea. I went to the door and opened it. "We have to wait for the tea," he persisted. I went outside and walked back up the little path and down the street. I had no idea where I was but I found a white taxi along a curb and climbed in.

"Mrs. Kay's bed and breakfast please," I said.

The driver turned around and looked at me. "You're the singer's always calling for a ride at the X.L. nightclub now aren't you?" I said I was, yes. "Our company owner said if ever I got you in one of our taxis again I was sure to bring you to his house for a drink...what about that? Will you go?" I leaned back against the leather seat.

"Well I don't know," I began.... "Who is he?"

"Oh, a fine man. A fine man," the driver said. "So we'll go there, shall we?" And I said all right, why not, we'll go there.

* * * * * *

No, after all this time, I realized Charles the shoemaker was not the first Charles I ever knew. Funny how one forgets these other Charleses, these other people who float in and out of your life like a leaf from a tree...slowly, flip flop, over and done. So there have been two Charles.

The taxi took me about forty miles out of town to a massive house set high on a hill, with a great modern front door and modern entrance way. "There you go...no, no charge...it's on him, this one. Ta love." And he sped away. I rang the bell. An American-looking man opened the door and as he had been on the radio with the taxi driver he was expecting me. He gave me a martini with ice in it.

"Pleased to make acquaintance...shall we sit in the living room? It's only one of many," he said. We stepped into a great hall filled with red leather couches and black artwork hanging on the walls. There were heads of animals and people everywhere.... "I collect shrunken heads," he explained, sitting me down on a plush garish couch. He flipped several switches on the wall and the lights dimmed, the curtains drew themselves, and a loud music came from nowhere... "Madame Butter-fly," he said. He sat beside me and draped an arm along the sofa back. I don't remember his name but it wasn't Charles.

My landlady at the bed and breakfast had nothing but contempt for me. "Eee, if I was you," she'd say, sitting down by the coke fire with me and sipping a newcastle brown ale. "I'd do my hair in ringlets and put on a low-cut gown and off I'd go to the nice discos. I used to do that, me. Eee, the fellas thought I was daft, but they liked me well enough....they always said, 'Irene, how do you look so lovely?' Oh I was quite the looker me. But I never brought one home like that fella you drug here the other afternoon. What a mess *he* was." She was referring to Charles the bar-tender who lived with his mother. I had only seen him once after that time in his house. He had been fired from his job and was selling newspapers on the street. When I passed him I almost looked away, he was limping up to me carrying a load of papers under one arm.

"You there! You the American...." He had forgotten my name.

"Oh, hello," I called, as cheerful as I could sound. "What are those?"

"Socialist newspapers...I got fired you know. All on account of you...they didn't believe you were my girlfriend. I didn't care for that job anyway. My mum always said I shouldn't work there." I bought a paper from him. "Have you ever met Frank Sinatra?" he called after me, as I was continuing on down the street. "I had a friend met him..." he said. He was following me. I hurried away. I didn't even call out good bye. He had the same shoes on as when I first noticed his club foot. Brown hospital shoes. "Paper!" he shouted. "Get your paper! You there." I rushed onto a nearby double-decker bus and rode on down the street.

"Now me, I'd never bring a fella home wasn't rich as a lord. Eee, they say all that stuff about royal blood...what d'you think of that, royal blood? What a load of trash. I've got as much blue blood in me as Prince Charles has in him, I'd say. Personally I don't think there's much to it. No, I'd leave my men right there on the dance floor and I'd say, 'THANK YOU VERY MUCH BUT I'M OFF NOW,' and they'd say, 'Oh must you go, Irene?' They like me. Oh, I was fun you see. They'd had enough of those women who didn't want to have any fun. I gave them a good time...always one with a joke or a lark. That was me, they'd say 'you're so much fun, Irene,' and I was. But I'd never bring 'em home like you. Wouldn't do, to do that!" My landlady sniffed at me. Then we had another beer together and she went off to make her husband dinner and I rang for a taxi to take me to the X.L. My hair was never in ringlets and I didn't leave them on the dance floor but the fellas like me too.

* * * * * *

No, I'm not one bit sorry I had these twins. I know my life will always be rough because of it, bringing up three children is no picnic alone but I don't suppose it's any picnic with a man either. Their father was terrified of the whole prospect. When I called him on the phone, he lived in New York with his parents, he was a weak nervous man, he said, "Twins!! Are you really going to have twins? My god, you poor thing. That's great, though. I'm here reading Dylan Thomas."

I said, "Are you going to tell your parents?" He was in his late twenties, but he was slight and very attached to his mother and father.

"Tell them?" he echoed.

"About the twins...."

There was a silence on the phone. Then he said, "I'm not coming back you know."

I was filled with a helpless rage. "I know that," I answered icily. "But are you going to tell them anyway?"

He signed a relieved sort of sigh, "Yes. I wish you all the luck. I'll send you a tape of me reading Dylan Thomas...would you like that? And perhaps something from my new sonata. I'm very busy these days. Take care...you will take care." I said I would be sure and take care. Then I hung up and wrote four letters to him, all full of vicious sentiments. But I never mailed them. No, I'm glad I have the babies. They're charming and someday they will be an inspiration to me. Someday they will say all kinds of things, other than "Mama? mama? ba ba mama...Mama?"

I'm here on a sunny street, spring has come and robins are on the grass outside my kitchen window. I have a new car that my mother bought me, complete with car seats and a place in back for the dog. I have lost a good deal of weight and have a boyfriend who actually holds down a job. What more could I want? I am fulfilled, am I not? My children are healthy other than runny noses, my daughter Regina has plenty of friends, my cat catches mice. So where does this feeling of fear come from? Why am I filled with a sense of depression and boredom? It is that my trials are over and I am now left with nothing to do? No little this and that to gripe over? Maybe I am the sort of person who thrives on sorrow and pain. Maybe having life go well for me is deadening to my senses. Or maybe I am spoiled and always want more more more...nothing is ever good enough...why can't my house be LARGE, why can't my children be picked up in the morning and dropped off at night by a fine day care, why can't my boyfriend be RICH? Why can't I weigh less and less? And why, ever why, am I still coughing blood?

* * * * * *

There are several kinds of abortions. All of them are slightly gruesome, the best being the stick suction, where I guess it's suctioned by something like a turkey baster, out of you, whoosh, zip zip, takes about three minutes they tell me on the phone. This is done during the first six weeks of pregnancy. After that one moves up the ladder to the machine suction, a more painful, more lengthy process which makes a lot of noise. I am still sick with the pox and can now look forward to the latter, ladder, whatever. Oh hell kite!

Charles said to me, "Are you just having this abortion so you can go out on a date with that construction worker?" A construction worker has expressed to my sister an interest in me.

"Je suis toujours fidele," I said.

He gave me that grey-eyed look of his, an all-knowing "see into the future and it's sad" kind of gaze. "Oh, sweetheart," he said, sighing. "I can see it all happening...."

* * * * * *

I turned on the Donahue show but it was about nuclear war and I will say it again, I can't bear to hear any more about it. What can I do? what can I do? We will all be burned to rubble and die with melting faces and what can I do? Nothing. I can do nothing. Maybe lay in a supply of pain killers.

* * * * * *

At midnight Charles's beeper went off. We were asleep, my leg between his, me wrapped up against him, with my clothes still on, I had fallen asleep by mistake...it cracked first..."Kkkkkkkkkkkbeeper fifty-one," the woman's voice called. Charles sat up. "Beeper fifty-one," it repeated. "Code three. Testing. Beeper fifty-one. Code three. See the woman having chest pains...." He switched on the light.

"Is that your old girlfriend?" I asked.

"Go to sleep," he said. He got up and put on his clothes, turned off the light, and disappeared through the babies' room, down the stairs, into the night, in his silver Volkswagon. I didn't see him again until this morning, when he came back carrying cheese croissants and looking tired. The babies were throwing things down the stairs, they say that is testing depth perception. Regina was loading her backpack with cabbage patch kid clothes and her lunch.

"Bye mom!" she called out as Charles came up the stairs. She had Alvina Florida, her preemie, under one arm.

"How are you doing?" Charles asked her as she passed him.

"Okay, I guess. I sort of don't want to go to school today...we're having to watch another sam goodbody movie and I hate them."

"Oh yeah?" I heard Charles say, "have you seen it before?"

"We've had to watch about four of them...yesterday sam was talking about skin and he didn't even have any on! He's just the inside of a person...yuck."

Charles came into the kitchen as Regina slammed the front door. "Hello, sweetheart," he said. I was eating a bagel. I sort of shoved it under Dear Theo so he wouldn't see. I tend to feel guilty about eating. It must stem from my childhood. All these little guilts and hangups in your older age stem from your childhood.   At least that's what my old psychiatrist thought. He was a Freudian therapist with a touch of the modern reparenting style. I used to go into his small damp office (he was located in the basement of the community church building) and sit on his sagging tweed checked couch. "Nobody understands," I would say, fingering the strap of my purse. He stared at me from under his dark eyebrows and heavy beard. He was going bald. "I miss my father. I miss being little. I wish I was little." His name was Jeffrey.

He sat quietly for a moment after this beginning sentence and then said, "You mean you would like to lose weight?"

"Well, that too. Yeah I'd like to be small. If I was small everyone would love me." He smiled.

"I see," he said. "Would you like me to help you attain that? We might to able to get you started by way of hypnosis." In his office there were little knickknacks brought to him by his other patients. I always avoided looking at them because it made me jealous. "If I was small I would be beautiful," I said.

"When someone loves you, you ARE beautiful," he said. We were both quiet for a moment after this revealing statement. I thought it was revealing...who knows what he thought? He often spoke in riddles. Like once in response to my saying "What if I run away from you?" he said, "It would hurt me very deeply if you took away your baby self, and that's no impotent threat...." I found that a rather exposing remark. Jeffrey told my family he was fashioning his therapy with me after the book *The Less Traveled Road,* which is about a doctor who loves his patients and shows them he loves them in various ways. My family was pretty skeptical. I would see them after a session with Jeffrey, I would be swollen from crying and warm from being held by him, and they would say "are you all right?" and I would say "No. no I'll never be all right...if only I was small!!" and they would peer at me anxiously, both my sisters and my mother; they were obviously disturbed by my violent change. Jeffrey did help me lose weight. He hypnotized me and I lost thirty pounds pronto, almost overnight, I didn't eat for days at a time, sometimes weeks, and when I did eat I made myself throw up by taking some hideous stuff called Ipacac. I first discovered Ipacac when my sister had to give it to her son for eating a plant. It made him throw up within five minutes. When I saw that, I went to the drugstore, bought some, went home, baked a huge strawberry shortcake with whipped cream, ate the whole thing and took two tablespoons of Ipacac. I threw up all night and the next day I had lost five pounds.

"Whatcha eating there?" Charles asked, lifting Van Gogh's letters off my bagel. The page was stained with butter. "Why sweetheart! Why did you put your book on your breakfast?" I was smoldering with rage. How dare he snoop around like that? Was he some sort of policeman? Did I have to answer to him every time I ate something? My psychiatrist used to bring in a peach and a yogurt during our session together and eat while I cried. He weighed 130. Whenever I get intimate with someone it's the first thing I ask, "How much do YOU weigh?" and then I hold my breath...what if they weigh less than me? What if they ask what I weigh? I am nearly always disappointed. Men these days are getting lighter...Charles for instance weighs only 145 with all his clothes on in the evening. Weight can be confusing. In a man it means strength and power. In a woman it means slothfulness and lack of will. In a baby it means health, in a child it means neglect, in a cat it means a good temper and in a dog it means old age. So depending on your age and species, you can be almost anything if the scale tips one way or the other. For my part, I get up every morning and rush to the scale. It is like my master, this small cold box on the bathroom floor, with one bulbous eye in the center, with numbers for pupils. If it says such and such I get off and smile in the mirror. Yes, I'm beautiful. If it says otherwise, I go in and yell at Regina or tell Charles to get out of my life.

"So, you don't want a cheese croissant now do you?" Charles asked, putting a bag from the bakery down beside me. "Had another call this morning...an eighty-year-old woman with a strangulated hernia." I picked up a croissant and bit into it.

When I used to see Jeffrey, I always ate ice cream after the session. We would sit for two hours on his couch, sometimes he would read to me from *Dubliners* by James Joyce, and while he read he would stroke my head, my face, stopping sometimes to look into my eyes as I lay with my head in his lap....

"It is, yes, a form of reparenting if you will," he had said to my mother. She sat across the room from him, furious and silent. "Maybe it's more than that...it is a giving. It is something I can't really describe to you in this one hour that we have set aside to discuss your daughter...I understand your concerns...I don't know really how to set your mind at ease...I think maybe we should all decide here and now not to discuss what goes on in here with each other. I think you shouldn't ask and your daughter shouldn't tell you." My mother laughed shortly. "Huh!" she said.

"Sweetheart," Charles repeated, "are you listening? I said I'm going to run after work so don't expect me 'til around eight. Then I have an ambulance meeting at eight-thirty...." I look up from my croissant.

"So?" I said.

"So I'm telling you, that's all. I don't want you getting all upset when I don't come in at six, thinking I'm off with somebody else...like you do...."

I brushed crumbs from my hair. "So run," I said. I was thinking how my psychiatrist used to run. How he would come to our meetings with his headband on, his jogging suit crumpled in a corner of his office, his running shoes unlaced.

"When I run I think of you," he had said once.

"You do?"

"Yes. I think how you are like a deer, how sometimes I feel I am the hunter...." To this day, reading James Joyce always reminds me of his damp cool basement room, his soft brown eyes that stared down at me from over the pages of *Dubliners*. Though now when I see him on the street we both look away perhaps because of all that reparenting; I still carry with me the things he said, "When you love someone," he told me, "they ARE beautiful."

* * * * * *

And so? And so what does one do in a case like this, when one is falling in love with a shoemaker who doesn't care for the impressionists. Who doesn't answer when I say "Oh, poor Van Gogh!" What does one do when one's whole life has been man after man, each year remembered and marked by the man she lived with, 1981 was the year I got into bluegrass because that's what Regina's father was into. The year of the grave digger, the year of the catholic, the year of the sailor, God I know a lot about oil tankers if anyone needs any information...the year I spent with the pianist, and now I can run a heel cutting machine, will probably learn how to repair suitcases, might even glue soles if we stay together long enough.

Where does all this know-how get me? I know a sonata from an opus, a rig from a tanker, a clawhammer from a five string, a boot from a shoe but so what? Who cares? And more than that, have I ever really loved? Because to love, musn't one stay with one person and be devoted for years and years, much like learning a craft? Shouldn't you be as involved with your mate as you are with your work? I sometimes think we are all so interchangeable that it doesn't matter who we are, if we have names or not, a susy is a janet, a woman is a woman, if you have all your body parts where lies the difference? Our brains? If you strip us all down to our birthday suits, we come out sam goodbodies every one.

* * * * * *

I left the babies momentarily in the car a few days ago while I rushed
into my sister's downtown store to make a phone call. I used to work for
her before the twins were born so I have my own key. She sells old clothes
and the phone hangs right in the window, by the victorian white dresses.
I know the number of the gynecologist by heart. "Hello? Dr Water's
office," the nurse said.

"I'm calling to see when I can bring in a urine sample," I began. I was
watching the babies out the window. They were in their car seats, each
with its own bottle.

"First morning specimen," the nurse said. "Now is this for
pregnancy?"

Someone was opening the door of my car. I hung up the phone.
"Hey!" I shouted, hurrying over to my vista. It was a woman with a
triplet mobile. Another woman with a twin mobile came up beside her.
"Gee," I said, "is this a multiple birth club?"

"We're from the day care. We were concerned about the children in the
car...."

"I was making a phone call," I said.

"Don't have a phone yet?" It always surprises me how everyone knows
who I am and knows that I don't have a phone...

"Well," I said, trying to sound airy, "you know how it is. I hate the
intrusion of a phone...so I use my sister's...or I go to a phone booth."

One of the women was leaning into my car touching my son on the
hand. "How you doing little fella? It isn't safe to leave them in the car,"
the woman persisted.

"I had my binoculars to the window," I said.

"How are your chicken pox? You don't look too bad." I said they were
better. "Well, we were just wondering why they were there...." The
triplet mobile pusher moved the carriage forward.

"Thank you so much," I called. I always say thank you after I talk to
someone. It's automatic. I drove home with the babies and took a Tupperware midget from the kitchen and put it upstairs in the bathroom for
the next day's sample. I got it as a door prize once when I went to a
Tupperware party. It's a small container with an airtight lid. I lay
upstairs with a rollicking headache. At first, I left the babies in the
kitchen but then I worried some person would come to the kitchen door
and see them in there alone so I got up and moved them upstairs to their

playroom where they badgered me through the gate.

"Mama? mama? Out. Mamamaaaa? Out! NO! NO! MAMA!"

I put my hand on my forehead and tried to clear my mind of those women. Who are THEY to judge me? I bet they weren't single parents of twins.

"Mama? Bababa. Out. No no."

They were the very day care that had finally accepted my childrens' applications. Starting in two weeks my twins would go to them full-time, I would get a job, life would become more and more pedestrian. Except if they are going to hassle me over every little thing....

"Oh oh! NO!"

With all the rotten parents in the world it seems so peculiar that they would choose ME to find fault with. My head was throbbing.

"Hi mama. Hi mama."

I lay on the futon waiting. The babies shook the gate and yelled at me, threw their bottles at me and then cried because they couldn't reach their bottles. I wonder if Jane Pauley ever leaves her twins in the car. Probably not. Probably she has a caregiver that goes everywhere with her. And then the Doonsbury guy to come home to at night. Why couldn't my life be like Jane Pauley's?

* * * * * *

Early in the morning I peed into the Tupperware midget, clamped the airtight lid on it, put it in the refrigerator, and began making Regina's lunch. Charles had had a class on heart valves the night before and then some sort of game, he plays a lot of games—I don't try to keep track. Anyway, he had dropped by in the night and left me a note on a kleenex. It was draped over my coffee pot: "Goodnight, sweetheart." He has the key to my house now, since taking the door off. You won't be able to lock me out anymore," he had said, removing my key from the key chain.

"But, Charles, how will I get back in?"

"Don't lock your door," he said.

Regina came into the kitchen wearing her pink sleeper suit. "Don't make me peanut butter and jelly again," she said irritably. I was making her a peanut butter and jelly sandwich.

"How about this trail mix Charles left here for snack?"

"UGH! I can't stand that stuff. There's no salt on it...make me a cheese and mayonnaise or a tuna fish and lettuce...and do we have any more granola bars?"

I dropped the knife. "Make your own lunch," I snarled. Regina opened the refrigerator.

"NO JUICE?" she said. Then she picked up the Tupperware container. "Is this juice?"

"Leave that alone!" I shouted. She closed the refrigerator door.

"Can Susie Waldorf come over after school today? Her mother said it would be all right. She doen't have dance on Wednesdays...Please?"

I got out the cereal. "How about cereal for breakfast?" I said. It was always a trial to have Susie Waldorf come over because her parents were wealthy and I had to make sure the house was all cleaned when the mother came to pick her up.

"Eggs," Regina said. "Can she?" And would you clean my room while I'm gone?" I put the cereal into a bowl and got out the milk. The babies were crying upstairs. They needed their diapers changed. Regina got dressed while I sat by the window drinking coffee. Nausea. Dizziness. Headache. Short temper. Exhaustion. These were all symptoms of pregnancy.

"Wear a dress!" I shouted. I was what, two weeks late? Three? And then the weight gain. Five pounds. But that could have been all the ice cream.

"It's gym today. Gotta wear pants," Regina said, coming into the kitchen in Osh Kosh B'Gosh overalls. All the kids in town wear Osh Kosh B'Gosh overalls. They all carry back packs and wear velcro sneakers and have C.B. jackets which are very expensive. "Did you make my lunch? I said I wanted egg!" I finished my coffee and thought how difficult she was at age seven. What then would she be like at fifteen?

* * * * * *

"Now is this first morning urine?" the nurse said loudly, taking my Tupperwear container and setting it down by her phone.

"Yes," I whispered.

"Do you still have your medicaid card?" she went on, her voice booming around the room.

"Yes," I whispered.

"May I see it please?" I recognized some of the women sitting in the waiting room. Susie Waldorf's mother was in the corner, trying not to look at me, reading an *American Baby* magazine. I wondered if she was pregnant too. "We are swamped right now," the nurse was saying. "If you'll call a little later in the day to find out the results of the pregnancy test." Was it my imagination or did she shout the word pregnancy? "Is your last name still the same?"

"Yes," I whispered. Then I opened the door softly and crept out.

The babies were waiting in the car. I looked around to see if anybody had noticed but the parking lot was empty. I got in and drove away. Something deep within me was embarrassed. Somewhere inside, I was humbled and it didn't feel at all good. I stopped at the store and bought a container of Heathbar Crunch ice cream, paying for it with food stamps. The woman at the counter was very sweet. "Aren't those children a joy?" she said, pointing to my babies who were in the store's playpen looking at all the shelves of food.

"Out," my son called.

"Precious," the woman said.

"They really are," I said, automatically.

"But I bet it gets hard sometimes," the woman said putting my ice cream in a bag.

"Yes...it does," I answered. "It's hard but it's worth it. They are so much fun."

"Just precious," the woman repeated.

* * * * * *

Ten-thirty I couldn't stand waiting any longer. "Hello? I'm calling about the results of the pregnancy test...are you sure? I see. Yes, Thursday would be fine. Three-thirty. Thank you very much." I hung up. It was negative.

Headache. Nausea. Dizziness. Weight gain. Pain in my left ovary. Of course it was clear as daylight. I have a tumor and it's growing faster than a weed. It must be the size of a grapefruit by now. And getting bigger every day. Just precious.

I went right to the shoemaker's store and parked in front, left the babies in their car seats, rushed in with a little note, "Buy a bottle of champagne, I'm not, isn't that great?"

A woman was standing at the counter holding a pair of shoes. Charles was in the back whirling away on his heel cutting machine. "Hello there," he called. I looked at him gloomily.   Why not make him worry a little? "How is everything?" he wanted to know, significantly. He knew I had taken in the Tupperware midget.

"I'll see you later," I said, my eyes downcast.

The woman with the shoes said, "Is my purse finished?"

"Haven't had a chance to get to that yet," Charles called from the back. "Could you come back for it at noon? I'll do those shoes for you too...."

I went out. I could hear the woman saying, "Looks as if you have quite a lot of work to do in here...."

Sometimes I get jealous because Charles stands there in that shoe repair shop all day working with women's feet. It bothers me when I see him fingering the heel of a boot that is still on some woman. "This here is all shot," he'll be saying, bending over where the woman is sitting and touching her foot. "See the leather is all frayed there...and you could use another heel too. Yeah, see that?"

The woman will bend down with him, looking at her foot. "Ohhh," she'll say, "I never think much about my shoes."

"That's obvious," Charles will say. The woman will laugh. It drives me crazy to think about it.

"Close the door and let's go upstairs," Charles said, pressing against me the next morning. "Come on...I'm going to do something to you...."

"What?" I asked, feeling faint, with pleasure or else with the tumor.

"What?" he repeated. "Come on and I'll show you...." He had been about to leave, he had his keys out and the door opened and then when he kissed me goodbye we leaned into each other and....

"I can't," I said, pulling away. "The babies are crying...."

He shook his keys. "Go take care of them. I'll wait." I went upstairs and made them each a bottle even though the doctor told me they were overweight from too much milk. Then I went to the bathroom and discovered—sacrebleu!—that I was having my period.

"You're gonna need a whole new sole for that boot," he said to my girlfriend the other day, while she held her foot up in the air for Charles to inspect. It's almost like being a gynecologist.

"How much will THAT be?" my girlfriend asked, laughing, but leaving her foot suspended in the air for Charles to hold.

"Don't worry about that," he said. He was running his hand along the bottom of her boot. "I won't charge you too much." I laughed nervously.

"How much though? I don't want to pay more than the boots were...." My girlfriend looked at me, smiling.

"Oh, I'm sure he won't charge you too much, will you Charles?" I asked. I was beginning to get very jealous.

"You could standa cleaning too...some oil...." He was brushing her boot with his fingers, flicking away with the tips of his fingers.

"TEA ANYONE?" I said. I was breathing a little too fast, comes from my lung problem...or maybe from seeing him do that, to some other woman's foot.

Charles let go of my girlfriend and she stood up. "None for me thanks," she said, still looking at Charles.

"Leaving?" he wanted to know.

"Got to get back to work," she said. "Some people have to do that for a living." They both laughed.

I put the tea water on but I didn't want any either. "Could you fix my old shoes?" I said, holding up a pair of pumps.

"Not those things. Sell 'em," he said.

My girlfriend went down the stairs calling, "I'll see you two later. Don't want to be involved in your lovers' quarrel...." I put the shoes down.

"Make tea, sweetheart? Gonna make me some?" Charles put his arms around me and pressed against my hips. All the anger melted out of me. "Mmmm, gonna make me some tea? hmmm?" He kissed my face. His hands were rubbing methodically up and down the side of my body. "Yes?"

"Yes," I answered, completely affected. "Yes Charles."

"Yes Charles? Yes I'll make you tea? Yes? Yes? What is it sweetheart? Yes what?"

* * * * * *

Of course one wonders why one's period didn't come until AFTER one humiliated oneself in front of many important figures in the town. It is curious why my period held out that last twenty-four hours, making me take in a sample of urine to the town gynecologist who also happens to be the father of one of Regina's friends. And then to know Susie Waldorf's mother heard the nurse calling out "MEDICAID card"...I guess I couldn't hide my poverty forever but it grinds away at you, the use of food stamps and having to slink in and out of doctors' offices, after the receptionist shouts, "I'll have to see your medicaid card for this month!" The humbling, the crow. Having to eat all that crow.

Naturally, it would occur to anyone in my present position, I've thought perhaps it isn't my period but the tumor itself which is bleeding. The possibility that it may be my insides are all bleeding, not the walls of some future baby's home, but the very essence of ME, the very walls of my sam goodbody.

* * * * * *

"Today sam showed us about bones. Do you know what a femur bone is?" Regina stood in the kitchen with me, her coat on the chair, her backpack on the floor, her lunch box on the table, a Cabbage Patch Kid in corduroy overalls and a raincoat thrown in a corner of the room.

"Tell me. What's a femur bone? And why didn't Susie come over today?"

"THIS is your femur bone. This is your spinal column...sam goodbody was just a skeleton today. He never has any skin on but sometimes he has kidneys and a liver and stuff. Today it didn't bother me as much because there wasn't any of the muscles. This is a collar bone here. Susie's mother came and picked her up at school. I don't know why." I of course knew why. I didn't mention it to Regina but I knew it was because of the urine sample.

This morning Charles said, "Some painter died last night...you'd know him I bet."

"Who?" I asked, turning the radio to Robert J. Lertzimer.

"I don't know WHO sweetheart...some painter. A Russian I think." Robert J. Lertzimer was saying,"...died today at the age of ninety-seven. Chagal was...."

"CHAGALLL! Oh no! I love Chagal," I said. "I have his painting 'The Lovers' hanging in my cabin. He was my favorite painter for years...."

Charles sighed. "I've got to leave sweetheart," he said. He always get disinterested when I talk about painters or writers.

"Oh, Chagal," I went on.

Charles picked up a baby and said, "Watcha doing? Huh? You like that apple? Zat good? I've got to leave, sweetheart. Got a lot I have to do today." I watched him drive away, his silver Volkswagon glinting in the sun. I thought about Chagal. I bought "The Lovers" painting of his, a rather good reproduction, at a yard sale in Kentucky. I was out walking Regina in her pram down a pleasant street and there were pictures all over someone's yard, leaning against trees. I got Picasso's "The Lovers" there too. I guess all painters have a picture called "The Lovers." I wonder what Van Gogh's would be like. Rooty and sharp, with zigzagging colors and shocked faces staring into the lens of his paintbrush. I love to look at Van Gogh's portrait of a mother and child, the baby being held up in front of the mother, its big dumb wondering face, its placid acceptance of everything, the very essence of a baby captured.

* * * * * *

I have a group of women friends in this neighborhood now. They met me through Tupperware parties and basket parties. I attend these get-togethers to be sociable and to appear average. One of my friends, Corrine, invited me to go out with the group to a bar. I brought Charles along, and we met them in a dark booth.

"I just had two bowls of popcorn," my friend June said, lifting a drink up to greet us.

"Hi, how are you doing?" Charles said to someone passing the booth. We sat down, I sat beside a thin balding man who kept rubbing his face.

"This is Bill," June told me. She is a divorcee with children who lives up the street from me. She sometimes stops in while her laundry is drying at the laundromat and we have wine. They were all having vodka tonics.

"You got a sister in town here?" Bill wanted to know.

"Yes...two of them," I said.

"I thought so...geez you look just like them."

I ordered a vodka tonic. Charles ordered tea. "Hi, how you doing?" Charles said to the waitress.

"You better come visit me," the waitress answered, poking Charles in the side. "Where've you been keeping yourself?"

I tried to make conversation with Bill and ignore Charles, who was beaming at the waitress. "Boy I hate my job," June began. There were five of us sitting there. Corrine was wearing a summery linen outfit, she is also divorced or in the process, she was supposed to be on a blind date with Bill.

"You seem upset," I said to Bill as he rubbed his head.

"Yeah, I got troubles. My wife took me...Jesus she took me for a ride. I'm paying support, she's got the kids...Jesus she really did a number. My daughter don't even talk. She hasn't said a word to anybody from day one, 'cept her mother and maybe two other people. That bugs me. But what can you do? I tried twisting her arm but that don't work...Jesus." He scratched his head.

"Where's that waitress?" June demanded, leaning against the side of the booth. "I've got to have another. I've been trying all week to put my house on the market. Golly, you know I love it but I can't make the payments. And that son of a—well, you know, won't give enough child support to pay beans. He's got it too. But I never see any."

Charles was stirring his tea. "So you're putting your house on the market. Don't you work?"

June sat up and stared across the table at Charles. "YES I WORK! Cripes I work my tail off, my boss says anytime you need anything, June, just ask. But I can't do that. I've got to take care of it myself, you know. If I can just sell the damn house and get out from under those awful payments.... I'm so loaned out I can't possibly take another loan...And that man! with his new wife and new set of kids. I don't think he cared a darn about his own kids...I really don't."

"Hi...what are you up to?" Charles said to the woman in the next booth.

"So," I went on to Bill, "is your wife nice to your daughter? I mean, why doesn't she talk? How old is she?"

"Huh?" Bill said.

"How old is your daughter that doesn't talk?" I repeated.

"Oh, she's six. Goes to kindergarten. I tried twistin' her arm but that don't work. You can'd do that...."

"No," I said. Bill ordered another drink and slumped further down in his seat. I tried talking to Corrine. "How's the old divorce?"

"Ohhhh, don't ask," she laughed. "Do you know he says if I try and get the house he'll leave the country and I won't get a penny? He said that. So, I'll be happy if I just get it over with. I don't know. I can't worry about it...."

"Hey listen," June said to Charles, who was leaning over the back of the booth and talking to a blond woman, "could you fix a pair of green shoes for me?" Her voice was slightly slurred.

"Green shoes? What color green? Turquoise?"

"Green shoes...they got sucked up in a vacuum cleaner."

"Green what? Green blue? Dark green?" Charles said.

"I left them under my desk at work, I always do that 'cause I wear my boots home...and the stupid...ohh I'm telling you he was retarded, Corrine knew him, the janitor at work sucked them up in his vacuum cleaner...." June sipped her vodka from a straw. "I got a call one night at home...and it was this janitor. I didn't know who it was...I said, WHO IS THIS? and he said, 'It's the janitor at work. I've got your green shoes.' Well I didn't know...I thought it was weird that he knew my number...I said, 'How did you get my phone number?'"

"If they're turquoise green I'll fix them," Charles said. He was fooling around with Corrine, putting honey into her vodka.

"Cut that out," Corrine said, slapping his hand. I ordered another drink.

"I don't know what color green. They're a mess I can tell you that. They got sucked up...so he said meet him at work and he'd give me the shoes...well, he's that guy that had a growth on his cheek and they had to operate and they screwed up somehow and his face was ruined. He looked like this," June said, and twisted her face into a snarled look. "Well, when I saw him I said, "EEEwww!" and grabbed my shoes. I was never so disgusted in my whole life. And do you know that awful man followed me to my desk and asked for a date??? He did. THE NERVE! I said, 'Get away from me and don't ever come near me again.' He said, 'They were under your desk and I was vacuuming and I sucked 'em right up....' Oh he was so ugly!" June paused and put the straw in her mouth. "I need another."

"Me too," Charles said. "I'll have more hot water," he said to the waitress. "And what are you drinking, Corrine?" he didn't ask me what I was drinking.

"You buying?" Corrine said, smoothing her linen jacket.

"Yeah, I'll get you drunk," he said. I stood up. "Where do you think you're going?" Charles wanted to know.

I glared at him. "To get another drink," I said.

"Well go ahead," he said. We never get along when we go out. I think it's because he is a horrible flirt, but he says it's because I get grouchy in public.

"So I went to my boss," June said, still with the straw in her mouth. "And I said keep that man AWAY from me. I mean, if I'm found dead someday, you'll know who did it. The janitor."

"He was awful," Corrine agreed. "I knew him. He was awful. Just as well he died."

"He died?" I said, interested.

"Well, he called me again the next night. 'Wanna go out on a date, babe?' I screamed and hung up the phone. I was scared, lemmie tell you. I'm a single woman with two kids, I can't have weirdos knowing my phone number. And at work he was following me around with the damn vacuum cleaner, wherever I went that damn machine behind me, whhrrrrrrrrr, so I went to my boss and I said, 'Hey this isn't funny, old June is being pursued by a retarded creep and if you don't get him off my back I'll be dead in a week sure as anything...and what are you going to do when my kids find me strangled in my house somewhere?' Well that got my boss going and do you know they brought him in and I had to SIT there WITH the creep while they talked to him??? I mean, UGH he was so ugly...."

Charles was looking at the blonde woman's foot. "I could fix that. Bring it in tomorrow," he was saying.

"So what do you know but next week the old bastard had a heart attack and by god I don't care I was glad...isn't that awful? But I was."

"He was really ucky," Corrine said. We all ordered another round. Other than the blonde woman and a few old men at the bar the room was empty.

"We didn't go to the funeral...my company didn't even send flowers to the funeral. I tell you we were glad to be rid of the creep."

"Yeah, I drove the ambulance to get him after his heart attack," Charles put in, turning from the blonde for a moment and dropping a spoon into his empty teacup.

"I've got to sell my house.... If I can get out from this debt I'll be okay...get away from that damn ex of mine. Doesn't even care about his own kids, treats us all any old way he pleases...."

I got up and stood by the bar for a while, looking into the huge mirror behind all the whiskey bottles. My face looked puffy, the way it does after too many mixed drinks. I could hear Charles laughing, the sound of the blonde woman giggling over something. Probably her foot. And June's voice, getting softer as she finished her vodka, and Corrine saying, "No it's true...her kids don't lift a finger...." I looked at all the old depressed men sitting on bar stools. They all looked at me briefly and then turned back to their drinks. We were in some terrible way, in the same boat, the old sinking ship, the sorry crew, humans floating in a bar, waiting for something to occur which would change the course of the wind, set us all straight and happy, make the world go round for us again

* * * * * *

My daughter said yesterday, "I'm afraid to move."

I said, "Why? What do you mean?" We were in the kitchen. She had on her Osh Kosh B'Gosh corduroy overalls and a Ronald McDonald House sweatshirt that I bought her when I stayed at the Ronald McDonald House during my son's spinal meningitis.

"I'm afraid to move because of sam goodbody," she said. "Ever since I saw all the parts about your bones now I'm afraid to move. People are delicate. You could break your femur bone or your wrist bone or your kidneys...."

"Kidneys aren't bones," I said. I put my arm around her. "You don't need to be afraid," I told her. "I won't let you break."

"I KNOW kidneys aren't bones," she said. "But you have two of them anyway, and they could get hurt and we have so many bones it would be easy to break one. So now I'm afraid to move." She opened the refrigerator. "Can we go to McDonalds?" she said.

* * * * * *

I read in the paper today that a twenty-three year old man was arrested for beatingup a one-year old baby. The pediatrician turned him in. It said he was being held on $25,000 bail. "God, I knew that guy," Charles said when I read it to him. "I used to give him hockey lessons. Taught him everything he knew...did you hear that, sweetheart?" Charles turned to the window...."Hear that sound?"

"Yes," I said, going over to him and kneeling by his chair. "What is it?"

"That's crows...hear that? Crows." He put his hand on my face. "Getting ready for the spring crops," he said.

* * * * * *

Rent's due today. I haven't seen my landlord since the wind blew my front door window out. I called him about it and he said, "My father ought to be coming over to get some of those things taken care of," but no one ever showed up. The place is beginning to have little problems here and there. Oh little irritants, like the stove won't work, the hall light is screwed up, the front window blew out in a windstorm, back door doesn't have a knob, minor problems...but I think the landlord knows how poor I am and he isn't in any hurry to repair things. I think he knows all about me from June because one evening as she was leaving my house after a glass of Inglenook she said, "Your landlord is such a sweetie pie. He said to me the other day, 'June, if ever you need ANYTHING just call...you name it'...isn't that nice? I told him I was trying to sell my house and just RENT a place...you know, get out from under all these bills...he's such a SWEET MAN."

So probably he will evict me and rent my house to June. More crow. More crow.

When we got home that night after drinking at the bar I screamed at Charles. "You are a horrible flirt and I hate you. Get out of my life!" I was shaking with rage.

Charles starting laughing. "I'm not a flirt," he said, taking off his coat.

"GET OUT, do you hear?" I repeated.

"I'm not a flirt," he said again.

"Why don't you listen to me? I want you to leave. I want my key back. You can't stay here. This is MY house." I sat down in a chair and covered my face with my hands. Charles put on tea water.

"I'm not leaving," he said.

"Get out."

"You don't know what you're saying. You're irrational." He took two cups from the cupboard. "Do you want some tea?" I refused to answer. "What a little brat," he said. "God, I can't take you anywhere."

"When are you going?" I said, trying to sound icey and calm. I was shaking all over.

"Never," he said. "So go on up to bed. I'll be up in a while."

This is how it is here on this quiet street with calm little ordinary houses along the side of the road, there is no sidewalk along my house but there are pretty lawns and the woman next door walks her dog when the weather is nice. This is how it is here. Up the street June, divorced. Across the street the auctioneer owns a mansion and rents out rooms to skiers. A little further down Corrine lives with her three children, and waits for her husband to come home from his meandering. And me, me with the rent due and my bills, my children and my bills...here in this little house that needs some repairs. I got a bill today from the breast pump company, I had to rent a breast pump when the twins were born because they were too small to nurse, and the letter said, "Your account, of one hundred dollars, payable on the first of every month, is now severely in arrears. Please remit." Here we all are. The great middle class.

* * * * * *

So you wonder where Donahue is? Me too.

Sometimes I think I see the father of the twins walking along the street and I surge forward in my Vista with the babies, my foot hard pressed to the gas pedal, hoping I will catch his eye, his foot, but then I look again and it is not him. Just an innocent red-haired man humming along the sidewalk, crossing the street; I let him pass.

The babies, God love them, are destructive. While I am in the kitchen cleaning, they are in the basement in their "playroom," as I so gently call it to outsiders, shredding newspaper. They get together and form a human ladder, climbing on top of each other to reach shelves and pull out all the Christmas trimmings, smash balls and run around the room throwing tinsel. They step on the smashed balls, and I find them with bloodied feet, sitting amongst the newsprint, the little boy hitting the little girl on the head rhythmically. (My grandfather was a drummer.)

And so much missed by merely not having someone to watch them! Today I could have gone to Regina's school and attended a meeting on a "Spring Fling" they are putting on this month. They wrote me a letter saying they would like my fresh ideas and talent and would I participate? But it was a meeting during the day and since I had chicken pox the day care won't let the babies come back for ten days so I can't go anywhere. I put them upstairs in their room and did the dishes, looking out on the lady next door's lawn. The little dog that she sometimes takes out for walks was peeing on a bush. I waved to the postman. I got down on my hands and knees and washed the kitchen floor with a sponge. I listened at the foot of the stairs to the sound of the babies moving their cribs around the room. They have taken to moving furniture. They sound like U Haul or something, the little boy shouting "AAAAAHHHHHH" and the little girl saying "Baby baby uhhhhhhhh baby," both of them pushing a crib in unison, scraping the paint off the floor as they go. Sometimes, yes, I will admit it, life seems not worth the terrible grueling effort. Sometimes, yes, yes, it is all work and no play and I feel like Jack, the dull boy.

June came over this week and said after two glasses of beer, "I told my kids, 'Kids, life is not fun. Life is work, and work is no fun. You do it because you have to do it, because you are supposed to do it.' I mean they make school FUN these days, do you believe it? I told them in no uncertain terms, 'Kids, school is not supposed to be fun. School is supposed to be work and work is not fun. You get up in the morning when you don't want to, you get dressed into something you don't want to wear, you go to school and you sit there all day when you don't want to...and it isn't *fun*, it's *work*. And gee whiz, work is not fun. Work is work.'"

Once I worked in a factory. I had to get up every morning at five a.m. and be at work at seven. It took me a whole pot of coffee to wake up that early. When I got there I put a card into a machine, this is called *punching in*. Then I took my brown paper bag with my lunch in it and sat down at my table and drank my cup of coffee that I bought on the way. On my table would be wires and boards, and I had to put the right wires on the right parts of the board and solder them together. There were no men working there except one man who brought in boxes of wires for the women to work with. The woman next to me was going through a divorce and she used to talk with the woman next to her about it. I listened to them while I soldered.

"I told him I was about ready to go to the lawyers this week. Boy, I don't know. He won't TALK to me. He sits there and I say 'Why the hell don't you talk to me?' and he says 'Nothing to say.' So I am. I'm going to the lawyers this week. Do you have the G-52 board there? Where are the numbers for it?" The woman at the next table had no bottom teeth. She had a set of upper false teeth and not bottom ones so her lower lip sucked in. The women next to me called her motor mouth. "Hey Motor Mouth, how was your hot date last night?"

Motor Mouth laughed all the time, even while she was working. "Not too bad," she said.

"Did it glow in the dark, Motor Mouth?" I never knew what they were talking about, but I liked to listen to them. They were so intimate and somehow shared some secret happiness.

"So I said to him, I'm going to get some of those japanese things that you put on and—what are they called? Those things advertised in the backs of dirty magazines? You know, Motor Mouth, what are those japanese things called?"

Every morning we would all give a quarter to the lottery and someone at the end of the day would win the money. I won. It was twenty-five dollars. It made me nervous to win because the women there didn't like me much and the least little thing could set them off. One night, after I had been given a better job and moved ahead of Motor Mouth, who had been there two years longer than me, she drove me up to my house with two other workers in her souped-up Camero. I lived with my mother. They beeped and jumped out of the car, it was midnight, I went outside. "Hi," I said, stupidly.

One of them they called The Indian shouted, "Come over here big shot and let us take care of that dumb face."

My mother came outside and said, "What's going on? Where's Charlie?" Charlie was her dog.

"He's inside, Mother...go back to bed."

"Come on you chicken, come over here to the car, we've got a little something to give you." The other two girls laughed.

"Stupid bitch," one of them said. My mother leaped toward their car.

"WHAT'S GOING ON???" she shouted, grabbing The Indian by her hair.

"Hey, it's HER we want," The Indian said, pulling away.

"GET OUT OF HERE. MY DAUGHTER IS SWEET. What's the matter with you?"

"You don't know your daughter," they said. Motor Mouth started to push my mother. My mother shoved her against the car. "Let's go," the Indian called, and they all piled back in and drove away.

My mother came back to the house shaking. "What horrible women," she said. "Don't work there anymore." So I quit my job. I think Motor Mouth quit around the same time because now she works in the grocery store arranging the fruits and vegetables. I never shop there. Not because of her but because I don't live in that town anymore.

* * * * * *

Nine o'clock every morning Donahue comes on channel five out of the studio in New York City, relocated to be near Marlo Thomas, I wonder how his relationship is going with her. I wonder if she is satisfied now that he has moved in with her. It is very hard to remain satisfied these days. One continues to want MORE and MORE, nothing seems to be quite enough, life is always short of perfect, bordering on dreary, if only such and such would alter just an iota.

I am that way. I said to Charles just this morning when he brought me a pot of mums, I said, "If only you weren't such a flirt we could be so happy. But since you're a flirt I can't live with you. I can't let you be my boyfriend." Charles sat down with his cup of coffee and picked up the free press newspaper.

"Sweetheart, will you shut up about that?"

* * * * * *

I wake up at six so it isn't that. I have Regina off to school by eight a.m. and the twins in the basement by eight-thirty. Charles leaves at nine fifteen, he should leave at nine, but we always take a long time to kiss goodbye. No, if I really wanted to, I could watch the second half of the Donahue show every morning. But something is keeping me from it. It's all a matter of discovering WHAT. WHY am I not watching the Donahue show anymore? Why? So what. So what. I think I may be cracking up.

* * * * * *

I have an appointment with my gynecologist this week. That should prove to be interesting...after all, he saw me through the miscarriage, the twins, the urine sample last week, and now he'll see me through a new diaphragm so I can be without worry with Charles.

Diaphragms are a form of birth control that date back to the Cleopatra era. They are always sliding out of your hand and shooting across the room when you try and insert them. That's what they call it when you put on your diaphragm, "inserting the diaphragm." They give you a little booklet with your kit explaining how it is done. "Put one foot on the edge of the bathtub," the book reads, "holding the diaphragm with your forefinger and your thumb, insert carefully after filling with jelly, pushing until you feel it behind the first bone." What would the second bone be? "Once the diaphragm is securely in place, intercourse should be performed no longer than twelve hours later. Should intercourse be performed a second time, use the applicator contained in your kit." After reading the booklet one ought to lose the desire for sex altogether, thus making the diaphragm a foolproof prevention device. Anyway, they show a drawn picture of a skinny girl with one leg on the edge of a bathtub, inserting her diaphragm and smiling. HER diaphragm is not shooting across the room covered with jelly.

* * * * * *

Dear Theo is getting terribly sad. Van Gogh is in an asylum and is very depressed. He feels guilty for being a burden on his brother.... The book is nearly finished, he will commit suicide in the end. Yesterday I heard a song on the radio about him. Starry Starry Night. I sat in my Vista and cried listening to it while I waited for a prescription to be filled. The babies cried too because their pants were wet. My mother was with me. "Ohhh, ohh," my mother kept saying, "it's so terrible...it's so damn sad..." and Don Maclean sang.

"This world was never meant for one as beautiful as youuuu," which of course reaches everyone because we all feel that way, do we not? We do. We are all beautiful, we are all suffering so because no one realizes how beautiful we are. Today on the Donahue show there were disfigured people on stage telling about how they coped with being ugly.

"On the trains it's the worst," a woman with some fibrosis disease said, her face was covered with bumps and knots, her mouth was twisted. "They won't sit next to you on the trains, they think they're going to catch something from you...."

"And who may I ask is the worst to you? Which group treats you the worst?" Donahue asks her, putting a hand on her shoulder. Brave, I think, of him.

"I couldn't say," she answered, "because they might be worse if I said. Next time I got on the train after being on this show they'd really let me have it." The audience laughs. The audience is made up of deformed people.

"Teenage males are pretty bad, aren't they?" Donahue probes, "I mean they can be really cruel.... I know they are to me...they say 'Hey Phil, gonna put us on your show Phil?' I mean these people are...it's like dealing with people with arrested development, isn't it?" The audience claps. They are very appreciative.

"Yes, they can be awful. They cover their mouths and act like they're going to throw up when they see me," the woman says. "They ask me if I'm from Mars...."

Don Maclean sings, "How you suffered for your sanity, and how you tried to set them free...they would not listen, they're not listening still...perhaps they never will."

My mother, who had met me in town to give me my rent money, turned and hugged me. "It's going to work out," she said, we were both still crying, my tears were bitter tears, how could this world treat one so? "Don't worry, you're going to make it...and I promise I'll live to see you do well."

I shook my head. "What if I never get anywhere?," I cried. "Vincent never did in his lifetime...he was forever ashamed of himself, do you know he wouldn't ever sign his paintings? Because it embarrassed him. He didn't feel worthy. And when he gave little paintings to people as gifts, they often returned them.... That Tersteeg guy...they were so mean to him...."

My mother patted me, she had stopped crying and was looking at me intently. "My mother would have helped ME," she said in defense of my position. "If I had needed her help she would have come through...don't you worry."

"I had a form of skin cancer and they removed a third of my nose," a woman in the audience said, standing up. "So for a short time I knew what it was like to be disfigured...and I'm one of the lucky ones. I was able to have surgery and hopefully now I'm pretty again." The audience claps. The audience always claps after a moving remark.

"Starry Starry Night...paintings hung in empty halls...." God that is just how I feel sometimes...that all my work sits in the closet under the Christmas tree trimmings, that the twins drop popsicles on it, that no one, other than my mother, see its. And I know there is a world of people out there who have worlds of work that is seen by no one. We are so wrapped up in ourselves that seldom do we look out of our own bodies and see the good in the world around us. For instance, I wonder what ever happened to Don Maclean?

One of the very distressing things to discover is that along the Petite Boulevard, where Vincent Van Gogh and Toulouse Lautrec and Gaugin hung out, there were hundreds of other painters, all just as good, maybe some even better, who were never catapulted to fame. They sank into oblivion after spending their lives pounding powder into paint, spending days outside with their canvases...there is only so much room at the top and so few are chosen, perhaps those with some connections, or those with particularly moving histories...the rest? They loved their work, but they are forgotten.

"So do you limit yourself because of your disfigurement? I mean do you go to the A&P or do you send someone else because of the hassle it involves?" Donahue is in the audience, surrounded by fibrosis victims.

The woman says, "Ohh sometimes I feel like staying in a closet. But then I think, 'Why should I ruin my life just because people don't want to look at me?' No, I go to the grocery." The audience goes wild with applause.

Donahue has his arm around her, holding the mike. "Good for you," he says. "And I promise I'll give you a chance," he says to someone out of the view of the cameras. "Right after this.... The Donahue show music comes on and it fades to a commercial about blindness.

"If you know someone who is blind or if you are blind, call this number and find out how YOU can help...."

I wonder if we human beings are falling apart at the seams. There is so much publicity on problems in humans. The radio talk shows are always on cancer, the news is full of new diseases, and now this peculiar disease that covers you with bumps and lumps and ruins your life because everyone thinks you're from Mars. It's all very upsetting.

* * * * * *

"We are writing about sam goodbody. Me and Anita are going to do our paper on the femur bone. It's the biggest bone in your body."

"Really?" I say, passing my daughter in the kitchen and letting the dog outside. It is snowing again. "Which bone is that?"

"I think it's the bone on your leg," she says, "but I'm not sure. Anyway, me and Anita are doing the paper together.... And mommy do you know we have a sort of puzzle in our room of sam goodbody...it's not really a puzzle but pieces fit together sort of...Like there is a heart on a stand...it doesn't come apart though...and lungs over by Eric's desk, I think they're lungs...."

Regina climbs on the counter and pulls the crackers off a shelf. "Hey watch out," I say.

"Couple of kidneys," she goes on, getting out the peanut butter. "It isn't really sam goodbody because he's all apart all over the room...and you can't put him back together...but we call it that...Me and Anita are making up a song for the talent show. I'm wearing her socks."

Susie's mother came over and asked if I would babysit for Susie once a week. I was going to say "I saw you in the gynecologist's office...," but I didn't. One never knows what will embarrass some people. "I'd love to babysit for her," I said. "She and Regina have great fun together."

The mother stared at my kitchen floor. I can't help it if the babies grind everything into the linoleum. I'm always sponging up cottage cheese and applesauce. "I'll pay you," the mother offered.

"Oh no," I said, even though I could really use the money, "she's no problem."

The mother looked around the room and then peered into my livingroom. "Well, Tuesday then..." she said uncertainly. "Come Susie...." They both left, climbing into their new Toyota Tercel, and driving away. Everyone here in town that has money has a Toyota Tercel. They are all the rage, just like Osh Kosh B'Gosh and down coats. The middle class people drive Dodge wagons, the rich drive Tercels, and the poor? We can be found in almost anything.

* * * * * *

When one is writing a novel, my sister told me, one should come to some sort of realization...at the start there should be doors to open, and each chapter a door which when left ajar shows some more insight into the problem or the situation until finally, at the end of the book, the last door reveals the obvious and one says, "Oh, of course...I knew that...I understand now." But this piece here has no chapters to speak of, no locks, no keys, no doors, no final resolvement (is there such a word?) and if I may say so right now, I don't think a person will come out of this saying, "Oh, yes, it's all clear to me now." Rather I think a person will come of of this saying, "Whew, long-winded. Confusing. Jumps around a lot. Covers a lot of territory," and maybe, "What the hell was that supposed to mean?" It's possible though that a reader might say, "Ahhh, the world is a sad and funny place" when they finish with this. That's providing that I finish with this, which at this point is dubious.

* * * * * *

This morning Charles came over early. He had played some game the night before, basketball I think, and when he came over this morning he brought an infant nasal aspirator with him and squirted water around the sink with it. He's always coming over with ambulance gadgets. On his belt he carries a pair of large scissors to cut seat belts with in case someone is stuck in a car. And he has a pick sort of thing that he wears on his belt. This is for breaking windshields. Last week I went to the home and garden show to watch him with the rest of the ambulance squad cut up a car. They had a new machine they were trying out called Jaws. Charles had on a fireman's outfit. He went under the car and attached a chain to the underneath and pulled the front of the car away and cut it up with this jaws thing. There were a lot of people standing around watching and two ambulances sitting there with drivers waiting in case somebody got hurt. It was, to me, very erotic, but then, everything is erotic with Charles.

* * * * * *

"Right this way," the disfigured nurse said, ushering me into my gynecologist's back room. "We need a urine sample first."

"No, I don't need one of those," I said, smiling. "I had my period."

"That's nice. But we do need one to check your sugar, please." I went to the bathroom and peed into a small paper cup. Men don't realize the problems women have peeing into a paper cup the size of a shot glass. I put the cup into the little door in the wall and went out. The nurse opened the little door from her side and removed the cup. Why don't they just have you hand them the damn thing? "On the scale please," she said, dipping something into my urine and holding it up to the light. I got on the scale. It is always humiliating for me to have my doctors know what I weigh. Little hang up of mine.

While I was standing there with her moving the metal bar further and further up the numbers, my doctor strolled by. "Well, hello," he said.

"Hello," I answered, stepping down. The nurse took me into one of his offices. He has several and in each one a naked woman waits.

"Take everything off. He is going to want to do a breast exam too.

There's the sheet." I looked to where she was pointing and picked up the small blue sheet, the size of a pillowcase. "You can put that over you," she said, and left.

I took off my jeans and my hand-knit sweater and my white blouse and my pink glittery bra and my old purple sneakers and climbed onto the table stark naked except for my striped purple socks, ankle length. I sat on the edge, down near the stirrups with the blue pillowcase wrapped around my breasts. Once they have you in the little waiting room they don't mind leaving you for half an hour at a stretch. Something about being naked in a doctor's office that brings cancer to mind, stuffs fear down your throat. I concentrated on a *Family Circle* magazine lying on a table. My doctor came in. "Hello, there!" he said as if he hadn't seen me on the scale earlier. He sat on the edge of a table casually, reading my chart and glancing at me occasionally. "Okay dear," he said, putting a hand on my knee. He pulled me forward on the table.

I said, "I think I have cancer. It would be unlikely for someone my age, wouldn't it?" My doctor is about my age.

"Yes," he said, probing.

"Ow, that hurts," I said.

"Everything feels fine," he went on. "Are you using any form of birth control?"

"Yes...do I feel pregnant?" I asked him, trying to sit up.

"Just relax," he said. "You aren't pregnant.... I'm going to put in a diaphragm now...how are those twins?" This is one peculiar job, I thought as he chatted to me while inserting a diaphragm. "A little snug...I think I'll try one smaller...." I was pleased to hear this. "Are you going to have any more children?" he asked. I said I wasn't sure. "We can always opt for tubal ligation," he told me.

"No, I think I'll just take a diaphragm for now," I said.

"You feel real good. Everything nice and smooth," he said, pulling me to a sitting position. I couldn't imagine saying that to someone. I couldn't imagine having an occupation where you spent all day with naked members of the opposite sex. I couldn't even imagine being married to a man who spent all day going in and out of little rooms where women sat on tables nude. My doctor is handsome, tall and strong-looking, and I guess he is what one might call erotic. Yes, one might, especially if it's me. I've been calling everyone that lately.

"I want you to do a breast check every month. Promise now? Here is a booklet on how to do them. You're fine now, but who's to say in a month, huh? So do that. And here is your diaphragm and kit and a booklet on how to use it. Be good." He handed me everything and patted my bare knee.

"Thank you," I said, holding the pamphlets and trying to keep the pillowcase on as he left the room. When the door closed I leaped up and threw on my clothes and rushed outside. One feels liberated after an internal exam that has come out well. If the pap smear is negative I can rest assured for another six months that I am not being attacked internally by some dreaded killer disease. Of course it all hangs on what the results of the pap smear are to be, but it seems unlikely that, and yet, still, there is no telling at this point.

How to examine your own breasts. Including X-ray mammography. Ugh. I can't stand reading another line.

Charles said to me today, "Sweetheart, if you can't say *no* to a man, what are we going to do?"

I said, "Oh I can say no, Charles."

He said, "Oh really? When he's doing this to you?" and then he put one hand on my breast and I looked into his light grey eyes and leaned my face against his scratchy beard and the whole room melted into a blurr. It was just Charles and me and his hand on my breast.

The average woman has one chance in eleven or about nine percent of developing breast cancer during her lifetime. Breasts come in all shapes and sizes. Yuck and I mean yuck. Sam goodbody could never be so upsetting....

This morning the little girl from up the street stops in wearing a yellow raincoat and carrying a knapsack. She, like many of them, comes from a broken home. They call them broken homes because the parents broke up. "Look," she says, "Mommy did my hair today." This is in reference to the other day when she came to my door carrying her barrettes and saying, "Mommy has a hangover and doesn't want to do my hair today.... Will you do it for me?" She has a winning way about her, chubby arms and long silky brown hair, almost the sort of child one might have painted in the eighteenth century. She's quite a bit older than my daughter. "I didn't have much breakfast," she says, eyeing my piece of toast.

"Here," I offer, "want a bite?" She takes the toast and wanders around the room.

"I love watching the news in the morning with mommy," she tells me. She is a very disarming girl.

"Regina! Time for school," I call up the stairs. Charles is having a cup of coffee and reading my journal. "Charles, don't do that," I say.

His beeper begins to hiss. "Kkkkkkkkk, beeper fifty-one," it shouts into the room.

"Shit," Charles says.

The twins are having eggs at their short table. They look up at the beeper. "Uh ohh," they say.

"Beeper fifty-one...code three. Possible miscarriage in Washburn... code three...."

Charles begins lacing up his boots. "Gotta go," he says. I watch him put on his coat. I hope the woman has clothes on.

"What will you do with her?" I want to know.

"Take her to the hospital," he says. He goes out the door. He does not kiss me goodbye. I guess a miscarriage is more exciting than a heart attack.

"Regina!" I say again. "Hurry up."

The girl from up the street is saying, "Actually, all I had this morning was a pear...." She is hovering near the babies' soft-boiled eggs.

"Mommy? juice," the twins say over and over. "Juice. Juice. Mommy." They have juice on their table.

"Yes. Good juice," I tell them.

Regina comes into the kitchen and picks up my booklet on how to insert a diaphragm. "Hey...what's this?" she wants to know. "Mrs. Modern wants us to bring in anything we have on the body."

"That's the inside of a vagina," I say, looking at the picture she is pointing to. It looks like a portion of the globe, with countries and lakes, mountain ridges....

"Ohh," she says, dropping the pamphlet. "We are studying the body but...I don't think we will be studying THAT part."

"Mrs. Modern would probably be shocked," I agree.

"Is it okay," the girl from up the street says, "if I eat Regina's eggs? She doesn't want any more...." I don't know, but maybe I'm coming down with something....

******

Mammography is not for everyone, part one.... Boy I'll say. If I thought I would ever get breast cancer I'd finish off the old body here and now...why wait for all those x-rays and machines and lying naked in little white rooms? Why? Why? "Many women find it convenient to schedule this exam at the same time as their test for cervical cancer." Now they're talking about the pap smear. I wonder if the results are back yet? I wonder if they're in the office deciding just how they're going to lower the old boom.

"Hello? We are trying to get in touch with your sister...her test results are...well, back, and we would like her to come in immediately.... No, we can't tell you why...could you drive over and get her?" I wouldn't go in, no not me. I'd hack off my head first.

******

When I was little my sister and I used to play a game; "what would be the worst way to die?" I think it came from the fact that our father had died and our mother worried all the time about different diseases and problems the could arise. Our mother wouldn't let us ride on school buses or drive in cars with other kids' parents because of accidents on the road. She wouldn't let us eat tuna fish or liverwurst unless we were at home and she could smell the can or give us wine in case it was spoiled. You know there were those women that had a tea party and ate tuna fish sandwiches and they would have all died except they gave some to the dog earlier in the day and the dog died so they knew it was full of botulism. Fortunately they made it to the hospital in time to be saved but my god...tuna fish is nothing to fool around with.

My sister and I were also not allowed to go swimming without our mother being with us because there was always the chance that the mother we would go with might not notice us drowning. There was the fear of kidnappers, of being cut up by the lawnmower. Our mother didn't mow the lawn much because she was worried something might get caught in the lawnmower and it would buck and rip off a leg or something. So my sister and I would often spend hours out under the apple trees in the summer talking about which way to go would be the gruesomest. "I'd hate to be locked in a truck of a car by a kidnapper and left to suffocate," I'd say.

"Ugh, that would be terrible but how about going down in a plane? That would be the worst. You'd know you were dying for about three minutes and there would be nothing you could do....and everybody would be screaming...."

I shivered. "Yeah," I said, "that is the worst. I've always been afraid of being zipping up all the way in a sleeping bag...or what about getting knifed by a killer?"

"Kids!" our mother would inadvertably call from the screened-in back porch where she would be writing poetry and having wine, "everything OK back there? Don't go in the road!"

The little girl from up the street tries to fit in with the rest of the kids but is is hard for her. Her mother has wild black frizzy hair and just under five feet tall. She is the thinnest woman I've every seen. She wears buttons all over her long skirts that say "heroin" and "Bug off" and "C'mon baby lets get down." She smokes constantly and moves from apartment to apartment, always being evicted for wild parties and not paying her rent. She drops by here once in a while, I try to discourage her but she is relentless. "Like I said to my landlord, 'hey its not my fault I don't have the rent...my mother sent me a check man and where the hell am I supposed to cash that? And like welfare doesn't give you enough for food....' they don't know how hard it is bringing up a kid...they think man that I have all this bread or something. And like my internal organs are so screwed up man that I'm like living on codeine." She sits in one of my kitchen chairs holding her side and groaning. "Uhhh man it hurts. I was peeing blood when I first went in and like they called the ambulance...it was really funny. While they were loading me in I ripped off two prescription pads. Hey where's the shoemaker?" While she is visiting I try and clean up the house. I put on loud music and listen to her go on about her lovers and her money problems. She is beautiful. When I took her to the grocery (she doesn't drive) she stole a whole bunch of magazines. "Like they never say anything to me," she said, walking out of the store with Cosmo and the National Enquirer...." They think I'm too weird. Too spacey man. Do you wanna get drunk with me? I've got to get drunk and just forget all my problems. I'm worrying too much."

Yesterday while she was here, lounging in a chair, June came by to visit while her laundry was drying. She was obviously shocked. "Well I better not stay," June said the minute that she saw the frizzy-haired woman sitting in my kitchen. "I'm going to have a permanent this afternoon."

"Hey like wow....I could do it for you. Save you money. I do a better job than those flakes man."

June looked nervous. "I want it curly," June said, trying to be polite, "but I don't think I want it *that* curly."

"Oh hey...I was BORN this way," the frizzy-haired woman said and leaned back in her chair shrieking with laughter.

"I'll...I'll see you later," June whispered to me, and went out the back door.

"Hey where are all these people from anyway?" the frizzy-haired woman said, pointing out the window, "Mars?"

* * * * * *

This house I am in, this quiet nice house with peeling outer paint, is becoming a stopping spot for everyone on their way home. Charles comes by for tea at noon, Corrine stops by in the morning for breakfast, June comes over while her laundry is being done, and now the frizzy-haired woman drops in to see if I will give her a ride to the doctors, or to the grocery. I put a sign on the door saying "please come back later. I am very busy." Then I went upstairs and lay on Regina's bed and looked at the works of Van Gogh. I was going through his studies of the post-master's wife when someone came in.

"Hello! Just dropped by to visit awhile! Hello!"

So you see, signs don't work. Breast checks don't work. One has to just accept one's destiny with grace.

* * * * * *

My sister loaned me a book she has of every work Van Gogh ever did with a picture on the cover of that cornfield and the crows. So maybe it is true what Nabokov said of Van Gogh…"He is the darling of the middle class." After all, we all DO love that picture of the crows. Oh but so what. I have been depressed of late. I have been down in the dumps. That's more my style, down in the dumps. And more my style too, to love the picture Vincent did of the postmaster's baby, of the little naked girl sitting on a chair, bent quietly. I wonder whose child that was. And the sharp sad pictures of Sien, his lover for awhile…she was a prostitute that he found dying on the streets and brought back to health. But I think deep down inside he could never really forgive her for her past. That's what men often say, "I couldn't really ever forgive her for her past…you know, you try, but it's always there, you know?" And the new girlfriend, who is listening to the guy about the old girlfriend says,

"Yeah, that's too bad…that must have been awful" when really you are thinking,

"God I hope he never says that about me…what if he knew?"

The shoemaker sometimes tells me about old girlfriends. These days one has had many relationships when they finally find the RIGHT one. We're always finding the right one. Charles said one night, "She actually made a movie with her old boyfriend…and her…."

"Doing what?" I asked.

"Oh come on sweetheart," he said, "Doing It." IT means they were making a porno film. I've never done that. I did put my camera on a tripod once and take a nude picture of myself but it wasn't dirty…it was sort of arty.

I have a terrible headache.   Probably due to ovulation or pressure...Regina went off the school with a single chicken pox on her face, the babies had breakfast and were put in their room to play, I cleaned Regina's room and Charles washed his hair in the sink and said he would be away for the weekend. "Farm extracation," he explained, gathering his books together, the one of defibrillation, the one on emergency medical techniques and how to apply them to whatever...

"Farm extracation?" I said, a little too loudly. "What's that? Learning how to deliver calves or something? Why do you have to spend the night there?" I have a funny feeling he isn't all that faithful to me. Shoemakers have quite a bit of contact with women. Women's shoes are always needing repairs.

"More like learning how to remove people from hay balers and learning about pitch fork wounds....hopefully then I'll come back here and teach the rest of the squad..."

I was silent. I get so jealous I can hardly see straight.   "Well, I said finally, sitting down at the table with a cold cup of coffee and eating a jelly bean from Regina's basket, "You mean to tell me you're the only one going to this overnighter?"

Charles laughed. "Overnighter! Sweetheart, they called me up yesterday, they picked my from the squad to learn up in Randolfe so I can come back and teach the crew here. There's someone going from each area in the state..."

The babies called from their room something about juice. "Why can't someone else go? Why can't the president of the squad go?"

"Yeah his wife would really love that wouldn't she? If he went off somewhere overnight? Sweetheart, I'm going. They're going to pay for me to stay in a hotel..." Charles is like that, firm. He will never change his mind if he decides to do something. This is the way country men are. In the cities, like New York, a man like that might be considered stubborn, or macho, but here in the sticks it is normal. Charles began doing the dishes which I hate, there's nothing worse than some man doing your dishes while they are telling you they are going away for the weekend without you.

"You'll pick up some Randolfe chippy," I whined, pouring my coffee out. Its a cold cup of coffee every morning. All mothers drink it that way. "Maybe I'll have that guy over while you're gone...the one who likes me. The one who makes up all those voices..."

"Maybe you won't" Charles said, firm. He speaks softly, with a deep voice, but with a terrible confidence that is shattering. "You can bring the kids and come with me," he said, rinsing a plate.

"I ought to tell you how much I hate men who take out the garbage," I said, bitterly. "You seem to like to do the things I ask you not to do." The babies rattled the gate of their room.

"Ohhhhh mama???" The little girl called. "Juice mama..."

Charles rinsed a cup. "You left soap on it," I said.

"Just take care of your children," he told me.

When we first met I told him right away, "I hate weak men." I was thinking of Lymon, who cracked up over the least little thing and went rushing through the house in his jockey shorts saying,

"I think I better go to the hospital...you better take me to the hospital. I'm sick. I'm crazy...."

Regina hated him. "Mommy?" she'd whisper. "Do we have to go to the hospital?"

I had to calm him down all the time. "Oh cut it out," I'd begin, glaring at him. "You're no more crazy than I am. You're just a nine-year-old in a man's body." This was a compliment I thought, he had a nine year old body too, but I figured the more I boosted his ego, the more he would want to live up to his image of himself.

"I can't see! I can't feel anything. I'm dead inside. Help! Take me to the hospital, Mommy."

Regina would look at him then, with a clear stare and say, "That's not your mommy, that's MY mommy." Boy, Lymon was a mess.

"Eee," my English landlady would have said of him, "what a mess he is. I'd have him out the door spit spot and tell him 'Mr. so and so, don't you ever darken my doorway again." She said that of her former husband, I remember. Well, aren't we getting off the track here? It was Charles, and the farm extracation.

"You can come with me. Bring the playpen," he said. He was finished with the dish and had begun wiping the counter tops. I do that when I am really mad. You can tell if I've had a happy week or not by how clean the house is, as I usually only clean when I am furious.

"How can I come? Where would I stay? Everybody would laugh at me," I said. "Your ambulance crowd doesn't like me."

"Sweetheart," he said, wipe wipe, clean scrub, "They don't even know who you are." At this point, the little girl pushed the little boy between the gate and the door and shut the door so he was wedged at the gate.

"MAMAAAAA!" the little girl shouted, "door!"

"You mean to tell me that we've been together for two months now and they don't even know who I am???" I went to the counter and grabbed the sponge from his hand.

"Don't do that. Geez I can't win can I? If I said 'yeah they all know you and hate you' you'd be mad. If I say 'they don't know you' you're mad. What do you want me to say sweetheart? They don't know you. I don't go around talking about you to everybody...sure, the president of the squad knows about you cause he's a good friend of mine. Why? You want me to tell all the guys on a run, hey I've got this."

"Oh shut up," I shouted, "I don't want anything. I want you to get out of my life. You don't care about me...you have your own little life with your ballgames and your meetings and your overnight gigs with farm equipment...you've got all you need. Your damn shoe repair business will always bring you in a new woman to..."

"Here we go again," Charles said, and dropped the sponge in the sink. He turned to look at me. His eyes and his hair are sometimes the same color, a pale golden color like a lion. "Do you love me?" I said, going over to him and leaning into his volleyball teeshirt, his corduroy pants, his warm turtleneck shirt underneath it all.

"Yes, I love you. More than yesterday. More than last week. More than the sunflowers on Van Gogh's walls," he said.

* * * * * *

Spring is coming, Spring is coming. I can feel it. Even though it snowed yesterday, even though the wind blew like crazy on Easter day, I just know spring is on its way. Easter day was so meaningful. My mother came visiting from New York where she has been teaching, and I invited Corrine for Easter dinner because the shoemaker doesn't eat lamb or any meat for that matter. I've never lived with a man who ate meat. Does that reflect on something in me? I made a salad for the shoemaker with sunflower seeds and lettuce and carrots and cheese and little bits of this and that, the sort of thing a wild rabbit might eat, and he made himself a cabbage casserole which made the whole event seem rather Austrian, or Polish, and Corrine brought over some jello concoction and my mother brought stuffed bunnies for the children. Charles gave me a book on Mozart which is rather too technical but he wrote a beautiful inscription inside which said he wanted the whole world to know how much he loved me. "So tell your ambulance friends," I said. I gave him funny colored socks and vitamins because I don't think he eats well, one can't live on burritoes and seaweed forever, and I made him colored eggs which said "MR FLIRT" on them. The children played outside, they had new shoes for the occasion. It's the first time they ever wore shoes and the little boy had a hard time getting around in them. The little girl figured it out right away and tore off up the hill behind the house saying "out out

out". Charles tried to put up my tent for them to play in but some of the poles were missing. And we all had champagne. Really, it was a heartwarming experience after so many years of sad holidays. I felt loved.

Is this saying anything? Is it time to reevaluate the whole piece of work here and ask myself "what doors have you opened today? Where is the story line, and if it is leading to something, do we yet have an inkling of what that something is?" I used to send stories out to the New Yorker magazine. It had been my dream all my life to have a story in their pages. I suppose it is every young writer's dream. They would write me letters which I hung on my walls and showed to people passing thru...but they didn't accept anything for publication. "We feel sure you will one day be one of our new writers" some of the letters said...this was before they found Anne Beattie, another darling of the middle class. But that is my jealously venting there. Forgive me.

Anne Beattie has been compared over and over to J.D. Salinger. I love J.D. Salinger but I wouldn't want to write just like he writes. I would find that embarrassing to write like someone else. Apparently Anne Beattie doesn't mind though. And so where is Don Maclean? And now, come to think of it, where is Anne Beattie? I saw her on the street here in our town one day and I went over to her and said,

"I get letters from the New Yorker...what does William Shawn look like?" And she said,

"He is a sweet, sweet, small man" and she looked at me almost as though I were from...shall I say it, MARS.

* * * * * *

Is the narrator coming to some sort of conclusion? Does she have enough realizations in her pocket to throw around, a few each chapter? Is the story line one in which you can grab ahold and hang on, much like you would grab ahold of someones hips while they pulled you thru water? Is there a method to the rambling style? I look at John Updike's novels and think to myself how much of a novelist he is. Now there's a novel, I tell myself. It has a story line, the man is married to a dull woman and the man is sort of dull and they have drinks in the evening and the man goes to work and there's a storyline going on about the man's work and a storyline about the woman at home, going to the club, all that, and then the storyline about the man wanting to have an affair, some dreamy parts, a realization that all love is similar, and then the ending where nothing really changes therefore the reader discovers life is similar - all life all love, all couples interchangeable. A beginning a middle and an end. And he writes for the New Yorker to boot. Now THERE's someone I wish I could emmulate. Thats what Lymon was always saying. "Gee wilikers, I'd like to emulate HIM," he'd say of someone. Or, "That woman is so ingenuous, I would like to emulate her." Whatever that means. But what of it? So what if I can't find a middle to my writing? So who cares if there is no CERTAIN beginning? If all roads lead to Rome?

* * * * * *

Once I lived in the middle of the country in Illinois, in a flat town with flat highways where motorcycles roared thru cornfields, Van Gogh would have loved painting there, and I was a topless dancer. I lived with my sister...she had an apartment on a quiet flat street, I slept in a cupboard. It was like a bunk bed built into the wall. At night I put on my hot pants (remember hot pants?) pink and grey, and a tight low cut teeshirt and high heels and climb on the back of my boyfriends Harley Davidson and he would drive me thru the cornfields to this blinking flashing nightclub called the BEACON where I stood on stage with a band behind me and took off my shirt. They'd play WIPE OUT and I'd slowly pull my shirt up, keeping my eye on the bar, staring at the rum and cokes, and slowly over my head, and of course I didn't have a bra on, and then I'd throw it on the stage floor and dance. Its funny, you think of topless dancing as being really sexy and the crowd shrieking and hollering but it was just sort of stupid. There were couples sitting around at tables looking at me quietly while they drank, and once in a while somebody's wife would get up on stage with me and take HER shirt off and dance too. There was one frightening man who came every night that I danced and sat at the bar staring at me. During my breaks he would buy me rum and cokes. He'd sit beside me, not touching me, but saying "I'm going to take you home one of these days and put you in a cage I'm making for you and never let you out. I'll keep you there like a pretty little bird in my living room, and give you pretty things to put on...not clothes, but trinkets, and you will dance for me and when I want to I will take you out and put you in my bed." He scared me silly but the only way I could make tips, as they were called, is if someone bought me rum and cokes and the bartender held the rum and gave me the money instead. That way, I would never get drunk but I'd make a little extra for the night. The Beacon was full of men from a near by army base. Most of them brought their girlfriends with them, it was not a depressing place exactly, just peculiarly ordinary. I never expected a job so bizarre to be so ordinary. "I'll line the cage with soft material so you won't hurt yourself," the strange guy at the bar would say, "and I'll give you just enough to eat so you will stay beautiful and thin and always wanting." I only worked there three weeks.

Does the reader have a sense that the storyline is developing along proportionate lines? What does that mean? Are we to consider the narrator totally naive? Or is she merely following a pattern not always visible to the naked eye? Is, she shall we say, dancing to the beat of a different drum? What doors, if any, have been opened thus far?

I'll say one thing about my life. I'm certainly not isolated anymore. Back when the twins were tiny four pound mice I used to live in a cabin in the woods alone with them, and with Regina, and we had no water or heat or phone...we slept in a great pile of blankets on the floor and saw no one for weeks at a time. I weighed more than Charles and the children put together and all we ever did was watch soap operas and eat popcorn and drink milk. They drank milk. I drank lets see, what did I drink? Sherry? Well, in any case, that is no longer so anymore. I haven't seen a soap opera in ages, I lost thirty pounds, I live on a nice street and I have about a million friends who come over continuously, like a stream of cars at a wedding, like a troupe of actors at an audition. This morning Corrine came over while I was typing. "Hello? Just thought I'd drop by," she said, climbing the stairs, carrying her daughter's Cabbage Patch Kid under one arm. She sat down and we drank a pot of coffee together making that my second pot as Charles had just left after we polished off the first. The minute Corrine left, a truck drove up and my old high school girlfriend arrived, bringing a canvas bag she had designed, swinging it in her hand casually, she was on her way to the hospital to visit a dying relation. I can't bear to hear about dying relations but it seems these days everybody's dying. I still have that headache by the way. Then when she was leaving, the frizzy-haired woman appeared at my back door like a black haired ghost, her thin body wrapped in a white knit shirt to her boots, her jean jacket hanging loosely on her, her jewelry clattering like bones.

"Man, I'm in pain...can you take me to the pharmacy?" she asked, her eyes were full of tears.

"I guess I can," I said I bundled the babies and shoved them into the Vista, and we went to the drugstore. On the way I said "don't steal anything or I won't take you again."

She was bent over and moaning, "man, this is serious," lighting a cigarette. A police car passed us and she ducked. "Feds," she said. Yes, one could say I'm no longer isolated. But sometimes, surely, I miss the woods.

The house is beginning to look like a florist's shop I have so many flowers now. How is it I have become popular? I seemed only days ago that I was at a low ebb, dreaming away in my cabin in the woods, rocking a baby in my lap, listening to the sound of an occasional jeep passing. And now? Well, for instance, tonight a man who plays music is coming over to play music. Charles will be at volleyball. I have flowers here in front of me from a friend. There is that man in town who keeps asking my sister where I live. She said she wouldn't tell him because he might show up unannounced and around here that is very embarrassing. The babies are often naked, tearing thru the house like wind thru a cornfield, crows overhead, oh Van Gogh if you had been a woman I bet you wouldn't have painted half of what you did. The babies are here at my feet (I have to stand to type because they crawl on my lap), they are moving furniture around me. "Hello???" The little girl calls down the stairs. Fortunately no one is there. The little boy can't say much. He says baba mama and uggg. He cries a lot. They both cry a lot. They are both crying right now. They are a constant presence. That's what this musician guy said to me when he dropped by unannounced last night and I was in my old skirt and purple sneakers and the babies were shredding toilet paper in the middle of the kitchen floor, he walked in and said "you are a constant presence with me. You are my tender present." He's very poetic.

Charles says he worries that I won't be able to resist this man. "You could tell me not to see him" I said.

"I couldn't do that" Charles said, looking at me. "That would be selfish..." I guess because he sees so many women on his own. When I went to his shoe store one night to make a phone call, he wasn't there. I let myself in and while I waited for the line to stop being busy, I poked around in his letters and stuff hanging on the walls.

"Oh Charles," one letter read, "I'm so happy now! Now that I know you! My whole life has changed for the good. This is going to be a great, great summer!" I shoved the letter under a shoe. Not a great summer for you, I thought, reading on.

"Chuck...promise you'll call me? I miss youuuuuu."

"Hey Charlie, remember this time together. I think you're ducky." This letter was accompanied by a duck cut out of a newspaper. Another letter was from some girl in Florida. I skipped the phone call and went home.

When I got there Charles was sitting in my kitchen. "Make your call?" he wanted to know.

"You better tell that chick who thinks you're going to make her summer that you're not available" I said, my voice rising. "Because I'll bust your shop windows if you go out with her."

He laughed. "Sweetheart, you shouldn't go thru my stuff."

"Ha! Are you going to go out with her? Do you like her better than me?"

"She's a married woman," he said, beginning to do the dishes. "I believe there is an unwritten code among men not to touch another man's woman." He was washing the plates and hardly rinsing them at all. I poured some wine.

"If she wasn't married who would you rather be with?" I demanded. "Me or her?"

"That's not fair," he said, "I'm not going to answer your dumb questions. Now sweetheart, why don't you finish your wine and go to bed? I'll be up. O.K.? Go on now." He is that way, sort of gently ordering me around. Changing the subject, hurrying me off to somewhere.

"WHO??" I shouted. "If you want to be with her then just say so."

"Go to bed," he said. His voice was not loud, but there was something in the way he said it that made me suddenly, well, sleepy. What's come over me? I never used to let anyone push me around. I think I'm becoming a martian.

* * * * * *

Babies crying. Corrine visits. Charles. World moving in around me won't let me think. Can't think. Weight gained. No money. Oh world, oh this and that, oh Phil Donahue, what happened to your ENTHUSIASM? I think since he moved to New York he is not so enthused. When I see him briefly, just flicking the T.V. on and off at around nine, I see him looking poorly, tired, maybe he isn't getting along with Marlo. I hope they work things out, gee it would be a shame after that big move to break up.

Charles had an important meeting with the ambulance squad last night which he called in sick for. Instead, he took me to a play The Taming Of The Shrew. We went in my car. His car has no heat and I don't think it has a radio either. Right away a blonde blue eyed beautiful actress (who wasn't a very GOOD actress) came over to our seats and sat beside him. "Where are you from?" she asked, putting on hand on his arm.

"He's from where I'm from" I said. Actually, that's what I *should* have said, instead, I just grabbed his arm and glared at her.

"What are you doing after the show?" she went on.

"NOTHING!" I said, loudly. "He's doing absolutely nothing." It's annoying that this always happens with him. I think he may smile at these women that approach him...maybe when I'm not looking he gives them his meaningful smile...maybe he'll go back there tonight without me and ask her for a date. Maybe I should go down to his store right now and tell him to drop dead.

Tomorrow night is ambulance dance and I haven't lost the five pounds I wanted to lose. I wish I could just cut myself up sometimes...get rid of some of me. My old psychiatrist would have something to say to that. Maybe it isn't Phil, maybe its me that is not enthused anymore. Sometimes fighting with Charles about other women takes all the love out of me. Makes me feel small and alone and dead inside.

Charles said, "It went on and on, but I liked it. What did you think sweetheart? Did you like the play?" I said I did. I liked the taming part.... I like the thought of that man dragging the witchy wife off and making her behave.

Dishes. Diapers. Corrine comes over and tells me what her exhusband is up to. The frizzy-haired woman has taken to loafing around my house. She loafs around and smokes and rattles her jewelry. She is so thin. I feel very fat when she's here.

"You better go," I say, "I have a lot of work to do."

"Hey," she says, leaning back in my kitchen chair, "Anytime you need a babysitter like, I love kids...I'd be happy to come spend the day here. You could pay me whatever you would afford."

I clean around her. "Gee thanks," I say. "Maybe sometime I will ask you." Ha ha ha.

Babies cry. Cry Cry. All the time. Maybe its the flu. Maybe they have strep throat. Maybe I should call the doctor. What to do? A mother has to always be making these important decisions. To call? Or not to call?

Regina is having open house night at her school next week. This is where she and Anita will perform their femur bone song they have made up. It isn't very good. She sang it to me halting and making it up on the way...I try and get her to APPLY herself more to things but she isn't interested. "All the kids like it," she said, defensively, when I suggested she work on the song a little more. Oh well, if the kids like it, who cares what else? In fact, who cares about anything anymore? I ought to run an ad in the paper saying "WHO CARES? Please let me know. Address below. Confidential. No weirdos."

Van Gogh cared. But even he sometimes wondered what was the point. His paintings by the way are all very pointy. They have point and the ones he made in the end of his lifetime are actually pointy LOOK-ING. Spikey. Scarey. Heart wrenching.

Mozart cared.

It seems Phil Donahue cares. Why else would he be constantly trying to enlighten people? And there are cars in town that seem to have drivers who care because they have stickers on their bumpers that read "HAVE YOU HUGGED YOUR LAWYER TODAY? HAVE YOU HUGGED YOUR KID TODAY? NO MORE NUKES and of course Charles has me wear this button saying I care...."bread not bombs" the button states. I don't know if I would put it that way.

Oh world, I think I know why people don't live forever. It gets so boring after awhile. It becomes so endlessly quotidian, as the *New Yorker* once said of a story of mine.

"As always, your writing is fresh and you bring new insights into old subjects but we find the thing as a whole endlessly quotidian." They should say that about John Updike.

In Vermont, instead of saying "oh my god" or "good grief" they say "cripes!" Don't ask me where it originated from before I don't know. But they say it. Yup. Let me out. Just let me out of this cage someone built especially for me.   That guy in Beacon..."I will line it with soft material...so you won't hurt your pretty self." But I WANT to be hurt. I want to hurt. I want to FEEL. Oh world.

Can I throw in a little medical problem here? I'm having my period again. That's right, only ten days after my last one and this one is quite violent. You know how one period might be mild, like a cat coming in from outside, its fur up, its breath cold, winter morning, you forgot to let it in the night before? And how another period might be like an angry mother, smashing things and screaming...or like a drunk, falling, unable to get up, and put five dollars in his pocket on the street but he is unconscious, there is nothing you can do about it....it is God's will or something. Well, today my period is a drunk. A mean mountain mother with flying hair and a vicious face, brutalizing her dirty children, tearing her own hair from its roots, kicking the dog, etc. Its a bad one to be sure. Well, this is just another confirmation of the fact. Simply an additional symptom to be added to the list of THE WARNING SIGNALS OF CANCER - UNUSUAL BLEEDING OR DISCHARGE. I can almost laugh about it now, it is racing toward me so quickly. It is coming with a hammer, a little delicate hammer to beat me senseless over the head, just like I almost did to that mouse and I can almost find the humor in it. DEATH! Cancer! Goodbye all my sweethearts. I've been getting tired anyway.

Poor Charles. He gets the brunt of it when I have my period. I woke up early in the morning, not yet bleeding, but in a bad temper, I shouted at the babies who were calling meekly from their cribs. "Ohh mama? Out mama. Mama? Baba." The same old five or six words strung together to make me feel guilty.

"ALRIGHT!" I shouted. "JUST SHUT UP"

Charles rolled over and looked at me getting off the futon. "I don't remember you having a stomach stick out like that," he said. I glared down at him.

"Constant criticism" I said and left the room. The babies began crying when they saw me. I dragged them out of their cribs and put them on the floor, gave them juice and crackers, and disappeared downstairs to make coffee. But naturally on a day like that we were all out of coffee. I have asked Charles repeatedly to donate some money to the household but he has quietly NOT. I began thinking about that. "Never gives a dime....Well he takes me out and pays the sitter. But then he is supposed to...I can't afford another person living on what I get." By the time he came downstairs brushing his gold hair and rubbing his grey green eyes, his checkered shirt and corduroy pants just barely on him, I was furious. "Get out of my life!" I said. He looked surprised. "Can I have some coffee first?"

"There isn't any," I shrieked. I was shaking. I felt sick. And lonely. I was despairing. Everybody must feel that way once a week sometimes...."Get out. I can't stand your flirting anymore," I was saying. I refrained from asking him for money.

So he left. Just like that. Out the door. "Bring your kids shoes by the store when they break and I'll fix 'em," he said slamming the door, not hard, that wouldn't be like Charles, no, gently. He didn't say for free so I assume it would be a business relationship. Well, no one can say I fell in love with him for any other reasons than his pretty eyes, his pretty hair, his beard, his soft clothes, his holding me at night...his funny accent...no there were no ulterior motives...but I know in my heart he has gotten all those other women feeling just like I feel. Helpless in his presence.

I've thought about moving away but really where would I go? I've moved so many times. Over and over to Europe and the West Coast and the Mid-West; by the way I heard on the radio that women in the Mid-West spend more time in bed than any other women in the rest of the country. What with all those cornfields and basically nothing to do except sleep and topless dance or go to the malls.

* * * * * *

Tonight is the ambulance ball. Where couples will swing arm in broken arm (little hospital humor here) to the beat of what, a band? It is being held at some hall or other...one of those legion type places. Everyone will be dressed in Sunday go to meeting clothes...

Did I mention the fact that he missed the farm extraction? He was so disappointed. He looked so terribly sad, sitting in the kitchen chair while I yelled at him about flirting, and he had missed his trip over the mountain and oh didn't I feel like a mean mountain witch? With wicked long strings of dark hair and a glassy look in my eyes and long robes wrapped around me? Actually I had on Charles jeans and my soft blue sweater but I was hopping around the kitchen shrieking and saying "You flirt, you do, you have to admit it!" And he was sitting there, sad, and furious too, but he doesn't show much fury he just gets sick, and there we were till ten at night, both of us stuck in our roles....no way out. Oh God why did you make man and women so? Why are some men quiet while the women accuse? And the men angry when the women let down their guard? And the women cruel when the men love?

"You are the first woman that EVER said anything about flirting," he said.

"But did you not cheat on your two wives? And on this last girlfriend? Yes or no."

"Yeah...." relunctantly.

"AH HA! You see! So maybe I'm the first girlfriend to speak up is all."

"I'll say," he said, then lapsed into silence again.

God deliver me from this witch hunkered down in my body, waiting for the opportunity to jump out like a cat going up a screen door, like a mouse disappearing, quick as lightening, quick as sound traveling down the stairs..."Mamama????? Up up up!" Help me whoever, to be a better person. I have so much and nothing really, to lose.

Ambulance dance. It brings to mind flashing red lights, white suits, stretchers...actually there was only one woman there in a wheelchair.

In the morning before the dance, we took a ride with the children, went to my old cabin and dragged back a bed to sleep in, though the mice had eaten thru the mattress and we had to leave it. We set up the iron bed in my bedroom and put the futon on top of it. "What are you going to wear tonight sweetheart?" Charles said, screwing the brass knobs back into place and watching me throw a quilt over the futon.

I said, "I'll wear whatever you want me to wear." He hates purple sneakers. My green dress with white spots? It is a size eight and I am now a ten. My black velvet dress with beads on the collar?

"What's that glittery thing on the floor of the closet?" he wanted to know.

"Oh that's my old performing dress," I said. Back in England when I sang in nightclubs I had worn it with a black glittery jacket, sitting on stage with my guitar, pouring out dumb songs to a crowd of English admirers. I used to take lots of money and ride a double decker bus into the town and buy two or three evening gowns at a time, not even trying them on until I got home. That is why Charles sometimes finds dresses of mine lying around with the price tags still on them...they didn't fit. I never throw anything away so they are everywhere, in wrinkled heaps.

Charles had me try it on and he said I should wear it with the glittery jacket. I was a bit over-dressed for anything. I put on a rhinestone necklace and he dyed my white wedding shoes black and he even sewed my old black velvet purse for me. Then he disappeared and came back with white sweetheart roses because he calls me sweetheart. My hands shook. Why is that? After traveling around the world three times, after going from one side of the country to the other, after all the dances why should going to an ambulance dance make my hands shake? Who knows.

* * * * * *

Letter from Lymon. "Meet me at seven o'clock Wednesday night in the La Maisson Restaurant. If you will not, then drop this card in the mail with NO written on it. I guess this is what people did before they had phones."

* * * * * *

And my period rages on, cat fits, rat bites, hatred is just like love - love is like water - water is like blood - and here I am, bleeding all the time or never. That's my life alright. It comes in a flood...it dries up like a well. I wonder what it will be like to finally succumb to the cancer that must be ripping through me right this very moment? Oh Ollie, I'm afraid! That's what Laurel and Hardy used to say in those old movies. I remember going to this restaurant with peanuts all over the floor and watching their movies while eating huge hamburgers. My whole life is made up of memories connected with food. The time in London when Eddie, my rich boyfriend and I went to a restaurant and had steaks and they were awful and the rolls on the table were hard like stones and I stole a little tiny English creamer made of pewter. I still have it, it was so small that it fit in my jewelry box. The waiters glared at me when we left, I wasn't sure if they knew or if they just didn't approve of my red velvet evening dress and black basketball sneakers...the English are so polite! Eddie loved my basketball sneakers. He carried a photograph of them in his wallet for years after we broke up. True they were on some other girl (he didn't know her...she was from a magazine) but he said it was because he missed me so much. Even though he couldn't come back - I was too flighty for him - he missed me. And he loved my sneakers.

* * * * * *

Charles wore his tan corduroy jacket with suede elbow patches, and his green corduroy trousers, very elegant, and a blue shirt, and the soft leather shoes he made himself. I just adore his shoes. It's funny how one never thinks about what one adores in people until, well, like I notice how FOOT oriented I am now that I know the shoemaker.

Long lines of tables with white tableclothes, a place set up cafeteria style, with a roast, all sorts of food, a bar at the end of the room. When we walk in, people look up interested...he is so handsome, my shoemaker, and we are at the entrance, I see Corrine at the bar and hurry right over to her, my dress crackling slightly when I walk...it is so glittery that the lights make me shine. I am determined to carry it off with grace. It's as easy as climbing on a stage. "Don't you look nice!" Corrine says, she is standing with her date. He knows everybody. He takes Corrine everywhere but he won't make love to her. He says it would make him committed but I think it's because he is gay. There are pictures of flowers on the wall and photographs of Kennedy and the Pope. I notice some women wearing jeans. Behind the bar is an ordinary older man serving drinks. I wait for Charles to come up to me and then I say, "Please get me a martini with an olive." They don't have olives. I didn't think they would. Charles is so handsome. I want to kiss him but he is too proper to neck in public.

Corrine is having a rye and ginger. She points out Charles' old girlfriend, a dispatcher for the ambulance squad. She is sitting with her new boyfriend across the room. I can see her nose very clearly. Charles said it looked like someone had smashed it in and he was right. But there is something sweet about her, too. She has on a short white shirt...I can't tell what the rest of her is like yet. Her boyfriend is very fat and bored looking. He is eating something out of his drink. Maybe they just ran out of olives. "Hi, how're you doing?" Charles says to someone. I look at the photographs of Kennedy on the wall. What was so great about him? I read in a news article yesterday something about how all the women in the country had been taken in by Jackie Kennedy but they wouldn't be taken in by Jackie O.

"Hey Charles!" someone says. It is the president of the ambulance squad. We go to our table and sit down next to him. I sit with his wife. This town is very small...his wife was my coach when I delivered the twins.

"How are the babies doing?" she asked me. "Gee you look pretty. I almost wore a long skirt..."

I am on my second drink. I keep watching the old girlfriend, and the more I watch her the more I like her. I like the way she walks....it is a dumpy kind of gait, innocent. I whisper to Charles "How could she leave you for that awful guy?" and he says,

"What are you talking about sweetheart?" I don't answer. We eat and they clear the tables away to dance.

* * * * * *

Lymon, father of the twins. Could I meet him really? Could I show up at the La Maison and have a glass of wine and say really Lymon, you should give a little child support. Really Ly, you should leave us alone. Really Ly, you are a jerk and what do you want from me? More blood? Plenty of that.

When will my period end? Is it my period? Maybe it's my insides coming out, slowly, until one of these mornings I won't have anthing left and Charles will find me white as a sheet dead beside him in bed and he'll have to beep his old girlfriend on his beeper and say "beeper fifty one-...tech thirty eight...send the ambulance to high street....my girlfriend died in the night-bled to death." And his old girlfriend will say:

"Ten four, tech thirty eight. Saw you at the ambulance dance. Why didn't you say hi how're you doing?"

* * * * * *

We danced right next to her and her boyfriend. He danced like a buffalo, hardly moving, his head bent down. She danced like I figured she would in her brown corduroy skirt, her rear end swaying, bumping into me. At first I was swaying along with the music, moving all over, dancing around Charles in circles, until he whispered to me "Everybody's glaring at you...can't you quit bumping into people? You did the same thing the last time we went dancing". So I stood in the same place and moved my arms around like a sphinx, a many-armed Egyptian thing, afraid of being knocked around on all sides by other excited dancers; everyone was shoving everyone. "Gee it's like bumper cars in here," he said when we sat down. The president of the ambulance squad got up and made a speech...Charles got me another drink. The Pope looked down at all of us from high on the ceiling. Charles is Catholic, Lymon is Catholic. My only husband was Jewish.

"We've got a ten dollar bottle of the good stuff to give away up here...so get your tickets out and let's see who the winner is!" Everyone cheers. The man on stage holds up a bottle of wine and calls out a number. They are all used to numbers in this room...they all have code numbers and speak in numbers to each other on their beepers. "Tech fifteen give me a ten twenty one and call the hospital please...ten four."

"I got it! I got it!" someone shouts from the bar and an old man in a suit rushes up to the stage dancing to collect his bottle.

"So let's get back to dancing!" the announcer shouts.

"Do you wish you were with her Charles?" I ask nuzzling up to him during a slow song. We are still dancing next to his ex-girlfriend. I don't know who it is that sets it up...maybe Charles moves us closer to her.

"What are you talking about, sweetheart?" he wants to know. I don't answer. I watch my feet instead, making sure I do not bump into anyone. I carry with me one of the roses from Charles. Sometimes I tap him with it on the nose.

The first letter I got from Lymon after I had the babies was written on yellow lined paper like Regina uses in second grade. It said "Oh fie on it! Oh fie on it!" Hamlet.

A few months later I got one that said, "How painful to merely have sired your children! If you care to arrange a meeting you can reach me through the University (thirty miles away from me) English Department."

So it isn't the FIRST letter I've had from him, God no. After the oh fie on it one, I got quite a few.

My exhusband, the one who sailed on the ocean as a seamate, couldn't say the word *bathroom*. He said "fafffrooooom". He also could not tie his shoes. So he knotted them four times each and never unknotted them...he slipped in and out of them, they were all worn down and sloppy like he was. I saw him today in the park, crossing the street. He has been coming to Vermont every few weeks now and checking up on me for two years. He carries with him a camera, a pair of binoculars, a duffle bag. I'm afraid to death of him.

"The lawyer we're sitting with says he thinks you're cute and he wants to talk with you," Corrine whispers to me at the bar. The ambulance dance is going on late into the night, it's old rock and roll music and photographs of John F. Kennedy and somewhere, a group of drunk guys are singing Rudolf The Red Nosed Reindeer and laughing. One of their girlfriends gets disgusted and sits at our table beside Charles. Another large woman comes over to Charles while I stand at the bar and gives him a kiss. He looks up at me nervously.

"A lawyer?" I say to Corrine, interested. The lawyer comes over to us.

"I'm the one who sold you and your husband that house."

"Yes, I remember you," I say smiling.

"I just wanted you to know I've always liked you."

"I like you too," I say. I am having trouble focusing. Is it the drinks or the lawyer?

"Well, thank you" the lawyer says. He doesn't want to leave. His wife is motioning for him. Charles is now singing Peter Cottontail with the rest of the ambulance squad. And the band is about to come back from their break. I am overdressed. I am not dressed at all. I am always naked. For anyone who looks close enough.

* * * * * *

"Of course I'm going....I have to go....don't you see? I have to know what it is he wants. What do I want? I have to go at seven to La Maison."

We are in bed, Charles is putting his watch on the floor, putting his beeper on the floor. "I'm going with you," he says.

"No, you can't do that," I tell him. He begins touching me.

"Do what?" he says. "What can't I do?"

When I went with Eddie to Holland we traveled on a ship over the waves. We had bunk beds and I lay in the top bunk feeling the waves shoot carefully through me, rock rock rock a bye baby. Charles has this same affect on me. "What can't I do?" he repeats. The futon is hard, like a ship beneath us like a hard wave that hits our boat, rock a bye.

* * * * * *

Dear Mr. Donahue,

I hope you will not mind but I have been doing a little study on you, your television history, your move to New York, your public relationships...I don't mean to say I have been peering in your windows, (wherever you may be, probably the Hamptons) no, I have just been peering through the T.V. at you and accessing your karma...I have been interested in how you operate, how does one discuss all the things you discuss and not go completely mad with sorrow? It appears to me that you have a tough skin, you wear a New Yorker's leather jacket after all, but this is not what I am writing to you about. What I am writing to you about is to ask you whether you would mind my using your name NOW and again, and some of the things you and your audiences say, you know, sort of quoting what I remember....I am hoping to become a well-known public figure myself one of these days. Maybe we will meet at a cocktail party or at a gathering in my honor...or yours, if I am invited. Of course all this may be circumspect, is that the word? It all may be *irrelevant*; I may die of cancer before finishing this novel. I may die of some dreaded hideous disease which has never been heard of and which they will then name after me, like Lou Gehrig. How is your health by the way? You looked a little tired the last time I tuned you in. Hoping you will respond favorably, I remain a fan no matter what Marlo does.

* * * * * *

Frizzy-haired woman stopped by yesterday. Tears in her huge vacant eyes. "Man," she begins, "man I am so screwed up with pain. Like do you want to feel how hard it is right here? Feel this.." She held her side and pressed in.

"I believe you," I stepped back. I've always had a sneaking suspicion she might have aids. "Charles saw you out the window the other day and said you were favoring your right side."

She seemed to perk up. "Yeah? Well he's right man....like I am. I have to go to the doctors and they have GOT to check this out. I know what it is...it's either adhesions or a cyst or a tumor. I stuck it out through the week-end but wow, like I can't sleep without four sleeping pills! I nodded. She was dressed in skin tight jeans, skin tight sweater, a loose belt that hung almost to her non-existant thighs...necklaces everywhere, bangles to her elbows. "I'm going to write a letter to Sammy Davis. I think he's my father, man."

"You really think he's your father? You don't look black," I said opening the screen door and letting her in.

"Where do you think I got all this hair??? Like I'm not from Mars," she said.

I read an article in Rolling Stone about aids. A whole family got it, all except for the four-year-old daughter. That broke my heart. I wonder where my poor children will go when I succumb? Regina's father said he might take her if I died. I called him up when I had been coughing a lot of blood and said "I may be dying, Richard, do you think you'd want to keep Ginny?" And he said, "Ohh...really? Well, sure. When do you think all this will take place?" I was horrified at his callousness. But we can't all care about everyone, can we I mean, I think Charles would be sad if I died...and my mother and sisters but who's to say if anyone else would show up for a funeral?

Lymon, tomorrow night. I could see if he wanted the twins in case. No, I think I would give the babies to Charles. Would Charles want them? He said he would love to have a child, but would he love to have MINE? Without me? I can see him, repairing shoes, two playpens set up near the heel cutting machine, a couple of girlfriends hovering around saying "oh I just love your kids" like they all say about his dog. "I'm really into mothering" they'll say, patting MY babies on their orphaned heads. And Charles will have it made. He will find a couple of girls to babysit and love them, he will maybe even give his dog away, afterall, he'll have the kids as an attraction.

"So you like my kids?"

"Oh I love your kids. They look like you."

He will think this is funny but he won't laugh aloud, that might reveal something. Those dumb chicks that saunter into his store, taking care of MY kids - why the very thought. It's just sickening.

Still bleeding. Period that has lasted six days? This morning blood poured out of me, in great pools...in sad drops like tears, good bye body. Oh body, oh why MY body?

One night when my mother got drunk she said something about "that's the Sammy in you" and right away I knew Sammy Davis was my real father. I've always wanted to call him up. It's all so weird. Like I just want to get these adhesions taken care of before I do anything else....you know? I worry sometimes, am I like the frizzy-haired woman? Do I think I have adhesions? What ARE adhesions?

June came over later, after the frizzy-haired woman left, she was walking past my house on her way to the grocery. "June," I called from the back steps. Spring is really, really here, I kid you not, yesterday it was seventy-five degrees out, I put my couch in the back yard. "June!" I climbed over the rock wall and met her in the street. She was dressed in culottes and a sweater. She looked slightly disapprovingly at my bare feet. I know my feet are not my best feature. If I didn't know it before, I know it now, after living with the shoemaker. He says little remarks like,

"Boy you ought to have your shoes custom made for you...your feet are so big!"

How should I know? It's not something one can diet out of...you have to live with them. You can't say "I've been dieting for two weeks now to reduce the size." You just have to accept the fact that you (me) inherited your (my) father's foot size. C'est La Vie.

June stood by the side of the road while I sat on the rock wall. "I saw Paul last night and boy I was so mad at him...we had the big fight, you know. I don't know. I think I have spring fever. Did you see those men working in the trees?" I nodded yes. "Boy a couple of them weren't half bad. And considering my condition I'm ready to go for just about any-thing. I want my cake and eat it too. I told Paul that and he said it was fine with him, whatever I wanted. Gee he's so accomodating it's almost no fun." She had had her hair permed and it was nearly as frizzy as the black haired woman but much shorter and neater. And silver blonde.

"Well," I said, watching the twins climb the hill behind us, "Charles would never stand for me to have another lover. He doesn't even want me to see Lymon tomorrow night but I have to, don't I? I mean at least to see if he'll give some child support?" This is all divorced woman talk. It is this way with me, with Corrine, with June, even with the frizzy-haired woman although her talk is mixed in with a lot of "mans" and "likes" and codeines, we all wring the same lament...where are the men? Why are they not here? Where are the good men? Why do they leave? Why do we get stuck with the kids and no money? Why are the cute men always working in the trees?

"Did you see the guys fixing the cable T.V. wires yesterday?" I asked, picking up a rough rock off the wall and dropping it again. The whole wall is falling apart.

"No....I had to work. Gee you'd think after working all week, eight to five...sometimes eight to six, busting my butt that I'd have something to show for it, you know? I mean SOMETHING, but after the mortgage and the electricity and the food bill we've got nothing left for the next six days. While that man gets away scott free...with his new wife and his new set of kids. I'm telling you sometimes I get so mad I can't sleep at night." I wondered briefly if June ever took four sleeping pills like the frizzy-haired woman.

"I know" I said, reasurringly, picking up my part and carrying the conversation..."Regina's father has never given me a dime, not one red cent. Now his mother is going to start sending me twenty dollars a week? That buys milk and eggs maybe."

June laughed. "Right," she said, "or two bottles of wine which God knows we need after a hard day with working, with kids, with the laundry. Speaking of which I better get going. I left the troupe back there minding their own. You know neither one of those kids would come with me to help carry groceries?

I sighed. "Regina is snippy these days, too," I said. "Do you want me to drive you?"

"Oh God no! I want to see the men further down in the trees. They say they're going to widen the street...so we may get our chance yet!" June slung her purse over her shoulder and began walking away.

"Well, hang in," I called. "They don't realize what they're missing!"

"Or maybe we don't realize what WE'RE missing!," she called back. I hurried up the hill, the babies had both disappeared over the other side, into the wealthier neighborhood yards.

* * * * * *

Lymon was very rough in bed. This is common among men. Women are often passive in bed, almost nonexistant, according to Charles. He told me some of his girlfriends never moved or said anything. I was shocked.

"Did it feel good?" I wanted to know.

"Well sweetheart!" he answered, sounding irritated. "Of course it FELT good. But it probably didn't feel good to them. Least they didn't let on if it did." Charles has had a lot of lovers. He tells me about them some evenings when we are having tea and sitting around the kitchen with nothing better to do. It usually ends in a fight but for awhile it is fun to ask him things.

"So this girl Lucy you met at a mechanics class? She was good in bed?"

"Yeah, she was," he said. He stirred his tea with his index finger. Erotic, I thought.

"What's good in bed?" I wanted to know.

"What's good in bed?" he repeated. "Well, you. You're good in bed."

I listened to this. "So me and Lucy are good in bed?" I went on.

"Yeah you could say that." He crossed his arms. My guru boyfriend told me this means you are feeling insecure. Also, if you hold your thumbs in your fist you are insecure.

"So me and Lucy are interchangeable in bed."

Charles jumped up and went to the stove. "I didn't say that" he said. "Will you shut up about all this? Jees I get so damn sick of hearing the same thing every night....over and over....can't you just let the past rest? I know what I did..."

I crossed my arms. I was feeling insecure. "But you said Lucy was good and I was good so what's the difference? We're both good...right? Right. Get out." I turned away and stared out the window at the street. I could see the T.V. going in the auctioneer's house.

"You are really weird," he said, louder than usual. "You have these lightening changes. God, I don't believe you. What's HAPPENED to you?" I got up and stood beside him.

"What's good in bed?" I repeated. I leaned into his soft clothes, rubbing my head on his chest.

"Oh sweetheart" he signed, "You are, O.K.? You're good in bed."

But Lymon was rough in bed. He pushed me all over the place and knocked me around, and all the while he was saying things about Catholic girls in high school...pretending he was the headmaster. It was really odd. But maybe I shouldn't be saying all this. You never know who's going to sue you over some little insignificant remark.

Twins in the basement. Oh children, I make you, and carry you nine months, I bear you with grace and dignity, controlling my howls until you are nearly born, give you my body to eat and then I desert you to the basement so I can record it all and fool around with Charles. Aren't human beings basic?

Bleeding so much that I've lost two pounds. I find this all very terrifying and calming in the same moment. At least I know what my destiny will be. I know where I am going now and sometimes it depresses me and sometimes I am calmed by it...yes, headed for hospital and death and cold sheets and everyone afraid to visit because you look so terrible, ravaged by cancer, yellow with cancer. And yet something in all this is profoundly sweet. To face the great black cape, I want them to play Mozart at my funeral. I want them to mourn in black and bury me during the rainy season. I want my casket a pine hand made box, let Charles make it, let Regina carry flowers to my grave, let them arrive in black cars, and no wake please. No wine and desserts and talking about how swell I was, late into the night. No, let them bury me and play Mozart and cry some and then go home. Let them all go home alone, and nobody better make love with Charles that night or I will rise from the dead and strike you all with a little nifty hammer, hidden in my shroud.

Charles turned on his beeper last night just to listen to another ambulance crew in another town. We heard a lot of static and then they were transporting someone to a bigger hospital, "Tie one this is Tie six, get the E.R. ready for this code 66, patient in crit con, a code three on this, ten four." Charles could talk to me and listen to all that at the same time but I had a hard time hearing him. I was so worried the patient would die on the way to the hospital that I kept saying "what?" whenever he said something to me.

"Shall we go read Shakespeare in bed?" he said, finishing his tea.

"There's a blood pressure reading of 80 over kkkkkkkkk...patient is damp and warm to the touch - possible kkkkkkkkk"

"What?" I said to Charles.

"Sweetheart you don't listen to me. I've told you before you have to listen when I am talking to you."

"Ten four Tie one...is Tie six on first response or not? E.R. ready, bring 'em in."

"The Taming Of The Shrew," Charles was saying. "We are going to read it for one hour every night....remember?"

"Kkkkkkkkkkkk....arriving....kkkkk"

"Yes I remember," I said.

"Well? Let's go," Charles went on, picking up my book of Shakespeare's plays and turning off the beeper.

"Charles...what about the patient in the ambulance?"

"They're at the hospital and they're doing O.K.," he said.

"They are? How do you know?" I asked him.

"Sweetheart, you don't listen. If you listened you would have heard them. They arrived at the hospital at nine fifty two patient in improved condition....probably a heart attack...now let's GO." He pulled me up by

my arms and I followed him to bed, feeling the blood seep out of me and
onto my underpants.

* * * * * *

Phil, just a note to say how much I enjoy your show. The frizzy-haired
woman from up the street and I got to talking about you yesterday and
she stopped by on her way to deliver a specimen to her doctor, and she
told me her favorite show of yours dealt with prostitution. I missed that
one but she told me you had several real prostitutes on the stage speaking
candidly about their professions. I wonder, could you send me a
transcript of that? Every morning after you are on, they say you can get a
transcript of the whole show just be sending in an envelope...but
WHICH show? Do you ask for like, the one where the woman stood in
the shadows telling about her thirty five different personalities? In any
case, I think you are very good at what you do and if I were given the
choice between you and Clint Eastwood (they did a survey of that, did
you know?) I would pick you. But of course that would never happen
because you have Marlo......right? You DO have Marlo still, don't you?
Hoping you are enjoying the Hamptons, I remain a fan no matter
what.

* * * * * *

The frizzy-haired woman was here yesterday early. "Man, I have to
get some scripts from the pharmacy...will you let me catch a ride with
you?" she said. I was just pulling out with the babies strapped into their
seats singing in the back "ohhhh, rummm rummmmm." They were
meaning the sound of the engine but it could have been ha ha ha and a
bottle of rummmmmmm. I drove her to the pharmacy and waited in the
car while she went in. "Like this shouldn't take long," she said, rattling. I
waited. The day was beautiful..."Mama?" the little girl said.
    "I'm right here," I answered. They both had parts of a granola
bar.
    "Mama?"
    The frizzy-haired woman came back out twenty minutes later.
"Could you stop by the post office? I have to mail this specimen to my
doctor...would you mind taking me to the hospital on Thursday morning
man. They're going to do an upper G.I." We drove along, waving to the
cute guys that were working on the highway. I like summer...everyone
gets so friendly when the sun comes out. "I'll be right back," she said,

leaving us in front of the post office. She returned in fifteen minutes. "Jim is really a great guy...he's the postmaster...gives me free stamps...." she leaned back and laughed. The babies laughed with her. I looked at the town clock.

"I have to get back...Charles might come for lunch after he runs," I said, moving the vista toward home.

"Like stop at the electric company...I have to pay my bill. Those people don't realize how hard it is bringing up a kid. They think I'm made of money or something. I mean I go around in circles,man, trying to figure out how to work things out...ohh, this balloon in my bowels is killing me. They're gonna have to do something about it and quick..."

"Maybe they'll take the whole thing out," I said.

"That's what scares me," she said, looking wilder for a moment. "I mean like there's nothing left in there to remove...they've taken everything already...."

I pulled up in front of the Electric Company and left the motor idling. "Well, maybe they'll take out your bowels and you'll have to wear one of those little bags," I said.

When we got to my house, Charles was not there. I saw a grey shirt in the washing machine that hadn't been there earlier and there was a frying pan in the sink so I figured he had come and gone while I was at the store. We took beer and cheese and crackers and sat outside on the patio with the babies. "It's so loud out here," I said, checking the little boy's diaper. He was dry.

"Loud? Whatdoyamean?"

"The elements," I said, waving my arms around....pointing at the clouded sky...it had quit raining while she had been in the grocery, the wind was roaring and the traffic on the road heavier...probably the men in the trees taking lunch breaks. "You ought to find a nice older man and settle down before it's too late," I warned her, eating a cracker. "If you end up with a bag attached to you you might not have so many lovers...."

"There's no way I'll live like that," she said. She was not eating any of the cheese or crackers. That's probably why she is a size five and I am a size ten. "I couldn't. I don't want to live anyway," she said. This sounded a lot like me. I sounded a lot like all the divorced women on the street...I wondered if men ever talk this way. When we had finished the beer, a friend of Regina's, Susie, the girl I am now babysitting for on Tuesdays, arrived.

"Where's Regina?" I asked her. She had her Cabbage Patch Kid with her."

"She's walking with the other girls going to the birthday party across the street." Susie put her doll down.

"Who's that?" I asked and pointed to her doll.

"Tina."

"Hi Tina," I said.

"Hi," Susie said.

June walked up the driveway. "How about some wine?" I said.

"You twisted my arm," June answered, and sat on the stoop. I bet she's afraid of aids too. "Work work work," June began, when I returned with her wine and my wine and a granola bar for Susie. "And I'm still so upset about the siding on my house....have you seen it buckling? IT is and it's getting worse and I'm such a marshmallow I'm afraid to say anything...fifteen hundred bucks down the tube...."

"I never noticed," I said.

"Hey do you like the dress I got at the thrift shop?" the frizzy-haired woman asked, pulling out a gauzy white dress from her bag.

"Ohhh," June said. She was more interested in her wine. "Speaking of which....I have to go to a wedding next week and I don't have a thing to wear...I love your green dress with the dots...do you think...."

"Hey!" the frizzy-haired woman said, loudly, holding up her white dress. "Borrow this man...this is perfect for a wedding."

"You can't wear white to someone else's wedding," I argued. The sun was hot and we were all getting slurred speech. "More crackers?" I offered.

"No thanks," June said to the frizzy-haired woman..." I want to melt into the crowd, not stick out like a sore thumb."

"Hey this dress is worth money man," she said.

We all swallowed our wine and I passed around more crackers. "I wear a nine anyway," June said to me. "And I'd love to borrow your dress - could I?"

"Sure," I said.

"Oh you're a doll...Thank you. You know I hate the thought of going to that thing at the kid's school this week...I've got a doctor's appointment the same day...."

"Hey you want a good doctor?" the frizzy-haired woman offered. She lit a cigarette. "I have the most gorgeous doctor in town...Jack? You know him? He's new to the area...GOD he is gorgeous."

"Well, that's half the battle," June said, trying to be polite, "confidence in your doctor."

"Hey he is hot," the frizzy-haired woman added, lying back on the couch.

"How's the shoemaker?" June wanted to know.

"He's fine," I said, "you know I'm seeing Lymon tomorrow night...do you think thats right??"

"You have to," June agreed.

"Like I can't drink wine man," the frizzy-haired woman said to us, but we were not really paying much attention. "Smoking pot helps the pain...they give it to cancer patients for pain man."

June looked up at her, horrified. "You take drugs?"

"NO way. Pot, man. They give it to cancer patients," the frizzy-haired woman repeated. I was getting uncomfortable.

"My father died of cancer," June said, looking out at the hill where the twins were climbing on the grass. "They got special permission to give him some drug for his pain....you know how people say how thin they get? And awful looking? From the pain and all...oh, so they gave him this stuff."

"T.H.C.!" the frizzy-haired woman said, excitedly. "That's the main ingredient in pot. It's great for pain."

I noticed my yellow potted flowers were wilting in the sunlight. The babies had taken their shoes off and were digging up the yard, like my dog sometimes does. "I'm going to be taking Susie home soon," I said to the frizzy-haired woman..."so maybe you better too...I mean, won't your groceries get hot in the car?"

She stood up, wavering in the breeze...almost as though her frail body would tip sideways in the wind, be blown one way and then the other. I felt how much alike we three were, in our own womanly way...we were all similar vessels...how basic it all becomes!

"Hey, Thursday morning man...the hospital. I have that upper G.I."

I nodded, drunk on wine and sunlight. "I won't forget," I said.

"God he was in such pain. It was a blessing when he died," June said to herself.

"Hey drop by my house sometimes," the frizzy-haired woman said to June.

"Ohhh," June answered, "Sure thing...I'm pretty busy...."

Susie rode her bike home at five o'clock and somewhere around six or seven, Charles bounded up the stairs, well he doesn't really bound after doing shoes all day. The sun seemed like it was still out...the house was hot. The babies, retired to the basement, were dismantling the heating system that runs along the baseboards of the room. "RUUUMMM, amook mama? Baba..ohhh! Boom!" they shouted. I said to myself, tomorrow is Lymon. Tomorrow I see Lymon...for the first time in two years...I see Lymon, father of my twins, weak man that he is, I see him and what will I feel? All week I have felt dead inside, knowing he is coming...knowing he is on his way...La Maison-seven p.m. Of course, I will be there.

* * * * * *

Memo to Phil Donahue. Dear Phil, what about more shows on women personalities and less on gorgeous men? Boy George, Liberace, where are the female heroes? Where are our figures to look up to? I mean Raquel Welch sure, but what about say, oh, a struggling writer, trying to make it with three kids and no money...a real heroine type? I would be willing at absolutely no charge to visit your show and express my feelings...what say? Let me know soon as I have been having my period of seven days now and may be draining away completely. A fan no matter what Marlo ends up doing to you.....

* * * * * *

My daughter's Cabbage Patch Preemies don't fit the preemie clothes I had for the twins when they were born. Get this...the clothes are TOO SMALL for Alvina Florida and her other Cabbage Patch Kid. That's how little my twins were when they came home for the first time. After Lymon had dumped us in the hospital...after all that pain and suffering. After after. How could I even consider seeing him? How? Charles said that the ambulance guys say when a woman won't leave an unfaithful man, "He must have a big one".

* * * * * *

Lymon walked in wearing a sweater and pants...a tweed overcoat, hair shorter, no beard no mustache. I had my hands around a glass of wine, he held his arms out...stretched his hands toward me, suspended there for moments, then sat down. We looked at each other. "You came..." he said. "I thought after I stood you up, you would do the same to me..."

I was struck dumb by how much he looked like the little boy. He was identical. Oh, Phil Donahue, will you do a show on the wrenching experience of losing a lover? Of seeing your children's father sitting before you, having expresso, the night cold in the middle of spring, it snows?

Here is the crux of this piece of writing. It is the jelling point. More than crows, that pick over their food and leave nothing, take the whole sheebang with them, it is about loss. Love. Cruelty. And hope... Of course a novel should include a smattering of hope throughout....Will the narrator succeed in whatever she is trying to accomplish? Yes. She might. Will she bring together all the fathers and all the friends...all the children? Will she live to see the light of her losses?

"Lymon, I didn't want to hate you anymore," I blurted out. He grabbed onto my right hand and held it tightly...through the whole evening I had to drink my wine with my left hand...fortunately I wore a beige outfit so if I should have spilled anything it wouldn't show. Did I spill my life's blood then Lymon? Did I spill my guts and my blood and my heart out? Did I break my femur bone over you?

"I just want you to know," he said, pausing dramatically, "that a day had not gone by that I haven't thought of you....often...often throughout the day. I I...I love you. And I know my pain could never equal yours..."

Of course not, I think now. No pain could equal mine. I'm the pain expert. Me and the rest of the divorced women on this street. Me and the people on the Phil Donahue show. Me and the brown babies in rags, in dirt brown rags in Ethiopia. Me and the dead people on the N.B.C. News. And Lymon? Why he could have been Tom Brokaw. He was the reporter, looking at me curiously...

"How did you manage? I'm so glad to see you haven't lost your wonderful spirit..." he said.

Spirit Lymon? You mean like a ghost? Or like a glass of whiskey? You mean that which is keeping me glued together? In the face of blood and doctors? Today I received a bill for the pap smear...some lab bill. WE HAVE BILLED MEDICAID it said haughtily. Oh Lymon, what sorrow did I live through? I can't remember anymore. I can't recall any of it. All I know now is the bottles and the milk. The car seats and the money for the sitter. All I recognize is the old hollow face in the mirror, the cribs against the wall, the mess in Regina's room of Cabbage Patch accessories, the sound of the twins tearing up my Van Gogh prints, oh Lymon, who are you? Why am I alive today to say anything at all?

"Are you hungry? Would you like to have dinner?" he asked me, still holding onto my hand, me looking into his smooth, untroubled face.

Am I hungry? Why yes, I am. I am hungry for something which eludes me. It is not love, God forbid it is not love. I USED to think it was love, but no, it is not that. What, then? It eludes me, slips in and out of my memory bank. Am I hungry Lymon? For fish? For wine and fish?

"I could eat," I said. I could eat and eat and eat. I could eat up the table
we are sitting at, chewing the wood with a deadly grinding away. Oh good
bye body. I watched it float out the door...my old sweet body, and here I
was still. Mr. Donahue, what makes us tick?

Over dinner he held my hand, me eating with my left hand, fish and
bread and champagne. He stared into me, saying how brave how strong I
was...how weak he was. "Oh no," I lied, "You were strong to come
tonight".

"Ha," he said, bitterly. "I'm not strong so don't say I am. I know what
I am....a coward. A weakling. I could never compare to you, not in the
eyes of anyone."

But you could, Lymon. Anyone, and this is the secret to this novel,
anyone can compare to anyone.   We are interchangeable vessels,
whoever has the kids has the kids, whoever is the leaver is the leaver,
whoever fixes the shoes walks, and me? I ride in my Vista with my babies
and my daughter and I ride and ride and ride across the town, through
the New England hills. Over the water. We are all just alike. This is what
John Updike thinks, I bet. He knows that one woman is as good as
another, that one man is the same as—

So hang on to him Marlo, because they don't all LOOK alike.

"Please let me see them," he said, finally, when we were sufficiently
drunk and the meal was cleared away and the coffee wasn't working, I
could hardly hold my head up I was so drunk. We were back drinking
wine and I said,

"Oh alright...let's go in my car." I took him to my quiet little street...it
became an ugly scary little street when I drove down it carrying Lymon
beside me in the Vista like a dead body, a human form like they use in life
saving classes, those inflatable soft rubbery dummies that let you do
awful things to them and then passively wait for you to save them
...drown them...stick them with i.v.'s...they remain looking at you with a
blank face. "This is your son," I said, picking up the little boy from his
crib and handing him to Lymon. He was damp, his diaper must have
come lose...

Lymon said, "Hi there, fella."

I said, "Say hello, daddy," just for the drama of it but he felt no more
like a daddy than I did.

Stop here a minute. Where are the pieces falling? Are we coming together like lovers try and do, or is this all over creation and the narrator is off on a tangent...let me ask one question here...did I shut the door?

"That's your daughter in the crib there," I said, pointing to the other bed with a small dark face peering out of the bars. The room was black but one becomes accustomed to anything.

"Hi there," he said..."Boy you look like...." he was talking to her and his speech became quieter...I left the room and wandered around in the upstairs hall...

I stepped into Regina's messy room and saw her sleeping in her iron bed, looking like Richard. I went to the bathroom and looked in the mirror at my drunken self. When I went back into the children's room I said "come on Lymon, Charles will be back soon and I should take you to your car..."

"He came out, his face was stricken and he sobbed on my shoulder. "What am I going to do?" He cried.

"It doesn't matter," I said. I patted his red hair and held what felt like my son.

"What am I going to do?" he repeated, louder. "WHAT AM I GOING TO DO?????"

"It doesn't matter," I said again and again. It plain doesn't matter because of all the things we are and are not, we human beings are fallible and every mistake you make is similar to someone else's, and somebody somewhere forgives us. And here I am Lymon forgiving you. So maybe Charles will forgive us for what I did...I kissed him. I said, "You are dear...I will always love you." Then I drove him to his old beat up car in the parking lot behind La Maison and he went away, his face like the face of a life saving dummy. His eyes empty and small, his pretty hair and handsome body, everything, all naked as the day.

* * * * * *

I should never have gone to see him. It made my hands shake all week, gave me a different outlook on things, on Charles for example. When I look at him now, I think, what did Lymon mean when he said it was hopeless..! and then later he said "Oh I'll be back...I am going home to think about you." What was it he said about our life together? How we used to listen to Robert J. Lerzemer's birds in the morning? How we lived in the woods...how dear Regina was to him? I look at Charles and all this comes back to me...I don't think I could have Alzheimer's disease but then it's possible, being a storyline can always be altered.

Charles took me out with his ambulance partner one night. We met them in a dull restaurant and while we waited to be seated, the guy said "how's it going?" to everybody who came in. All the people there were dull looking. Is that unfair of me to say? Charles says I am too critical of people. I had on my linen skirt outfit, Charles in his corduroys, the other couple were dressed in something boring. The wife never said anything all through dinner. When we were seated, the couple Chris and Mary, ordered chicken fingers and milkshakes. Who in the world orders a milkshake for dinner? I haven't had a milkshake since I was twelve. For the entire evening we listened to Chris talk about ambulances and fires. He is a fireman too.

"Do you have any kids?" I asked, thinking, well, if nothing else, talk about kids.

"No I do not!" Mary said adjusting her round glasses. She was very small, almost like a twelve-year-old. "We decided a long time ago...no kids. I don't like them," she explained, looking at Charles.

"You decided, " Chris said briefly. He turned back to Charles, "Did you see the fire up on Frog mountain last night? Boy that sucker was burning like a whirlwind outa control. We dug all night, trenches you know, boy we were down there in the mud dust digging away...but I'll tell you, if that lightening had started the fire two days ago it'd been a lot worse. A LOT worse."

"I have a part-time husband," Mary said.

"And it wasn't even our territory...Brushmont said they knew it was going on but as long as our boys had it, why they weren't about to get dirty. And it was on Brushmont line too." Chris was buttering rolls while he talked. "You go to that accident down on route four today???" he asked Charles.

"No, I wasn't on call till six," Charles said. They both had beepers with them and during the evening there would be a sound and they'd take out their beepers and listen. There weren't any accidents all through dinner...Unfortunately...I wouldn't have minded having to leave them off at the ambulance shed...Once in a while I tried to respond to something Chris was saying, but it met with nothing. It was almost as if Mary and I were not there, and Mary didn't appear to be there anyway. She stared at her chicken fingers and drank her milkshake. After dinner I ordered coffee and they all had water...I have never been out with people like that.

"Boy, that car overturned on the woman and she broke her nose...cut her jaw up bad. But she didn't like it when I took the scissors to her blouse...I said how do you get into this thing? No she didn't like that a bit." We were all standing in the parking lot outside the restuarant, after eating, listening to Chris.

"Why did you have to cut off her blouse if it was just her nose that was hurt?," I wanted to know.

He was looking at Charles when he said, "Check for broken bones...her nose was broke bad...boy she was hurtin.."

"Kissed the windshield did she?" Charles said.

"Oh yeah...and that car was totaled...it was really nice. I mean seeing all that devastation...." Mary was glaring into the night, her tiny arms crossed across her flat chest.

"Well, we better be leaving...." Charles said for the fourth time.

All in all it had to be the most boring evening of my life. I had no idea people related to other people like that. I had no idea there was so much boring detail to discuss. Or that couples had such a blank life together. "We'll see you Charles," Chris finally called, as we moved toward our car. Nobody said goodbye to me. That is just as well, because really, I wasn't there. I was mulling over Lymon....the champagne we had together, his red hair bending to me, now what was it he had said?

But Lymon, what is it? Why am I weak in the knees and at a loss for what to do all of a sudden? Why do I feel as though I am waiting for something? Something to happen, that will change everything drastically? Why am I suspended, waiting, for you to come tear up my life again? "I was so worried," he had said, "that your spirit would have been broken.."

Charles took me to an exhibition of impressionist paintings not far from here yesterday....there were only four pictures, one Mary Cassat, two Eduard Manet's, one Degas. There was also a painting supposedly done by Rembrandt but it didn't look like a Rembrandt, it was too out of focus, too blurred, and underneath it there was a little plaque that said there was some dispute about whether or not it might be a fake, done by Rembrandt's student..."that's no Rembrandt," I said loudly. The other couple in the room turned and looked at me. Probably from Mars, was written on their faces, meaning me....Later, Charles took me to an outdoor cafe where we had a carafe of wine and talked...it was so romantic, like Paris, drinking and watching joggers...but do you notice how I say "Charles took me here" and Charles took me there? It sometimes feels as though I am only a bystander in this novel.

And while we're on the subject, AM I merely a bystander? Is there enough of the narrator in this piece to warrant it being a novel or is it something else? Maybe I have been all along, writing a long poem. What do they call them? Epics. Title: Crows or Poseys. Epic poem, file under; rambling. Disoriented. Often bantering. Subject: Woman roaming earth.

Regina's open house. She stood in front of all the kids in her class and all the parents and read a story she wrote about Cabbage Patch Kids.

"Hey mom," part of it went, "I want a Cabbage Patch Kid."

"Why?," said Mom.

"Because," said the little girl.

"Oh, O.K.," said Mom. "We'll go to the store and buy one later. I'm busy right now."

That embarrassed me. Not because it was unoriginal, everyone else's stuff was unoriginal too, they like it that way in school, but because the mother was busy. That's the way I am. Always too busy to listen to the little girl.

Meanwhile, Charles was standing in the back of the room with none other than his old girlfriend, a dispatcher for the ambulance squad...she was there to listen to her friend's child read some unoriginal work they had written. Charles and his old girlfriend both had on their ambulance jackets and talked through the whole thing. It felt like the school had hired them for safety measures, that there was a smoking ambulance waiting outside in the rain, in case a child had a heart attack while reading their story on stage.

I sat in the front row with Susie's mother, I was so upset about Charles flirting that I could hardly listen when Susie's mother said, "we'd like Regina to visit at our house on Mondays, and you take Susie on Wednesdays....I have a sitter there most of the week but I can't find one for Wednesdays. Vacation week is such a bother....There's the doctor's daughter..."

I sat there in the front row saying to myself, "afterall YOU went out with Lymon...YOU went out with the musician guy. YOU'RE the one kissing other men, he's not doing anything so bad. It's YOU that is doing bad stuff....HE'S just talking away with his old girlfriend...he's just having a good time letting the whole room know that he isn't necessarily with YOU." And by the time all the children had stumbled through their endlessly quotidian stories I was ready to strangle Charles, who came over innocently enough and said,

"Ready to go?"

"Get away from me," I whispered. "Go drop off a building."

We made our way through the crowds of parents who were laughing over their adorable children and calling "come now Matthew, mommy and daddy are leaving now..."Charles dropped behind and I heard him say,

"Hi, how're you doing?" to someone but I didn't even look back to see who. I was interested in getting a cupcake. I wanted ice cream. It's the same old story, like with my psychiatrist, the minute anything threatens me, I get hungry.

If only I hadn't gone to La Maison!! If only Lymon had not showed up, like a beautiful devil, red haired and taller than I remembered him, his tweed coat and his clean hands, his Shakespeare sonnets and his flattery. If only I hated him!

Charles said to me at the open air cafe while we drank wine, "I'm going to protect you. I don't think you can take care of yourself...you need someone to take care of you."

Well, that is true enough...but does it lend itself to the storyline? Is the narrator to this point in the novel, a woman unable to take care of herself? I always imagined her a world wise very intuitive type, but then, maybe I am too close to the whole thing to recognize her little failings...anyway, it was like Charles to say something like that.

Let's analyze the character *Charles*.

1. He is a busy man. He has classes and jobs and squads and leagues and associations he belongs to. Busy busy busy.

2. He is very good looking, flirtatious, likes women, doesn't worry all the time like the narrator does, isn't bleeding, not at this point anyway, but a few more flirtings like the open house one and he might be....

3. Parental. My psychiatrist always labelled people either "childlike" or "parental" so I would have to pick parental for Charles as he is definately not childlike.

4. Prone to selfishness.

5. Erotic, fun, intelligent, cold, unpredictable, kind, and loving. That's what is so confusing.

The twins are in bed. So what else is new? Well, not much to be honest. The frizzy-haired woman sent her daughter down here at one point to tell me she was sick.

"Mom wants Charles to come check her right away," she said, leaning against my screen door.

"CHARLES?? He drives an ambulance, he's not a doctor!," I said.

"Well mom wants him right away," the little girl persisted.

"Forget it. Tell your mother he isn't a doctor," I said.

I closed the screen and she walked away. "Tell your mother he isn't a doctor," I heard her mimic. Since then neither one of them have bothered me. I did dream I had an upper G.I. though...I DO *feel* for her, the frizzy-haired woman...it's just that my life is so mucked up with people, dull people, people wanting and demanding, it's like the whole world has become twins, clambering all over me.

* * * * * *

Egotistical. You have to be careful when doing a piece of writing that the subject does not become too SUBJECTIVE. The narrator, should there be one, (and thank God I'm not dead yet) should remain objective if not aloof, and should in no way impose her theories on the storyline. Something of an example would be "everybody there was dull." This is a statement that not everyone can associate with. For instance, what if a dull person were reading the work and came to that part? Would they say to themselves "why how dare she!"? or would they say "she must be talking about artists...all artists are dull." Therefore, turning her statement into something they are able to conceive of....

Having gone thus far let me say this, a writer should BLOCK out her moves, should be LEADING toward something, should have in mind a definite door opening...a celebration of the finale...in short, a writer should have an inkling of how the outcome will come about and naturally, WHAT the outcome will be.

Do I? Do I know where I'm going? Have I ever known? Am I headed up stream or down? Am I rollicking toward a grand exit or am I meandering away from the scene of the accident?

I read in the paper that a woman ran over a drunk man late one night and killed him. It was an accident, he just appeared out of nowhere and went under the wheels of her car. She stopped and turned around and a great crowd had gathered around the dead man. She was apparently, upset so she went home and didn't call the police until the next morning reporting that it was her who had killed the man. (The man had been taken away immediately to wherever they put dead people.) This woman is now serving a jail sentence, pregnant. I would find that a less bitter pill had there not been the day before in the paper an article about a man who had murdered his wife near here and was found innocent by reason of insanity. Is this state pro men or what? That's what my husband used to say. "So you going out or what?" "What are you doing classy chassis? Shoppin or what?" He was just awful.

* * * * * *

Yesterday Charles had a morning extracation class, an afternoon

mountain rescue class, and evening I.V. class...I got him to skip his
mountain rescue class to take me to the impressionist exhibit...actually
that is not true. I can't get Charles to skip anything...he does what he
wants and he offered to skip it to take me to the impressionist exhibit. He
almost skipped his I.V. class to take me to the Mozart movie again which
I love so much but the babysitter had to get home early. When we got
back the babysitter was sitting on one of the twins little chairs, waiting.
"Hi," I said, coming up the stairs, She said nothing. "Where are the
babies?" It was six o'clock.

"I put 'em to bed," the babysitter managed.

"YOU DID? Why how wonderful!" I said, enthusiastically. I try and
get her to talk by being very enthusiastic.

"Yup, put 'em both down couple minutes ago," she went on.

"Oh how great," I said. "Is there anything you can't do?" She stared at
me. Maybe I had layed it on too thick. "Did they eat?" I asked.

"Gave 'em half a peanut butter sandwich," she said. She was still sitting in the little chair, her great dark body well, she is not dark but she
gives an AURA of darkness, sitting utterly placid.

"Yeah," Regina said coming over to me with her jumprope, that's all
seven-year-olds do...jump rope, "they didn't want it so she ate the
sandwich." The babysitter batted Regina in what I suppose was a playful
move.

"Ohhh, how great," I continued. "Well, Charles will pay you and give
you a ride home..." Charles was in the kitchen collecting his books
for class.

"Ready?" he said to the babysitter. She stood up, silent, and lumbered
down the stairs.

"Bye! Thanks!" I called...

"You're welcome," Charles called back. They both climbed into his
little silver volkswagon and drove off down the street.

"Two four six eight. Who do we appreciate?" Regina said, jump jump
jump. "Look Mom, I can chinese jumprope now perfectly. Look....look
Mom!" I looked. She had strung the rope between two chairs and was
hopping all over the place. "Whoops, that didn't count," she said.
"Whoops...wait a minute. Look Mom! You're not looking. See? I can do
turnies too."

"Great," I said, with less enthusiasm than I had showered on the sitter. "Let's go to bed and watch T.V....."

"Wait but look Mom," Regina said again.

"Regina, I'm so tired, I'll look tomorrow..."

"You always say you'll look tomorrow...will you color with me?"

I poured a glass of wine and began turning out the lights. "Color?" I echoed. "Maybe later...let's go to bed..." Regina was jumping in the dark kitchen.

"Insies outsies backsies frontsies turn turn turn," she chanted. I left her downstairs, carrying my wine with me to my bedroom, through the twins room, switching on FAME, falling back into the futon, considering Lymon.

There is Mexican music on the radio and Charles has just left. He was angry. Mexican music reminds me of going with my mother over the border and dickering endlessly with a little man about a chess set. Now I wish we had bought it but at the time I didn't care. This is how I am. I am always sorry later. So who will I be sorry over next? Will I be sorry if I don't respond to Lymon's recent love letter? (Received yesterday? "darling what am I to do" he says.) Or will I be sorry if I see him and lose Charles? These are all questions that should be answered within the next couple of chapters. Actually, I think I will round up this triad fairly soon.

* * * * * *

Dear Phil, Life goes on here at the little peeling paint house of which you know nothing about. I was thinking, how about doing a show on just a regular person? You know, interviewing them, talking about their family life, showing baby pictures, and fooling the audience by telling them this is a famous person...see how they respond. I would be happy to be the guinea pig as I have spent my life being sort of an experiment. I sometimes feel as though I have been under glass, better put, I am straight from a lab - Mars. With fondness for the both of you, I remain living.

* * * * * *

Sick. Nausea. Weight gain. God what if I'm pregnant? Babies in the basement, Regina in her room (vacation time) over and over the life cycle, up, dress, eat, type, ride my bike, go to the store, worry, eat, sleep, make love, receive letters. Is life so dull as this? I sometimes wonder what would happen if I killed myself? I see Charles arriving for lunch, finding my note on the front door, "Tech 38...call the ambulance and don't come in because I am dead upstairs." The kids are all in the basement...and Charles would come in anyway, and walk heavily up the stairs, find me dressed politely for the viewing. He would lift my silent body up and maybe carry me downstairs, maybe not, and surely he would cry. He would say, "Oh I had a feeling but I thought no, she wouldn't...but I guess I should have known..." and then he would take me to where they take dead bodies...I guess the morgue? Is there a morgue in this area? The morgue man would say,

"Better go on and wait in the other room...this isn't very pleasant..." and Charles would say,

"I'm staying. I can run later..." because it would be his lunch hour and he always runs on his lunch hour. He can run five miles without stopping. I find that incredible. So the morgue man takes off my nice outfit and lifts me onto a table and checks me for what, spots? Adhesions? Mars marks? Finds it was an overdose of something...then heaves me onto a scale, do they weigh the deceased? I always decide not to kill myself when I come to this part...the man heaves me onto a scale and Charles reads the numbers with the man..."Gee," Charles says, somewhat horrified by the whole thing...."I never realized she weighed that much...." and his sorrow is hampered by his surprise at how dense I must be.

"Thick blood, heavy bones," the morgue man says, throwing a sheet over me. "Now where do you want this shipped?"

Charles signs some papers and leaves me cold on a slab of marble in a body refrigerator. Other bodies lie with me. Charles walks outside and does some warm up exercises. He bends his knees, touches his feet, stretches, and then light as a gazelle, my old boyfriend begins to run. While I am being chilled on marble, he thinks about us, thinks it is all a shame, but you can't (he has often said to me) stop living just because someone you love is gone...What would be the point of that? he has said many times. Well, I have argued, a certain reverence for the dead. A respect you know, for what other reason are we here on earth than to love and miss one another? I ask you, would you be comfortable with the thought that when your dead everybody's going to keep on playing cards?

Dear Mr. Donahue, I am writing to tell you how much I enjoy your show. I would like to know if you put the whole thing together or do you have help? I am rather inventive myself and thought if you ever need some fresh ideas I would be more than willing to accomodate. Afterall, I have been a fan of yours for months now and though I have been ill, possibly terminally, I still have fresh and thick blood in me and could reel out something for you if the need arose...I of late have been searching for a reason to go on living and I thought, why doing a Phil Donahue show might just do the trick...I write to you from a small ordinary town, an ordinary street, but I gleen from your shows that you are not afraid to embrace the average. I remain a fan, hoping Marlo sticks it out.

* * * * * *

My son runs pantsless through the kitchen while the little girl sleeps upstairs, she has some spots on her legs which I think might be measles but Regina says it's just dried Kool Aid. Regina is outside on the patio jumping rope with her three Cabbage Patch Kids. Do you wonder where we got three Cabbage Patch Kids? Canada. They have loads of them up there. As a matter of fact Charles is taking the whole family to Canada this week to the zoo. We are all very excited. I am dieting, Regina is jabbering about where will we see the giraffes, the twins know nothing about it but they are as always in a state of high pitch excitement anyway. Charles is taking the whole family, I think, except this morning when he left after I told him about Lymon's letter he seemed, well, irked. He said "NO SWEETHEART I'M NOT MAD" when I asked him but he sort of shouted it and slammed the front screen. I heard his little Volkswagon start up and I was shot through the heart with a stab of remorse. I guess I shouldn't have told him about the letter. I guess I should never have even seen Lymon. I guess the wheels are turning and it's too late to stop anything...as always, I am moving through my life as a bystander moves, I get out of the way and find myself in another section altogether.

* * * * * *

The character Lymon....1. Childish. Almost retarded in some areas, nine-year-old frame of mind.

2. Brilliant in some places. Recites like a dream, knows Mozart from Bach, from Bartok, teaches, reads dreams, talks.

3. Parasitical. Lives off women. Me, for example.

4. Selfish. Aren't we all?

5. Handsome, but too boyish. Looks like Christopher Reeves at age nine.

6. Trouble. Trouble trouble trouble.

I have to say that I know just what's going on here. This Lymon character has come into the novel to put tension between the narrator and the shoemaker. In a novel, there should be several strains of tension going on...between narrator and boyfriend...narrator and children... narrator and babysitter...narrator and world at large...and possible world tension, say starving Ethiopians and what to do? What to do?

The woman who was my coach when the twins were born, who is also the wife of the president of the ambulance squad, came over this morning to discuss Friday night plans. Friday night the ambulance squad is having their annual awards dinner and the wives, alas, are not invited. We thought of picketing the restaurant, I said I would carry a sign saying "TECH THIRTY EIGHT COME HOME!!" but really we'll get together and drink a bottle of champagne and speak in hurried voices about love, and longing, and waiting. Wives of ambulance drivers are good at waiting. We wait for them to come back from a run, we wait for them to return, to love us. Meanwhile, this dinner will be a spoof. Charles tells me these dinners are very dirty. They give out obscene awards I guess...his ex-girlfriend will be there...she belongs to the squad...sometimes I wish I did. I would like to wear a red jacket and rush around town but I don't like ill people...they frighten me. And so I sometimes frighten myself.

On the back of a raspberry patch tea box it says, "Keep away from the widsom which does not cry, the philosophy which does not laugh and the greatness which does not bow before children."

This is what I have been striving for in this piece. I have looked for the sorrow and the humor in life and, in truth, I have always had the children speak the greatness which the adults lacked...I have looked to put in exactly what this character KAHIL GIBRAN was saying on the back of this tea box. And so I came close, hip hip hibiscus, right?

Steeping tea. Babies asleep. Regina at the auctioneer's house jumping rope with the auctioneer's daughter who is also eight and who also spends her waking hours going up and down, up and down on the pavement outside her house. "Regina and Jeffrey sittin' on a fence - trying to make a dollar outa ninety-nine cents! TWO-TWO: FOUR-FOUR. Regina, you're cheating!" I can hear them across the street, hopping with an eight-year-old fever that is only topped by a sixteen-year-old passion...I remember when I was sixteen and fell in love for the first time with a guy whose last name was, guess? BLOOD. Now tell me life isn't all a matter of fate.

Charles knows all the doctors in town and he tells me about how terrible they are. This shatters my confidence in their diagnosis of me..."You're going to be just fine," the lung specialist said.

But Charles said last night, "yeah that lung specialist is a real jerk. He tells all his patients they're going to be fine and then he rakes in when

they have to be hospitalized for something he could have avoided if he'd
bothered to take the time out from golfing to look down there..."

I panic inside when I hear this. "But he said..."

"Yeah, that guy's a real flake," Charles says, not hearing me. Or one
day when he had been out on a run, this is what they call riding in the
ambulance, he said, "Boy Dr. Smith is a pain to work for. He doesn't care
when his patients die or anything! One day we had to call him out to a
farm where this guy had died on a baling machine and he showed up
drunk and yellin...he fell down twice crossing the field to where we
were...and there's this guy's family all crying and stuff...it was
TERRIBLE. Dr. Smith doesn't know what he's doing half the time."
Dr. Smith was the doctor who told me,

"Oh I wouldn't worry...all women at around thirty being thinking
they're dying. I wouldn't let it cross my mind anymore if I were you." It's
true when I left his office I noticed I had an odor about me of a
martini.

So who DO I trust: Who DOES know if I'm dying or not? I ask these
quacks and they all say they don't know, but they doubt it. Well, I'm not
playing cards here, I doubt it is a card game I'm playing life. I'm trying to
hang in till I get to Boardwalk if you'll pardon the introduction of that old
standby Monopoly. Many writers have compared their life to the board
game Monopoly. I guess if I had to choose which property would best
describe me I would pick those icky light blue ones right after GO and
maybe the orange ones, SAINT JAMES PLACE, and the other two
because I have two different worlds going at once. Icky and pretty
good.

* * * * * *

Remember that song HONEY about the woman who died while her
husband was at work? I used to sob buckets over that song little knowing
it could have been written for me. Not that I have a husband...or even
that I am looking for one. Actually I am afraid to enter into another
marriage. Not that it has come up...well, Lymon is supposed to be meeting me tomorrow night and Charles has decided it is high time he moved
in with me officially...but these are all ruffles that must be smoothed...however I have another symptom which I'd like to get off my
chest.

Lump on lower back (any lump or thickening in the breast or
elsewhere....) Last night Charles went to his Sunday night I.V. class
where he sticks needles into his classmates and they stick needles into

him in case in the future they have to stick a needle into an accident victim which Charles says is highly unlikely in this area. "Some areas," he told me, "have to do it all the time...New York...." He came to my house late and found me already in bed. Why do I use the word FOUND? As though I were dead? He came into my bedroom with bandaids on his wrists and one hand red and slightly swollen. I had been reading a romance book and drinking wine. He lay down beside me and began touching my face and lifting up my dress. "What are you doing in bed?" he said, kissing me, moving onto me.

"I don't know," I answered. The reason was that when I am dieting I go to bed early so I won't eat. That's the only way I can stay out of the refrigerator...if I am in bed. "What are you doing?" I asked.

"What am I doing? You tell me," he said. Then while he was doing what he was doing the bed fell in. It's an iron bed and the railing was against my back hurting me...

"Charles, you're hurting me," I said.

"I am?" He went on, not stopping.

"The bed!" I said. When he finally pulled me off the railing I had a bruised feeling on the lower part of my back...which today has turned into a lump or thickening. "Look at that!," I said, accusingly and pointed to the spot.

"I see it," he said. He seemed rather disinterested.

It's funny because I was just thinking how sometimes when he makes love to me I get afraid he will wreck my spinal column and I'll be in a wheelchair for the rest of my life. Would he stay with me if I got crippled from making love? Would he feel it was his fault and remain with me, be unfaithful occasionally, or would he leave me, saying, "it's not because you're in a wheelchair...really, that part of it doesn't bother me at all sweetheart...it's because we are so unsuited...we come from different worlds..."

This morning I said, "Charles what if this lump is from a fractured vertebrae and the swelling is trying to help it but I'll be unable to walk in a few days anyway?" He was reading the paper when I said this and having a bowl of health food cereal.

"Oh you're such a hypochondriac," he said, munching. But what if I'm NOT a hypochondriac? What if indeed, a few days from now I wake up stiffer and stiffer and suddenly I can no longer walk and the doctor says, "if you'd come in when it happened we might have been able to sodder that vertebrae together but at this point all we can offer you is a wheelchair..."

* * * * * *

I guess I know how HONEY must have felt when she was all alone
with her diagnosis. "I came home unexpectedly and found you crying
needlessly in the middle of the day..." Men never believe you when
you're sick. They assume you're a hypochondriac right away if you com-
plain of an ailment and even when the doctor gives you something for the
sickness they think you've just got the doctor wrapped around your
finger. When I went into labor in Kentucky way back when I lived with
Regina's father I woke him at four a.m. and said, "I'm in labor..." and he
said with a sneer in his voice, "Oh you are not. Go to sleep."

When I had my miscarriage and my husband called me on the ship's
radio the first thing he said was, "So what are you doing in the hospital?
Can't you be at home or what?" He was always saying OR WHAT after
everything he said.

"I just lost a lot of blood," I said, irritated.

"So are you still bleeding or what? Can't you go home now? It's not
the expense of the hospital stay....we'll cross that bridge when we come to
it, but uhhh....so when are you going home?"

Of course it's true a lot of women do feel sick all the time. They have all
sorts of disorders and problems which they tell in detail to their horrified
husbands, men are afraid of vaginas I think, even though they love making love, they are afraid to discuss or become too involved in that part of a
woman. It's all that blood and birthing and life that goes on down there
that scares them. That's why gynecologists are so peculiar.

* * * * * *

A few days ago the president of the ambulance squad dropped his wife
off at my house to spend the evening while he and Charles went to the
annual-ambulance-squad-awards-dinner. Just as they were leaving,
Charles got a call on his beeper and had to take someone to a hospital in
another town so he missed most of it. I don't know if he would have told
me what went on there anyway. I sat in the kitchen drinking champagne
with the president's wife and talking about psychiatrists. It was eerie how
her experience with Norman, her psychiatrist in New York, was almost
identical to my experience with Jeffrey, my psychiatrist. I saw Jeffrey
during my married days just as she saw Norman. And just as Jeffrey did,
Nor man held her and hugged her and told her how special she was, he
even offered to be her daddy like Jeffrey did. I guess the evening was

revealing about women and love but for the most part we wolfed down cheese and pineapple and drank ourselves under the table. Charles once said to me, "sweetheart you can drink me under the table any day..." and I was so hurt. It sounded like he was commenting on my size.

Article in Cosmo magazine..."Couple of the year award goes to Phil Donahue and his lovely wife Marlo Thomas....says Phil, 'Marlo is the most important woman in my life.'" I don't know why but this depressed me for days. Is it that my relationships never stay together or is it that I secretly was in love with Phil myself? Neither, I guess. I guess it's just the disease that's bringing me down. The lump on my lower back, the cough, the sad realization that we all fall down. We all fall down comes from the nursery rhyme:

Ring around the rosy
a pocket full or posey
ashes ashes
we all fall down.

I'm sure everybody knows this but that came from the plague years, when people rotted away and had to carry flowers in their pockets to keep from smelling so badly. The ring around the rosy was the first symptom of the disease...much like ring worm I think. And ashes ashes was from the great bonfires they burned of the dead victims. Half the world fell down during the plague...now it's aids we've got to worry about.

There is a man somewhere here in our town who has aids. He went to New York the story goes, and came back with it. You don't even know you have it for two years. God I could have it right now and not know it. I could have already infected my children....Charles, my mother, my whole family....or they could have infected me! And in two years we'll all die. That's a more comforting thought....taking the whole family with you rather than going down alone.

I see the woman next door outside digging a flower bed in the sun. She looks like she has gained some weight. Maybe she WON'T die of the cancer that was eating her up. Maybe she will live, giving us all hope here at the house with peeling paint. Afterall, hope is essential to life. Without it, anyone can keel over.

Charles says it's time we lived together officially. He says he will help with the rent and the electric bill and all the rest, he will change diapers and clean up. But he will not give up the ambulance squad or running. "All the other stuff...the volleyball, the meetings...they can go..." he said.

But for some reason I am balking. I am terrified of something....what is it? "Why am I afraid Charles?" I asked him.

And he said "I don't know sweetheart." He took me to a waterfall yesterday while I left the babies with the sitter. We walked down a hill and sat by the roaring water on a dead log. He said "I'm ready to be really committed..." and I thought, that's sometimes how I feel...only committed always meant a nuthouse to me. So on my door it still says, "Welcome to the maison fou!"

"And honey I'll miss you...and I'm being good. And I'd love to be with you. If only I could..."

Men have a way of getting over dead wives. My mother never remarried after my father died but the minute her sister died, her sister's husband began seeing another woman and five years after the funeral he's been married something like three times. Charles told me his father was seeing another woman after his mother died, and I guess they would have gotten married except that woman died too and then Charles father died. Poof. God how we all die.

When we were sitting by the waterfall I said to Charles..."See that bridge up there? I used to walk the twins in the twinmobile over that bridge and have the overwhelming desire...fear...to throw them over the side."

Charles seemed genuinely surprised. "You've felt that way too?" he asks. "I wonder what would happen if you didn't STOP feeling that way?" We looked into each other's eyes, his are so pretty and blue green...he almost looked like the water was reflecting in them...and he said, "It's up to you sweetheart...you know how I feel. I want to live with you, and be a family." I shivered then because the wind came up and sprays of water reached us....the dog had jumped out of the car and was wandering around down the slope. I said,

"We should get the dog before she gets run over."

* * * * * *

Regina is finished with bone structure and her class has now moved on to Laplanders. I know this because when we saw a camper trailer go by it had the word NOMAD written on the side of it and she said, "Nomads live in Lapland." This impressed me.

"I didn't know that," I said.

Novel review. What happened to earlier characters? Where is the connection between nomads, illness, the narrator, the shoemaker, and Phil Donahue? With what tools and tricks do you plan to tie up the novel's ending? How will the issue of Ethiopia and the narrator's continuous bleeding end up? Will aids spread? Will Lymon come back? Does the narrator have a feel for what she is going through? Does the writer know where the shoemaker is right now? Look for possible way out of this whole mess.

1. Lymon comes back and the narrator settles down with him.
2. The shoemaker moves in and the narrator quits bleeding.
3. The narrator adopts a family from Ethiopia.
4. The narrator dies and the novel is finished by the shoemaker.

* * * * * *

I am a human body. I am real. What is real? It is the same thing as love. Charles said last night "I don't know" when I asked him what love meant. Real is something in your head too. When I was little my sister and I used to play a game of reality. We would stare at a table and say...that's not a really a table. It's just MATTER. Matter is everywhere and this has been dubbed TABLE but really it could be WINDOW or DOOR. Which reminds me...the twins have learned a new word. DOOR. They go around all day calling DOOR to each other, and pointing to various closets and cupboards. To them, reality is gates and closed doors...when a door is closed they say "AHHHH!," as if suddenly everything has jelled which is just what this novel needs...a jelling point.

Yesterday, June came by for a drink just after I received another letter from Lymon stating that he would not meet me at La Maison or anywhere else...he said "I will not end up like Mozart." This is the epitomy of the character Lymon.

"Ah so what," June said when I poured her a gin and tonic, telling her about the letter. "You learn from your experiences...and you go through it. Now tell me, isn't it easier this time around with him? You cry less, right?"

I cut a lime up. "Yeah," I said, taking my drink to the table and sitting down.

"Turn it around," she said. "Make it work for you. Turn it around." I was watching the babies out the window, in their new pen Charles has made them. Charles is very kind to me. He criticizes me quite a bit but this is really his only drawback, other than the flirting which he promises has stopped....And all women are criticized by their men I guess. I think all human beings criticize each other which brings me back to the point, "I am a human being. I am a body." Regina has been studying the eye in school. She tells me that the iris of your eye opens and closes to let in the required amount of light needed to see. It is much like the opening and closing of a door.

Has there been any door openings this chapter?

Will there be a party in my honor upon completion of this work.

To think that Mozart travelled around most of his youth playing concerts and composing. But to think of Mozart anymore at all is almost boringly repetitive. Afterall, he has been a discovered genius. The middle class knows him now since Amadeus. And when the middle class gets hold of an artist forget it. Look what happened to Barry Manilow! Look what's happening to Phil Donahue! Of course he always had his middle class audience but now he's headlines everywhere! I can't seem to write about anything without the whole country taking it up, just as if I were waiting in line for a ride down the slide and when I get to the ladder somebody else shoots down and the slide breaks and there I am, after all that waiting....For instance, I heard from June that Phil Donahue is very good friends with Mario Cuomo, who is the new democrat-for-tomorrow sort of guy, a real homebody nice man with morals but not too many morals - like the silent morals, or is that the silent majority? One can't recall every new action group that comes along. Anyway, June thinks Phil Donahue might well run for some office next election. This sounds good to me. I think Marlo would deserve as much. She used to work very hard at THAT GIRL. It seems like it ran on T.V. for a long time.

This is not getting us anywhere. What are we trying to achieve here?

Well, Charles has moved in, given me his half of the rent and hung his toothbrush next to Regina's in the bathroom which he says makes it REAL. But I say, what is real? So it's a toothbrush. It could well be a table. It is just solid air, and solid air is matter and matter is anything so his moving in is reduced to nothing. Merely air shuffling around, matter replacing space, space being another sort of matter. Weird isn't it that we are all made from stars? According to my mother, a star burst and made all of us. I can believe that. Sometimes I think I will burst...fly out of myself in a rage or a bloody pool and cry long, loud wails...Lymon oh Lymon I could say, you did it to me again!

* * * * * *

Dear Phil, my whole point in dragging you into this mess is to prove a point. But like your show, the point is left up to the people. THEY must decide what it is, whether or not it is valid, and what to do with it once that have grabbed hold. I know you may be thinking that you have producers and directors that help the audience along with their decision and give a clear picture the audience can see to make a decision on, and you maybe thinking that this whole piece needs a director and that I have not filled that role. But I have tried and isn't it the new feeling in this country that as long as you try and try you should be given a medal no matter how it turns out? I am writing to ask you for a medal, a small quiet place on your show. I promise you I won't say anything adverse...Please Phil, help me out. My ex-boyfriend Lymon didn't show up for our meeting in which I was going to politely come out victorious, and once again I have been foiled and fooled and hurt by everything. What I need now is some reassurance that this will turn out beneficial...you know, will the narrator find happiness in a world of turmoil? Will Africa survive the drought? Will the shoemaker leave the narrator because she has lost her sparkle? It's true, Charles said, "I love looking at women's bodies...the first thing I look at is their teeth, then their feet..." and my heart sank because those, Phil, are my worst features. Hoping this letter comes at a good time in your marriage, I remain sincere.

* * * * * *

Charles had to pick up number one in Brainwater this afternoon. Number one is the green ambulance, and he took me and the twins along because he had no other way to get there. At first the sun was shining and we drove thru little towns with churches and pretty houses....I was laughing and the twins were saying "Door! door!" and pointing to the car doors the whole way. Then I noticed Charles had on a shirt from one of his many women admirers and I said,

"I don't want you to wear that shirt, Charles...it's from that woman in your I.V. class, isn't it?"

He admitted that it was. "I'll give it to Regina," he said, whipping around a corner and terrifying me. I hate driving like we are headed to the scene of an accident.

"I have a better idea...I'll wear it," I said. I was thinking how that would bother the girl he got it from, seeing me in it.

"YOU!" Charles laughed. "YOU wouldn't fit it! You're too big!"

After that, the scenery went grey and I sat with tears rolling down my cheeks the whole way to Brainwater, and when we arrived and he climbed into Number One, I drove home in silence, listening to the sound of the engine and the twins calling "DOOR! Mamama!!! Door."

He is not for me. Lymon, Charles. My father. My old psychiatrist. My guru. The one who worked in the graveyard. Funny how I've had a gravedigger boyfriend and an ambulance driver. Now all I need to make it complete is a funeral parlor man. A mortician. A body stuffer. One of those creepy types that shoot dead bodies up with formaldehyde and apply make up to dead faces, dress cold, stiff, bodies, lay out the flowers and drive the black car. Then I will have gone through the whole death cycle. The ambulance, the funeral, the grave, and finally the music played at the wake, by Regina's father or by the twins' father, I need a hankerchief manufacturer. I need a chauffeur for a hearse. I need a preacher, a graveyard mower, and something else...No, thank God it is not love. Let it be fear, let my mind wander to Phil Donahue, my body melt in great red waves of loss, but knowing that reality is just a burst star, this makes my words sunflowers, and God knows we are short of impressions.

* * * * * *

On Saturday evening I am having a great good bye party. I have invited Regina's father who is coming, the president of the ambulance squad and his wife and child, they are coming, all these people are coming, my sister the painter, my sister the guidance counselor, the shoemaker, my old girlfriend from high school who used to sunbath with me, several couples from town, Corrine, June, and the woman who is dying of cancer next door. I am looking forward to this party as if it were my last. I am thinking of it as sort of a wake. I am saying good bye to this piece of work and to a life that I somehow managed to get through (this is the hopeful ending). I am settled here on this middle class street and settled with Charles, critical and flirtatious as he may be. I am thinner, older, more worn down and still sickly but I am alive.

I am here to say that life is a hell and a hurdle, that women and men are so unalike and that all human beings are so similar that it can make you sick if you think about it too much.

This party will mean the death of the old life and the start of the new. I am going to be normal beginning on Saturday. I am going to keep a clean house, sit on a clean floor and play Creative Playthings with my twins, they will no longer have to whine at the door in the basement, they will grow better this way. I read recently that if you withhold love from a child it will stunt its growth. I am going to load on the love and the cleaning. Maybe Charles will marry me someday and I'll be a part of a nuclear family. This whole novel is over and I too am over in some respects. Bleeding and limping, with a lump or thickening in the back and elsewhere, I hand this up to Phil and the public. I really didn't think I would live to see this page. Hoping this comes at a good time, I remain.

* * * * * *

Where does this novel end? Well, to begin with, there should be a wrap up on the characters. Shall we bump of the narrator? Then who will end it?

"The narrator is dead now, but I promised her as she lay in the hospital calling wildly to someone named Phil, that I would end this saga for her."

"Will you make sure it ends happy?" she asked, taking her six o'clock morphine and leaning back into the white hospital sheets, her face rosy and grey all at once, her arms and legs thin, the tumors, no, this is no good.

What say we finish it like this...Charles came into the house this morning and discovered me crying needlessly, in the middle of the day...no that's been done.

I, being of sound mind and body, do hereby ask the general public and the public at large to end this piece FOR me, as I am no longer able to keep abreast, a grasp, of the situation.

I sang for Regina's school, a song about the femur bone and about her charming class. The audience thought it was "cute." Can I hope for that response to this piece? Probably I'll never become more than a hill of beans. Or maybe not that. What if the shoemaker glues shoes to my feet? What if I fall and break my femur bone? How about if I get the rich boyfriend to donate all his assets to Ethiopia? What if the narrator continues on as if nothing had happened? And that's the crux of the whole situation. There is no end for this. I realize now what I am looking for is a pat answer to life. There are pats, but no pat endings. As an editor once wrote to me about a piece,

"Thank you for letting us read your article although its not appropriate." I send you my regards, from Mars, from the Phil show, from yet another open door and I remain,

inappropriately yours.